"You look like one of those angels on top of a Christmas tree,"

Roman told her.

'That's a nice compliment. I remember the one we had when I was a little girl. My parents let me help trim the tree, but I was never allowed to touch the angel."

Roman smiled. "Are you trying to tell me something?"

"Would it do any good?" Noelle asked lightly.

"You must know I want to kiss you." He moved closer and lifted her chin in his palm.

Excitement raced through Noelle as she gazed into his brilliant eyes. She was very conscious of Roman's firm mouth only inches from hers. It was tempting— *too* tempting. The attraction between them had the potential to turn into an avalanche, carrying her away. But she couldn't afford to get involved. Not when it might scuttle her whole mission.

Giving a shaky laugh, she told Roman, "I only kiss on a first date."

"Fortunately, I don't have the same reservations."

Dear Reader,

Welcome to Silhouette **Special Edition**, where each month, we publish six novels with *you* in mind—stories of love and life, tales that you can identify with.

Last year, I requested your opinions on our books. Thank you for the many thoughtful comments. I'd like to share with you quotes from those letters. This seems very appropriate now, while we are in the midst of the THAT SPECIAL WOMAN! promotion. Each one of our readers is a *special* woman, as heroic as the heroines in our books.

We have some wonderful books in store for you this June. *A Winter's Rose* by Erica Spindler is our THAT SPECIAL WOMAN! title and it introduces Erica's wonderful new series, BLOSSOMS OF THE SOUTH. Not to be missed this month is *Heart of the Wolf,* by Lindsay McKenna. This exciting tale begins MORGAN'S MERCENARIES.

Wrapping up this month are books from other favorite authors: Gina Ferris (*Fair and Wise* is the third tale in FAMILY FOUND!), Tracy Sinclair, Laurey Bright and Trisha Alexander.

I hope you enjoy this book, and all of the stories to come!

Sincerely,

Tara Gavin
Senior Editor
Silhouette Books

Quote of the Month: "Why do I read romances? I maintain a positive outlook to life—do not allow negative thoughts to enter my life—but when my willpower wears, a good romance novel gets me back on track fast! The romance novel is adding much to the New Age mentality— keep a positive mind, create a positive world!"

—E.J.W. Fahner
Michigan

TRACY SINCLAIR

ROMANCE ON THE MENU

Silhouette®

SPECIAL EDITION®

Published by Silhouette Books New York

America's Publisher of Contemporary Romance

SILHOUETTE BOOKS
300 East 42nd St., New York, N.Y. 10017

ROMANCE ON THE MENU

Copyright © 1993 by Tracy Sinclair

All rights reserved. Except for use in any review, the reproduction or utilization of this work in whole or in part in any form by any electronic, mechanical or other means, now known or hereafter invented, including xerography, photocopying and recording, or in any information storage or retrieval system, is forbidden without the permission of the publisher, Silhouette Books, 300 E. 42nd St., New York, N.Y. 10017

ISBN: 0-373-09821-9

First Silhouette Books printing June 1993

All the characters in this book have no existence outside the imagination of the author and have no relation whatsoever to anyone bearing the same name or names. They are not even distantly inspired by any individual known or unknown to the author, and all incidents are pure invention.

®: Trademark used under license and registered in the United States Patent and Trademark Office and in other countries.

Printed in the U.S.A.

Books by Tracy Sinclair

TRACY SINCLAIR,

author of more than thirty-five Silhouette novels, also contributes to various magazines and newspapers. An extensive traveler and a dedicated volunteer worker, this California resident has accumulated countless fascinating experiences, settings and acquaintances to draw on in plotting her romances.

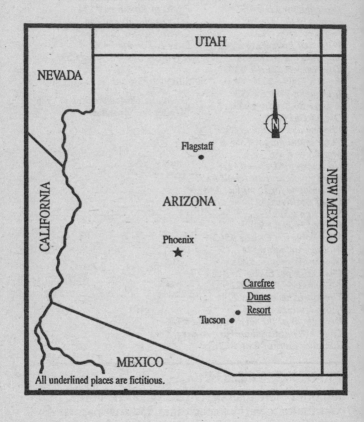

UTAH

NEVADA

CALIFORNIA

ARIZONA

Flagstaff

Phoenix ★

Carefree
Dunes
Resort

Tucson ●

NEW MEXICO

MEXICO

All underlined places are fictitious.

Chapter One

Noelle Bartlett was doing her morning exercises when the telephone rang. Even with her long, honey-blond hair piled haphazardly on top of her head and no makeup, she was remarkably beautiful.

Crossing the room with a dancer's grace, she picked up the phone. The voice on the other end made her smile. "What are you doing up this early in the morning, Diane? The idle rich are supposed to sleep late."

Diane didn't waste time on pleasantries. "I have to talk to you, Noelle. Can I come over right now?"

"I'm not showered or dressed yet, and I have a couple of errands to do. How about meeting for lunch?"

"I can't wait that long."

Noelle's smile vanished as the tension in her friend's voice registered. "Is something wrong?"

"My entire life is coming apart at the seams, that's all!"

"What happened?" Noelle asked in alarm.

"It's a long story. I don't want to go into it over the phone."

"Then by all means, come right over. Unless you'd rather I came to you."

"No, I have to get out of the house. I don't want to break down in front of Rosa." That was Diane's housekeeper. "I'll be there as soon as possible."

Noelle's thickly fringed blue eyes held concern as she cradled the receiver. What could be upsetting Diane to this extent? She seemed to have it all—a rich, handsome husband she adored, a captivating child. Diane had even had a successful career, which she'd given up voluntarily to marry Drew Vanderhoff and devote herself to raising their daughter, Christine. It was hard to believe Crissie was five years old already.

Diane had never achieved stardom, but she'd been a well-known supporting actress. Noelle's first big break on Broadway had been dancing in the chorus of a musical in which Diane had the second lead.

Unlike many successful actresses, Diane treated the lesser members of the cast as equals. She'd singled Noelle out for special encouragement, sensing her insecurity among the more seasoned dancers. They worked together in several shows after that, and their professional relationship developed into a warm friendship that continued after Diane left the stage.

Noelle was deeply troubled as she went into the kitchen to make a pot of fresh coffee.

Diane wasn't eye-catchingly beautiful like Noelle. Striking was the word that most often came to mind. Her black hair was always perfectly groomed, and she possessed great poise and a charming, gracious manner.

The woman who arrived that morning was shockingly changed. Dark circles ringed her eyes, and her hair looked as if it hadn't been combed in days. Diane was obviously under great stress.

Noelle didn't bother with preliminaries. "I've been imagining all sorts of things since you called. What on earth is the matter?"

"I'm in terrible trouble," Diane answered. "I need your help."

"Of course! Anything at all. Just tell me what's wrong."

"I'm being blackmailed."

Noelle's mouth dropped open. That was the last thing she'd expected. "You must be joking! What could anyone possibly have on you? Your life is a fairy tale."

"That's the image I've been keeping up," Diane said somberly. "Actually, Drew and I...our marriage has been rocky for some time."

"I can't believe it! You've always seemed so happy."

Diane smiled sardonically. "I'm an actress, remember?"

"An awfully good one. I never guessed. Do you want to talk about it?" Noelle asked hesitantly.

"It's the same old story. The only difference is that Drew got the seven-year itch a year ahead of time."

"He's having an affair?" Noelle's surprise showed. Drew had always seemed like the perfect husband.

"That's all I thought it was at first. Not that I wasn't crushed when I found out, but I'm not naive. Men are more insecure than women. No matter how handsome and successful they are, they still need to be assured of their virility."

"You're very understanding." Noelle wasn't sure *she* would be, but now wasn't the time to say so.

"I love him," Diane answered simply. "I gave up my career for Drew, and I've never regretted it."

"Then hang in there. I can see what this is doing to you, but it will all blow over."

"You don't understand. He wants a divorce."

"How can he even consider such a thing? What about Crissie? Did you remind him that he'd be walking out on her, too?"

"He's trading her in for a slightly older version," Diane replied bitterly. "His not-so-blushing bride is a twenty-year-old. How does that grab you?"

"It sounds as if Drew is going through a midlife crisis. He needs a psychiatrist or a marriage counselor, somebody who will make him realize what he's throwing away. Have you suggested that to him?"

"We can't communicate anymore. He's a different person." Diane paced the floor distractedly. "Do you know what it's like to have your husband look at you with complete indifference? It's all over. At least the marriage is. I just wish to God that's *all* I had to be sorry for."

Noelle was abruptly reminded of Diane's dramatic announcement earlier. It didn't make sense after what she'd just revealed. Drew was the one who'd been unfaithful. "Why are *you* being blackmailed?"

"Because I was a fool." Diane ran shaking fingers through her disheveled hair. "You can't imagine what a blow this was to my self-esteem. Drew's rejection made me feel dowdy and undesirable. My self-confidence was completely destroyed. I just wanted to go somewhere and hide."

"Was that why you went to the spa in Arizona?" Diane had only recently returned from what Noelle thought was a vacation.

"Carefree Dunes," Diane said with bitter mockery. "Where rich women like me go to be pampered. That's where I met Troy Slattery, a physical-fitness trainer with the body of a lifeguard and the morals of a snake. You can guess the rest. I had a sordid, one-night stand with him, like some cheap little tart. How could I have been such a fool!"

"Don't be so hard on yourself. You were terribly vulnerable."

"Exactly. And that creep capitalized on it. His attention made me feel desirable again, like the woman I used to be. When he invited me to his room for a drink, I accepted, but I never intended to get involved with him, I swear!"

"I believe you," Noelle said soothingly.

"Somehow, things got out of hand. I honestly don't know how. I only remember having one drink." Diane's long nails bit into her damp palms. "The next thing I knew, we were in bed together."

"Do you think he put something in your drink?"

"I wouldn't put anything past him. The next morning I woke up filled with disgust. I checked out and flew home, telling myself I had to forget about what happened, it was over. Only it isn't over."

Noelle had a sinking feeling in the pit of her stomach. "He's the one who's blackmailing you?"

Diane nodded. "He took pictures with a hidden camera, and he's threatening to sell them to the tabloids if I don't pay up. When the news gets out that Drew and I are getting a divorce, everybody will think it's because I was having a sleazy affair."

"Not the people who know you," Noelle answered loyally.

"When the story is accompanied by pictures? It would be terribly humiliating, but Christine is the one I'm worried about. Imagine what it would do to her if the kids at school started repeating what their parents were saying at home. I can't let Troy sell those photos."

"I understand how you feel, but paying a blackmailer is no solution. Once you start, there's no end to it. He'll bleed you like a leech."

"I'm aware of that. My only hope is to destroy his evidence."

Noelle paused, unwilling to dash her friend's hopes. But Diane wasn't thinking clearly. "I'm sure it made you feel better to tear them up, but it doesn't really help. He'll simply print more."

"I was talking about the negatives. I have to get them away from him."

"How can you do that?"

"*I* can't, but you might be able to." As Noelle registered shock, Diane rushed on without giving her a chance to speak. "You're my only hope. I can't trust anyone else. For Christine's sake, you can't turn me down."

"You know I'd do anything for you and Crissie, but how can *I* help?"

"You can check into Carefree Dunes," Diane said eagerly. "Troy wouldn't have any reason to suspect you weren't just another guest."

"And then what? I assume you want me to steal the negatives, but how would I go about it? They're small and flat. He could hide them just about any place. I'd have no idea where to look."

"There's an easier way. Troy will come on to you immediately—I know him. Just string him along. When his guard is down, you can trick him into telling you where they are."

"You're grasping at straws," Noelle said impatiently. "I'm flattered that you think I'm so irresistible, but this jerk sleeps with women for a living. He isn't some teenager with raging hormones. He'd be more likely to set me up as his next victim."

"You can at least get friendly with him. If that doesn't get results, you can sneak in and search his room."

"What if he caught me at it? I could wind up in jail! I'd like to help you, but the whole idea is preposterous," Noelle said flatly.

"Then I might as well kill myself and get it over with."

Noelle gazed at her friend uncertainly. Diane had a flair for the dramatic, but she was undeniably under intense strain.

"You don't mean that." Noelle's soothing tone covered considerable fear. "We'll figure something out."

"I've thought about nothing else for days, and those are the only two alternatives." Diane's ravished face was almost calm, as though she'd made her decision.

After a long pause, Noelle sighed. "This is probably the craziest thing I've ever agreed to, but okay, I'll do it."

Another meeting was taking place in the editorial offices of *Style* magazine, a slick publication that catered to the upper-income group.

Roman Wilding's rangy body was slumped in a chair, his long legs stretched out and crossed at the ankles. Amusement crinkled the corners of his gray eyes as he gazed at the woman behind the desk.

"You have to be kidding, Nora."

"Wait till you hear what I'm prepared to offer," Nora Crandall, the editor-in-chief, answered.

"It doesn't matter. I'm an investigative reporter, not a society columnist. No offense, but I don't do puff pieces."

"I'm not asking you to. We want this article to have some depth."

He laughed derisively. "How deep does it get at a reducing spa for over-privileged women? Maybe I can find out they've been tampering with the scales."

"These spas are big business, Rome. It's a cultural phenomenon of our times that women are willing to pay thousands of dollars to starve themselves into shape. The meals total only about five or six hundred calories a day."

He shook his head in amazement. "That's hard to believe."

"You could do a story about what goes on at a place like Carefree Dunes. Is the cost defensible in our present economic climate?" Nora watched him shrewdly. "You have to admit it's a subject with substance."

Roman looked thoughtful. "It could be. But why me? This is an assignment for a woman. You'd have to get inside to find out exactly what goes on. I don't get my information secondhand."

"You wouldn't have to. One week a year they open the spa to men only. It's coming up shortly. You could register under an assumed name and check out their operation for yourself. Consider it a vacation."

"On six hundred calories a day?" he asked mockingly.

"Men only go on the diet plan if they choose to."

"Why else would they go there?"

"For a complete change. As I understand it, the male guests are high-powered types who need to unwind—get away from telephones, meetings and the pressure that goes with their jobs. For one week they can just vegetate and recharge their batteries."

Roman flexed his powerful shoulder muscles. "I could use a rest."

"This is made to order for you, Rome," Nora said urgently, seizing the slight advantage.

"Except that I'd be working," he pointed out.

"Technically, but mainly you'd be soaking up the atmosphere and observing. It would be a piece of cake for you after that undercover government investigation you just finished."

"Even so, I can think of another objection. You want a story about what goes on at a fat farm that caters to rich women. What good would it do me to hang out with a bunch of men?"

"You could see how the place operates. They have the same staff for men and women. While you're checking out the facilities, you can make some contacts among the employees. I don't have to tell *you* how to turn on the old charm."

Nora gazed with frank admiration at the man across the desk. Roman was a magnificent male animal with the added wallop of charm and intelligence. His splendid physique was enhanced by a rugged face. The combination of high cheekbones, penetrating gray eyes and a square jaw indicated a man who could be dangerous if provoked. But his firm, yet sensuous mouth would tempt many women to take that chance.

He was regarding her with a sardonic expression. "I wish that's all there was to investigative reporting. I've been working twelve hours a day digging into dusty files for nothing."

"That's the beauty of this assignment. It's a change of pace for you. What's so bad about being waited on hand and foot—and getting paid for it?"

He smiled. "That's the part that just might convince me."

"Then you'll do it?" Nora asked eagerly.

"Let's say I'm willing to discuss it. If I agree to do the story, I'm not going to pull any punches," he warned.

"I don't want you to. Just tell it like it is."

"What if somebody recognizes me?"

"That isn't likely to happen. The few pictures I've seen of you in the newspapers either showed you in army fatigues with a baseball cap shading your face, or else you were looking away from the camera."

"I try to stay out of photos whenever possible."

"And you never appear on TV. There's almost no chance of anyone identifying you. Just pass yourself off as a stressed-out businessman. Nobody will suspect differently."

"What business am I in?"

Nora waved a dismissive hand. "It doesn't matter."

"That's where you're wrong. Before going undercover you invent a complete persona for yourself. I think I'll be an advertising executive," he said thoughtfully. "It's a high-stress job and I know enough about the business to get by."

"That sounds fine. I'll take care of your reservation and plane ticket." She was obviously anxious to make all the arrangements before he changed his mind.

"How soon do I have to be there?"

"Men's week starts on Sunday, the twelfth. You'll just have time to go out and buy some bathing trunks."

"I was thinking about a complete resort wardrobe on the expense account." He grinned. "You want me to look dashing when I turn on the charm for the staff, don't you?"

"You'll get even further in your bathing trunks," Nora answered dryly.

Diane was pathetically grateful. To cut short her fevered expressions of indebtedness, Noelle beckoned her into the kitchen.

"I've made fresh coffee," she said. "Would you like some toast to go with it? I'll bet you didn't have breakfast."

"I haven't been able to eat since I got those photographs. It was like a nightmare! And then when Troy phoned and demanded money, I just fell apart." Diane's hand was shaking badly as she picked up her cup.

"What did you say to him? Did you agree to pay?"

"I didn't know what to do. At first I told him I needed time to think it over, but he said if I didn't get the money to him immediately, he'd send the pictures to the *National Informer*. So then I agreed to his terms, but I said it would take time—a week, anyway—to get that much cash together." Diane's mouth twisted. "Blackmailers don't take checks."

"It's a good thing, or you might have sent him one."

"I would have. I'd do anything to stop him!"

Diane was becoming agitated again, so Noelle was relieved when the slices of bread in the toaster popped up. Placing butter and jam on the table, she said, "It won't help matters to make yourself sick. Have some toast and calm down."

"I feel much better now that I've talked about it." Some of the strain left Diane's face. "I only hope I'm not messing up *your* life. Will it be a problem for you to get away?"

"No, the timing is right, anyway. I got the part in Michael Shelby's new production, but we don't go into rehearsal for a month."

"You see?" Diane exclaimed. "Everything's working out perfectly. It's a good omen."

"Don't get your hopes too high," Noelle warned. "I'll do what I can, but it's a long shot. A week isn't very much time to locate those negatives."

"You can stay longer if you have to. I'll pay for everything, naturally."

"You told Troy you'd have the money in a week," Noelle reminded her.

"I can stall him if I have to. Besides—" Diane's smile held some of her former spirit "—you'll be providing a distraction. Your figure is as good as any of the aerobics teachers I saw."

Noelle stared at her contemplatively. "That might be an even better idea than being a guest. If I worked there, I'd have more freedom to snoop around the staff quarters. I wonder how hard it is to get a job at Carefree Dunes?"

"One of the masseuses told me that turnover is a big problem. The younger women, especially, get bored with the isolation and the lack of men."

Noelle chewed on her lower lip. "What about experience? I don't know if I could lead an aerobics class."

"Of course you could, if you'd really rather work there than be a guest. You're a dancer. Teach them the dance routines from your past shows. It would be something different and they'd love it."

"That might work," Noelle conceded. "It would give the manager some reason to hire me."

"Exactly." Diane reached across the table and squeezed Noelle's hand impulsively. "You've saved my life. I'll never forget what you're doing for me."

"Something tells me Carefree Dunes is going to remain in *my* memory, too," Noelle answered wryly.

Carefree Dunes was a green oasis in the Arizona desert. The closest city was Tucson, miles away, but a nearby small town catered to the health spa's needs. It had a dry cleaner, a movie theater, a restaurant and a lively bar that featured country-and-western music on the weekends. At other times an old-fashioned jukebox provided music for dancing.

In direct contrast, Carefree Dunes was the ultimate in restrained luxury, a secluded, sybaritic retreat far removed from the problems of the world. Green lawns and colorful flowers flourished in the midst of the arid desert.

A one-story white building with a red-tile roof was set in the middle of the lush greenery. Several smaller buildings surrounded the main guest house. A large swimming pool and two tennis courts were located far enough away so the noise wouldn't bother guests who wanted peace and tranquillity.

The lobby was delightfully cool after the desert heat outside. Noelle located the manager's office by a brass plaque on the door that read: Sybyll Ogilvie, Director of Guest Relations.

The woman sitting behind the desk was in her middle forties. She was tastefully dressed in a beige silk blouse and skirt, and her auburn hair was impeccably coiffed. Her gracious manner became all business when she discovered that Noelle wasn't a guest.

"We do have an opening for an aerobics teacher." The manager eyed her appraisingly. "What experience have you had?"

This was the sticky part. Sybyll wasn't impressed by her career as a dancer. Noelle was beginning to worry that her plan would never get off the ground. She anxiously renewed her argument that dance classes would be an "innovative change."

"That may very well be." The older woman's eyes narrowed. "However, I'm wondering if that's your real reason for being here."

"What other reason could I have?" Noelle asked warily.

"Your timing is rather suspicious. Does it have anything to do with the fact that we'll soon be hosting a group of highly successful men, some of them in the entertainment industry?"

"That never entered my mind," Noelle answered truthfully. "I'm fed up with show business. I want to get as far away from it as possible."

Sybyll frowned, trying to gauge the accuracy of that statement. "A lot of girls think this is a chance to advance their careers or find a rich husband. I can tell you right now, you'd be wasting your time."

"I'm not interested in either one," Noelle assured her.

"Well, we *are* dreadfully shorthanded at the moment. I'll take a chance on you." The manager looked past Noelle to a young woman who was crossing the lobby. "Erica, come here, please. This is Noelle Bartlett," she told the other woman. "She's our new aerobics instructor. Take her to the staff quarters and show her around."

Erica Jones was probably in her early twenties, but she seemed younger. Her light brown hair was caught into a ponytail, and her smooth skin and tight body were due to youth, not expensive cosmetics or dieting.

She gave Noelle a friendly smile as they walked out the front door together. "You're going to love it here. The air is clean and at night it's so quiet you can hear the coyotes howl."

"Is that supposed to be a recommendation?" Noelle asked.

Erica laughed. "You'll get used to it. Carefree Dunes is kind of like camping out with all the comforts of home—if you happen to live in a mansion."

"From the little I've seen, it's quite plush, but there don't seem to be many guests. Is this the off-season?"

"No, we're full up. Most of the ladies are having their massages or taking mineral baths at this hour. That's the reason the place seems deserted."

"It must take a lot of people to run a spa like this," Noelle remarked casually, trying to work the conversation around to Troy. "Are all the employees women?"

"Just about, except for our fitness trainer and the gardeners and service people—the men who take care of the pool and do maintenance work."

"Carefree Dunes sounds like a cross between a nunnery and a sorority house."

Erica flashed a gamin grin. "Troy Slattery would never be allowed within fifty miles of a nunnery. He's our resident body builder. The ladies adore him."

Before Noelle could pursue the subject, they reached their destination, one of the small buildings. A row of closed doors lined a corridor facing the path.

Unlocking and opening a door with a brass letter nine attached to the panel, Erica said, "This will be your room. Mine is right next door."

The room had the characterless look of a motel accommodation. In addition to a single bed covered with a flowered cotton spread, there was a dresser, a nightstand and two chairs, one straight-backed, the other more comfortable. Not exactly palatial, but at least it had a private bath.

"You have a nice big closet and plenty of drawer space," Erica said. "Where's your luggage?"

"I left it in the car." Noelle had rented a small compact at the airport. "I'll walk back and get it."

"I'll come with you. After we bring in your suitcase, I'll show you where to park. You'll have to leave your car in the employees' lot."

"I don't want to keep you from whatever you're supposed to be doing."

"No problem. I'm free until after lunch. Would you like to take a look around the place?"

"I'd love to," Noelle answered. "And while we're walking around, maybe you can fill me in on the people I'll be working with."

"They're a good group. Of course a lot of them come and go. There's not enough excitement here for some people."

"How long have *you* worked here?"

"Three years." In answer to the speculation she saw on Noelle's face, Erica added, "I'm twenty-one. I was nineteen when I started, not long out of school."

"You graduated college at nineteen?" Noelle asked in surprise.

"I meant high school. I never went to college. My parents couldn't afford to send me," Erica said matter-of-factly. "I have three younger brothers and sisters at home."

Noelle deeply regretted her words. "A lot of people spend four years in college without learning much more than how to party," she remarked dismissively.

"It would have been nice, but I try to make up for it. I take correspondence courses and I read a lot." Erica's wistful expression changed to an impish grin. "Did you know that President Woodrow Wilson's wife was the great granddaughter of Pocahontas?"

"No, really?"

Erica nodded. "I also read that the air on Mars is poisonous, although I don't know what I'll do with the information."

"No knowledge is wasted. If you see a little green man wearing a gas mask, you'll be able to identify where he came from."

They were laughing together, unaware of the man approaching until he blocked their path. Noelle glanced up and got her first look at Troy Slattery. It couldn't be anyone else. The tight white T-shirt and tennis shorts showed off an impressive body. He also had streaked-blond surfer's hair and a handsome face, although not one that appealed to Noelle. His mouth was too loose-lipped and his chin was weak. She could see where many women would be willing to overlook those flaws, however. Troy was undeniably sexy—even if he didn't possess the universal appeal he was obviously convinced he had. Noelle was turned off by the bold glance, only partially veiled by deference.

"Well, hello. I don't believe we've met." He extended his hand. "I'm Troy Slattery, the fitness trainer here. At your service."

Noelle was forced to shake his hand. "Noelle Bartlett," she answered with a fixed smile.

"Welcome to Carefree Dunes, Ms. Bartlett. This must be your first stay with us. I know I'd remember if you'd been here before."

"Save the phony charm," Erica told him. "Noelle is the new aerobics instructor."

His manner changed. The deference vanished and his eyes wandered over her curves insolently. "Well, well, you're a big improvement over the last one. She was a real drag."

"That means he struck out," Erica remarked.

"Is that what she told you?" He swiveled his hips suggestively and gazed at Noelle with a little smirk. "Do you believe that?"

She wanted to tell him exactly what she thought, but she couldn't allow herself the luxury. "I'm sure you're a major asset to Carefree Dunes," she answered evasively.

"Haven't had any complaints yet," he drawled.

"We'd love to stay and hear about how fantastic you are, but we're on our way to get Noelle's luggage," Erica said.

He didn't move out of the way. "Where are you from?" he asked Noelle.

"New York City," she answered.

"Great town. Why would you want to leave the Big Apple to come out to the boondocks?"

"I got tired of crowds."

"Then you came to the right place. Rush hour here is when four cars are on the highway at the same time."

"That sounds heavenly," Noelle commented.

"If you like being out of the action."

"Why do you stay if you don't like it?"

His eyes lit with secret amusement. "I've got a good thing going for me. The work is easy and the pay is good."

Noelle's nails bit into her palms as she forced a smile. "You can't ask for more than that."

"Oh, I don't know." His eyes held hers. "I can think of a couple of things."

"Congratulations," Erica said disgustedly. "You've just broken your own record for hitting on a new girl."

"So many women, so little time," he replied mockingly.

"Then you'd better go spread yourself around." Erica steered Noelle past him. When they were out of hearing distance, she asked, "What did you think of our local stud?"

"Does he always come on that strong?"

"Only to females between the ages of eight and eighty."

"Surely not to the paying customers?"

Erica shrugged. "He uses a little more finesse with them. Troy can act almost human when he wants to."

"What exactly does he do for them?"

"Anything they want, I suspect."

"That's hard to believe. The women who come here are all wealthy and cultured."

"That doesn't mean they don't have problems. Some have rotten marriages, others are afraid of growing old. There are dozens of reasons women starve themselves at a place like this and exercise till they drop."

"There are health reasons," Noelle pointed out.

"The majority of them come to keep in shape," Erica admitted. "But a lot are dissatisfied with their lives. Troy plays up to them and makes them feel like the prom queen again. Everybody's happy and nobody gets hurt."

Noelle's eyes darkened as she thought of Diane. "A woman with problems can be very vulnerable."

"I'm not saying that nothing shady ever goes on, but even if it does, they're all consenting adults. Troy is a grade-A jerk, but I'm sure he wouldn't take advantage of a paying customer. Sybyll would bounce him out of here so fast he'd get windburn."

"She doesn't know his hormones are on permanent simmer?" It had occurred to Noelle that the manager might be in on the blackmail scheme.

Erica snorted derisively. "Troy acts like a choirboy around Sybyll. That's the reason none of us ever bothers to lodge a sexual-harassment charge against him. He's smart when it comes to his own hide. None of the guests are going to complain, and Sybyll wouldn't believe *us*."

"So you have to put up with him?"

"We all think he's a joke. He won't bother you unless you encourage him. Troy isn't going to jeopardize his cushy job by getting too far out of line, so don't worry about him. You're really going to like it here."

"I'm sure I will," Noelle murmured politely.

"Did you teach aerobics in New York?"

"No, I was a dancer."

Noelle had decided to use her real name and be candid about her occupation. There would be less chance of a slip up that could cause someone to wonder about her. She'd merely pretend to be unemployed and disillusioned.

"How neat!" Erica exclaimed. "Why on earth would you want to give it up?"

"I got tired of going to casting calls and seeing the part go to the producer's girlfriend. How about you?" Noelle asked to head off any more questions. "Are you working toward some particular goal?"

Erica laughed. "I'm the feminists' despair. My ambition is to marry somebody wonderful and have lots of babies."

"That shouldn't be very difficult." Noelle glanced at the younger woman's lovely face and trim figure. "You must have had lots of offers."

"Not from the right man." Erica sighed. "I'm still waiting for whistles to blow and bells to ring."

"Aren't we all?" Noelle observed ruefully.

Erica gazed at her curiously. "You must have met some fabulous men in your business."

"The theater is very competitive. It's hard to get excited about somebody who's more interested in himself than he is in you."

That part was true, but it wasn't the whole story. Noelle had met perfectly suitable men—handsome, caring men who would probably have made model husbands. She had even been fond of a couple of them, but something was missing. A certain magic, the instant awareness that this man was special. She was as naive as Erica, Noelle thought disgustedly.

They reached her car and the subject was dropped. For the next half hour Noelle was busy unpacking and putting her things away. Erica sat on the bed and told her what to expect.

"You came at a good time," she said. "Next Monday is the start of men's week."

"Why is that good?" Noelle asked, putting lingerie into a drawer.

"We have a lot of free time. The men don't usually attend aerobics classes. I suppose they think it isn't macho. They work out in the gym, instead."

"Then what do we do all day?"

"We take them jogging or hiking. The ones who want to go. A lot of them just lie by the pool and kick back."

"Why do they need someone to take them jogging?" Noelle asked.

"They don't. We simply go along to keep an eye on them and see that they don't wander into the desert and get overheated."

"We act as nursemaids to grown men?"

"You might call it that." Erica laughed. "But don't knock it. Sometimes we have an entire afternoon to ourselves. All of us except Troy. He finally earns his salary during men's week."

"Doing what?"

"Everything. He supervises the gym and helps Thelma give massages. He also gives swimming and diving instructions on request, and he plays tennis with anybody who needs a partner."

"That's quite a full schedule."

Erica chuckled. "By the end of the day, Troy is too tired to be obnoxious. He's out early in the morning and doesn't finish work until dinnertime. The guys really keep him hopping, and they don't tell him how wonderful he is, either."

Noelle was lost in thought. With Troy out of the way, she'd have a perfect opportunity to search his room. "Does he bunk in this building like the rest of us?" she asked casually.

"At the end of the corridor. He has the corner room." Erica got up from the bed. "If you're all finished, would you like to see the grounds?"

"As soon as I make a telephone call. Is there a pay phone around?"

"There's a booth off the lobby, but you have a phone in here." Erica indicated the instrument on the nightstand.

"This is a long-distance call to my mother, and I don't want to start running up any charges on the phone." Noelle gave a little laugh. "I promised I'd let her know I arrived safely. You know how mothers are."

Diane picked up the phone on the first ring. "I've been waiting to hear from you," she said in a strained voice. "Did they hire you? Maybe we made a terrible mistake. How can you register as a guest after applying for work?"

"Relax. I got the job."

"You did? That's wonderful!" Diane went from anxiety to euphoria in an instant.

"It's a start, anyway." Noelle didn't share her friend's optimism.

"Have you met Troy?"

"Yes." Noelle tried but failed to keep her distaste from showing.

"I know what you're thinking," Diane said defensively. "How could I?"

"I'm not passing judgment. I just called to tell you everything is going according to plan so far. I probably won't have an opportunity to search Troy's room until next Monday, so don't expect to hear from me until then."

"I'll try to be patient." Diane sighed happily. "At least I know it's almost over."

"This is only the beginning," Noelle warned. "I can't predict what's going to happen. Maybe all I'll get here is a suntan."

"You can't fail. My entire future is at stake!"

"Mine, too, if I get caught," Noelle answered grimly.

Roman Wilding was in the same ambivalent mood. "How did I let myself get talked into this nonsense?" he asked himself irritably. "After a few days' rest I'll probably be bored silly." He sighed and massaged the back of his neck, muttering, "Oh well, how much difference can one week make in my life?"

Chapter Two

Roman glanced around the luxurious room assigned to him. Unlike the staff quarters, it was furnished with a king-size bed, a round table and four chairs, and both a desk and a dressing table. The pastel colors and quilted fabrics were excessively feminine, but he realized the management couldn't very well change the decor for one week out of the year.

The dainty pink-tiled bathroom amused him, but at least the tub was big enough to accommodate his long body. Roman turned on the taps and removed his clothes. Although he would normally have taken a shower, he decided a bath would be more relaxing after the plane ride and the dusty drive from the airport. With a sigh of satisfaction, he lowered himself into the tepid water.

Noelle was enjoying Carefree Dunes, in spite of her reason for being there. The scenery was breathtaking, the pace relaxed, and her dance workouts were enthusiastically received. So far, so good. Troy was really the only drawback. Noelle couldn't cut him down to size as she normally would have, so he made a real nuisance of himself.

"You're too nice," Erica scolded. "You should tell him what you think of him."

"I was taught not to use that kind of language," Noelle replied. "Besides, Troy won't be a problem this week. When do the men start arriving?"

"A couple are already here. I saw a Mercedes and a Cadillac in the parking lot. Most of them show up in the late afternoon, though."

Sybyll came out of her office, looking harried. "If it's not one thing it's another. Gertrude went home sick. I think she has a virus." Gertrude was one of the maids who lived in the village and commuted daily. "The worst of it is, housekeeping is already shorthanded. Would you girls mind helping out?"

"We don't do windows," Erica joked.

"Of course not," Sybyll said impatiently. "I just want you to stock the rooms with towels. And please hurry before the guests arrive."

Noelle followed Erica to the linen room where they each stacked their arms with towels. "I haven't seen any of the guest rooms," Noelle remarked.

"Get set for an envy attack," Erica advised. "You start at this end of the hall and I'll start at the other."

All of the elegantly appointed rooms were more or less alike. After leisurely inspecting the first few, Noelle realized time was flitting by. When she entered the next room, her attention was centered on the towels she was separating from the pile, so she didn't see the signs of occupancy.

Heading straight for the bathroom, she pushed open the door. Then stopped dead in her tracks.

The man in the tub gave her a startled glance that turned to interest. His eyes wandered over her flushed face to the O of her softly parted lips. After that they traveled over her slender figure. Noelle was wearing a halter top and brief shorts, so there was a lot to admire.

"I don't know what's called for in a situation like this except to say you're a very welcome surprise," Roman remarked pleasantly.

"I . . . I'm sorry," she stammered.

Her long lashes swept down, but his image was burned on her lids. She could still see his wide muscular shoulders and the droplets of water on his broad chest. They were like dew in the curling dark hair that tapered to a V— and then was joined by another patch submerged beneath the water. Making her equally uncomfortable was the total lack of embarrassment on his rugged face. Why not? He had a lot to be proud of!

As she backed toward the door, Roman called, "Don't go away with my towels."

"I'm sorry," she repeated. "I didn't know this room was occupied."

"We all make mistakes. *I* didn't notice there weren't any towels. Hand me one, will you?"

She held out a bath towel, still with her face averted.

"Could you come a little closer? Even Godzilla doesn't have arms that long."

"I'll just hang them on the bar." Out of nervousness, she spilled the entire pile on the floor.

As she knelt to retrieve them, Roman crossed his arms on the rim of the bathtub and rested his chin on them, gazing down at her. "Correct me if I'm wrong, but you seem excessively nervous."

Noelle was indignant. He was making a sticky situation worse by laughing at her! "I'm not used to barging in on a naked man," she answered stiffly.

"Once you've seen one, you've seen them all." His gray eyes danced with mischief. "You *have* seen a naked man, haven't you?"

"That's none of your business," she snapped.

"I suppose it *was* an intrusive question to ask a stranger. Let me introduce myself." He held out a wet hand. "I'm Roman Wi— Widenthal."

Noelle ignored his hand. She stood, turned her back to him and hastily hung an assortment of towels over the chrome bars. "I regret this intrusion, Mr. Widenthal. If you need anything further, please call the office."

"Do you make up my room regularly?"

"No, I'm an aerobics teacher here. We won't meet again."

"Your class is full?"

"Not many male guests are interested in aerobics," she answered primly. "We only hold classes on request."

"You've just been requested."

"You don't really want to take aerobics." She whirled around angrily, then quickly turned away.

"Well, no, but I'd like to see more of you. It seems only fair." He chuckled. "You've seen quite a lot of *me.*"

"Enjoy your stay, Mr. Widenthal." She headed for the door, barely restraining herself from running.

"Wait! You didn't tell me your name."

"Noelle Bartlett." She shot through the bedroom and out the front door.

Erica was approaching. She gave Noelle a curious look. "What's the matter? You look funny."

"I thought all of these rooms were empty, so I didn't knock. I walked right in on one of the guests!"

"So you caught him in his skivvies, big deal. I'm sure he didn't mind, and Jockey shorts aren't much different than bathing trunks. A big-city gal like you shouldn't be so shook up," Erica teased.

"City or country, men don't wear their shorts in the tub," Noelle answered crisply.

Erica gaped at her. "You walked in on him when he was in the bathtub? Was he at least taking a bubble bath?"

"No."

"Oh, my gosh, that's a real bummer. How did he react?"

"With a lot more poise than I showed. I stood there gawking like a teenage girl looking at a male-nude centerfold."

"He was that great?"

"The only thing he didn't have was a staple in his navel."

"Too bad you won't recognize him again." Erica grinned. "It doesn't sound as if you spent much time looking at his face."

"I only hope he doesn't remember *mine*."

Roman's door opened and he appeared in the entry. "A face like yours would be difficult to forget." He was barefoot and his dark hair was tousled, but he'd pulled on a pair of beige linen slacks and was buttoning a cream-colored silk shirt over his impressive chest.

Noelle's cheeks bloomed with renewed color. Although their voices had been hushed, neither she nor Erica had noticed that Roman's windows were open. Noelle was overwhelmed with embarrassment, and Erica was no help. She was staring at him in speechless admiration.

Roman broke the stunned silence. "Could either of you tell me where I can get something to eat? I just flew in from

Chicago and I didn't have lunch. You know what airline food is like.''

When Noelle didn't answer, Erica said, ''The dining room is closed at this hour, but you can call room service. They'll be glad to fix you something.''

''I can see why Carefree Dunes is so popular. Everything a man could want is provided—you might even say anticipated.'' He glanced at Noelle, his gray eyes sparkling with suppressed laughter.

''Excuse me. I have to finish my rounds,'' she muttered, hurrying away.

Roman spent a pleasant afternoon reading under a shady tree, a rare luxury for him. After several hours, his taut muscles began to relax and he felt better about the assignment he'd allowed himself to be talked into.

At dinnertime he strolled to the dining room, looking forward to the week ahead, instead of regarding it as time wasted. Did the presence of a long-legged blonde with cornflower-blue eyes add to the attraction? It certainly didn't hurt, he admitted. He'd known a lot of beautiful women, but there was something about this one that set his nerve ends tingling, the way they did when he stumbled across a major story. It was probably just the suggestiveness of their meeting, he thought dismissively.

The dining room held tables of varying sizes. Roman selected a table for two. Most of the other guests had arrived and were introducing themselves and exchanging personal histories, but Roman was reluctant to join them. He wanted one day of complete vacation.

As he was having a leisurely drink and gazing around the room, a young man appeared and paused on the threshold. He looked like a college student, rather than one of Carefree Dunes' high-powered clientele. At first, Roman thought he was part of the staff, but his uncertain manner seemed to indicate otherwise. He was like a freshman on enrollment day, not knowing where to go or what was expected of him.

Roman's interest was piqued. What was this youngster doing at a spa for stressed-out businessmen?

In spite of the solitude he'd promised himself, Roman asked, "Would you like to join me for dinner?"

The newcomer's face lit up. "That would be great." He walked over and held out his hand. "Jeff Mainwaring. I didn't know if they assigned you a table or you just picked one."

After supplying his own name, Roman said, "You can sit anywhere you like. Most of the men at the larger tables are here alone. You're welcome to join them."

"I'd prefer not to. Older men treat me like a kid."

Roman hid his amusement. "I'm afraid you won't find many of your contemporaries here this week."

"I didn't expect to." Jeff sighed.

"Then why did you come? You don't seem exactly enthused about the prospect."

"I'm not. It was my mother's idea. She thinks I need to network with mature males—her words, not mine."

Roman raised one eyebrow. "Any special reason?"

"I guess she's hoping their polish will rub off on me."

Roman gazed at the young man appraisingly. His casual sport coat and slacks were expertly tailored to his athletic body and he was well-groomed. Although Jeff lacked the assurance that came with age, he was charming and friendly, a thoroughly likable young man.

"You look perfectly presentable to me," Roman commented.

"But not someone you'd trust to make decisions. Would you offer me a seat on your board of directors?"

"Is that your goal?" Roman asked evasively.

"It's supposed to be when you're in banking."

Roman hesitated. "You're a teller?"

"No, I own the bank. At least my family does. I was being groomed to take over sometime in the future, but my father died suddenly last year. Now I'm expected to deal with people who still think of me as Herbert Mainwaring's kid."

"That's not too unusual when the parent is a strong person."

"Which parent are you talking about?" Jeff asked wryly. "My mother could run the bank better than I ever could. I keep telling her that."

"Don't sell yourself short." Roman was acquainted with that type of mother, the kind that dominated their offspring's lives, living vicariously through them.

Jeff gave a shamefaced smile. "You'll have to forgive me. I don't know why I'm dumping on a perfect stranger."

Roman returned his smile. "I'm not perfect, believe me. Shall we take a look at the menu?"

The small group of women around the table in the employees' dining room were discussing the current crop of guests.

"I took a peek at the list," Mitzi Rawlings, the beauty operator said. "A real bunch of movers and shakers. We have a producer, a plastic surgeon and a banker in the group."

"Do they have to give their occupation when they make a reservation?" Noelle asked.

"No, but Sybyll makes it her business to find out. She knows everything that goes on around here."

Noelle's earlier suspicions were revived. Maybe Troy *wasn't* working alone.

Erica interrupted her speculation. "Is there a movie star on the list? Noelle got a look at a man who could pass for one. In fact, she got a *good* look at him."

Before the others could ask questions, the door opened. All eyes focused with interest on Jeff, who looked startled.

"Oh...I'm sorry. I was looking for the, uh..." His voice trailed off.

"It's the door at the other end of the hall," Erica told him.

After he'd beaten a hasty retreat, Mitzi laughed. "Can you imagine a guy being embarrassed to ask where the men's room is? What a geek."

"That's not fair," Erica protested. "You'd be uncomfortable, too, if you had to ask a bunch of strange men for directions to the powder room."

"Maybe, but I'll bet he won't be coming in for a massage," Thelma commented.

"Not if he has to take his clothes off." Mitzi grinned. "We already know he's the shy type."

"Give the man a break," Erica said. "He's probably very nice."

"Okay, we'll back off and leave you a clear field," Mitzi teased. "You two would be perfect together—a regular Ken and Barbie."

"You'll eat those words after you find out he's a nuclear physicist, or one of those electronic whiz kids," Erica warned.

The conversation drifted to other topics, but as she and Noelle were walking back to their rooms after dinner, Erica brought up the subject again. "I'll bet he's a jogger."

Noelle didn't have to ask whom she meant. "You'll find out tomorrow morning. What happens if no one shows up?"

"We wait and see if anybody comes to aerobics class later in the day."

"So what we do all week is hurry up and wait."

"You got it," Erica answered. "See you at seven."

Noelle wasn't thrilled about getting up that early. It wasn't the norm in her profession. But once she'd showered, pulled on a pink warm-up suit and opened the drapes, her grumpiness disappeared.

The sky was a heavenly shade of blue with little puffy white clouds dotting the expanse. In the distance, austere mountains loomed over open desert land, contrasting with the spa's lush green lawns and colorful plants. Noelle took a deep breath of the flower-scented air on her way to the pool area, where any interested joggers were to gather.

Erica was already there, along with four men. Noelle felt her stomach muscles tense when she saw Roman was one of them. The young man of the dining-room incident was another.

"This is Noelle Bartlett," Erica announced. She introduced her to Jeff and the other two men.

"You forgot Roman," Jeff said when she omitted him.

"They've already met." Erica grinned.

"Unexpectedly, which made our meeting all the more memorable." Roman's eyes held a mischievous glint. "I know *I'll* never forget it."

Noelle ignored him, addressing herself to the others. "I'm sure you're all anxious to get started. Erica, you take Mr. Mainwaring and Mr. Widenthal. Mr. Moroni and Mr. Shelby can come with me."

As the two men she designated moved toward her, Roman remarked, "It said in my brochure that we have our choice of jogging or hiking. I'd prefer to hike. Anyone else care to join me?'' When they all declined, he said, "I guess we're a twosome, Ms. Bartlett.''

Noelle was annoyed. Why should *she* get stuck with him. He was only doing this to irritate her, but she didn't intend to let him get away with it.

"Erica knows much more about the countryside than I do," she said smoothly. "I'll take the joggers and she can show you the flora and fauna.''

Erica glared at her indignantly. "I'm better at jogging than I am at nature walks. *You* take Mr. Widenthal.''

"I didn't mean to create a problem," Roman said mildly. "I can go by myself.''

Noelle realized she was trapped. It was part of her job to be agreeable, no matter how difficult the guest. "It's no problem," she said, trying to sound gracious. "I'll be happy to walk with you.''

"It's all settled then.'' Erica led her group off at a trot.

Noelle and Roman followed at a more leisurely pace. After the silence had lasted for several minutes, he said, "This is a unique experience for me. I've never forced myself on a woman before.''

Noelle could easily believe that. Roman looked very virile in a gray warm-up suit that matched his eyes. The baggy outfit camouflaged the trimness of his body, but it didn't conceal his broad shoulders. The fleeting thought crossed her mind that he must have brought pleasure to a lot of women.

"I'm sorry you got that impression," she said evenly. "I'm here to make your stay at Carefree Dunes an enjoyable experience.''

"I've been audited by IRS people who were friendlier," he commented dryly. "Do you dislike men in general, or have you taken a dislike to me personally?''

"How could I? I don't even know you.''

"Precisely." He smiled engagingly. "I'm really a very nice person. Can't we be friends?"

His considerable charm melted her reserve. "I'm sorry for the way I've been acting. We got off to a bad start, but it certainly wasn't your fault."

"Consider the whole incident forgotten. Tell me about yourself," he said casually. "How long have you worked at Carefree Dunes?"

"Only a short time."

"Do you like it here?"

"Yes, it's beautiful country."

"What's the spa like normally? When the women are here."

"A lot different. Most of them come to lose weight. The food is the same as you're getting, except the portions are tiny. We try to keep them too busy to realize they're hungry." Noelle smiled.

"How do you do that?"

"With a full agenda. In the morning we offer jogging, aerobics classes and lectures. Then in the afternoon they can take a mineral bath and have a massage. After that they usually get their hair done and have a facial and manicure. It makes for a full day."

"I can see that. What's the average weight loss by the end of the week?"

Noelle was puzzled by Roman's interest in the spa. He continued to question her. Was he planning to open his own fitness center? She decided to ask some questions of her own.

"What business are *you* in?"

"Advertising." Before she could pursue the subject, he asked, "Are those goldfish in there?"

They'd reached a lovely little pool ringed by boulders and shaded by a weeping willow. It was an unlikely setting at the edge of the desert.

"What a pretty spot." Roman dropped to one knee and dabbled his fingers in the water.

"It's my favorite." Noelle perched on a rock. "I come here when I have free time."

He lowered himself to the grass and sat with his back propped against another rock, gazing at her curiously. "That doesn't sound very exciting. Carefree Dunes is pleasant for a week, but I can't imagine living here. Don't you get bored?"

"I'm too busy for that."

His eyes wandered from her long honey-blond hair to her delicate features. The only makeup she wore was a touch of pale pink lipstick, but her clear skin didn't need cosmetics, and her blue eyes were fringed by naturally thick lashes, much darker than her hair.

"I can't imagine a woman as beautiful as you being content in a place like this."

"You're very kind," she murmured.

"I wasn't trying to flatter you. I really don't get it. What do you do in your spare time—besides sitting by this pool?"

"We go into the town sometimes. It has a movie theater and a pub that's lots of fun. All the locals gather there."

"Who do you go with?" Roman asked.

"Some of the other women—a group of us, usually."

"Don't you ever date?"

Noelle smiled. "That would be a little difficult. The maintenance people are the only men around, and they're all married."

"It said in the brochure that the spa has a fitness trainer, Troy something. Is he married, too?"

"No, he's single." She stood. "Shall we continue our walk? Perhaps you'd like to see a little of the desert."

Roman complied, but he didn't drop the subject as she'd hoped. "It seems like an abnormal life for young women like you."

She shrugged. "It's an easy job and there are a lot of pluses. Look at this beautiful scenery." She waved an arm at the purple-and-gold landscape of mountains and sand dotted with saguaro cacti.

"You don't miss male companionship?" he persisted.

"I'm enjoying it right now," she said lightly.

He raised a dark eyebrow. "Are we so hard to take that once a year is enough?"

"Just like a man," she teased. "It hurts your macho pride to think a woman can't live without you."

"In your case, it's the terrible waste that bothers me." His inspection was openly admiring. "A face and figure like yours shouldn't be hidden away."

"That's very flattering, but nobody made me take this job. It was my own choice."

"What brought you here?"

"I heard there was an opening, and I'd never been to Arizona. I thought it would be interesting."

"What did you do before?"

"I was a dancer." Noelle looked at him uncertainly. "You sound like a detective. Why are you asking me all these questions?"

The sudden thought occurred to her that Diane's husband might have gotten wind of her affair and sent someone to snoop around for evidence.

Roman's reaction didn't reassure her. His intent expression became unreadable, but he answered smoothly, "It must be obvious that I'm interested in you."

"A man like you must have plenty of girlfriends at home. Where did you say you're from?" she asked offhandedly.

"Chicago." He didn't confirm or deny her first statement.

"I love that big museum you have there. On Diversey Street, isn't it?"

A little smile tilted his firm mouth. "I believe you're referring to the Chicago Art Institute, and it's on Michigan Avenue."

"Oh, yes, that's right." Noelle had a feeling he knew she was testing him.

"Where are *you* from?" he asked.

"New York City."

"Too bad I didn't know you when you lived there. I get to New York quite often. Do you miss the excitement?"

"Not yet. I'm enjoying the slower pace and wide open spaces. I'd never heard a coyote howl before."

"Was that what I heard last night?" Roman·glanced around the flat desert. "Where do they live?"

"In the mountains, but they come down at night to hunt. You hardly ever see a coyote out in the open, but sometimes you can catch a glimpse of a bighorn sheep silhouetted against the sky—way up there." Noelle was pointing at a cliff, not noticing the gopher hole in her path. She stepped in it and stumbled.

Roman caught her before she fell. Supporting her body against his, he asked, "Are you all right?"

The intimate contact rattled her. His hard body was so unmistakably male. "I'm fine," she mumbled. But when she disentangled herself and tried to stand alone, her leg buckled.

Roman caught her again and lowered her to the ground. "Let me take a look at that ankle. You might have sprained it."

"Oh no, I couldn't have! That would ruin everything."

"Relax, it isn't the end of the world. You'd just have to stay off your feet for a few days."

"I *can't!*" Noelle had counted on being able to search Troy's room this week. It would be her only safe opportunity.

"It's admirable to be conscientious, but aren't you overdoing it?" He had removed her shoe and was probing her ankle gently. "Does that hurt?"

She winced. "Yes."

"Let's get you out of this hot sun and then we'll see how bad it is." He scooped her up into his arms and started toward the spa.

"You can't carry me all the way back," she protested.

"This is *my* fringe benefit," he teased. "You wouldn't normally let me hold you like this."

In spite of her pain and worry, Noelle was acutely aware of his arms cradling her, and the hard chest pressing against her breast. His face was uncomfortably close, also. She could see each long spiky lash fringing his gray eyes, and when he turned his head to look at her, his lips almost grazed hers. Noelle had a sudden impulse to smooth the lock of dark hair off his tanned forehead. She bit her lip to control the urge.

Roman misunderstood. "Hang on, little one," he said gently. "We're almost there."

When they reached the pool, he carefully lowered her onto one of the rocks. After removing her sock, he guided her foot into the water.

"That feels good," she said.

"Let it soak for a few minutes. It will help reduce any swelling."

"I hope so," she answered fervently.

"Surely you're not worried about losing your job if you're laid up for a few days."

"You never know. I haven't been here very long."

"Can't Erica take over for you? Only four of us showed up for jogging this morning. Actually, we could have gone along—although the company wouldn't have been as pleasant." He smiled at her.

"You can say that after having to carry me home?" she asked ruefully.

"That was the best part." He tucked a strand of shining hair behind her ear.

The innocent gesture felt like a caress. Roman was only being gallant and she was used to male attention, so Noelle couldn't understand why she was reacting like an immature teenager.

Lifting her foot out of the water, she said, "I'd better find out how much damage I did."

"Hang on to me." He clasped her waist and helped her up.

Noelle placed her hands on his shoulders and gingerly put weight on her foot.

Roman watched her closely. "How does it feel?"

"A little sore, but nothing I can't handle." She smiled up at him. "All this fuss and it turns out I'm just a klutz."

"That isn't the word I'd use," he murmured. A twig snapped and they both turned their heads toward the sound.

Troy was standing a few feet away, leering at them. "Don't mind me, I was just passing by."

"The lady turned her ankle," Roman explained. "I was simply making sure she can stand on it."

"Whatever you say." Troy's unpleasant smile broadened.

"That *is* what I say," Roman answered ominously.

Troy's smirk disappeared and he turned obsequious. "I'm sorry I disturbed you. Please forgive the intrusion." He hurried off down the path.

"If I run across that guy again, we're going to have a long talk," Roman growled.

"It doesn't matter," Noelle said placatingly.

"The hell it doesn't!" He glared down the path, but when he turned back to her, his expression softened. "We weren't doing anything suspect—unfortunately."

"They say virtue is its own reward," she answered lightly.

He chuckled richly. "Don't you believe it."

Noelle let go of his shoulders and stepped back. "Well . . . I guess I'd better see if anybody feels like doing aerobics."

Roman fell into step beside her. "How are you going to jump around on that foot?"

"At least I can walk on it now. Anyway, I probably won't have a class, but I have to put in an appearance." She glanced over at him. "I don't suppose you'd be interested?"

"No thanks," he answered promptly.

"I didn't think *you'd* have hang-ups about your masculinity," she teased.

"I like to prove it in more rewarding ways. But that has nothing to do with my refusal. I came here for rest and relaxation. The next few days you'll find me flat on my back, reading a book."

"You aren't alone. A lot of the men here aren't looking for any more exercise than lifting a knife and fork."

"I'm not quite that lazy. I'll probably work out in the gym after I get my second wind."

"When you're ready for it, that's the gym straight ahead." Noelle pointed to the building Troy was going into.

Roman scowled. "Maybe I'll stop in right now and find out who that guy is."

"I'll save you the trouble. He's the spa's fitness trainer."

"You knew who he was?" Roman looked at her in surprise. "Why didn't you say so?"

"It didn't seem important."

"Does he always throw innuendoes like that around? Why don't you complain to the management?"

She shrugged. "It wouldn't help. The guests like him and that's what counts."

"Here's *one* guest who doesn't." Roman had a dangerous glint in his eyes. "I intend to teach that jerk how to act around a woman."

"No, don't!" The last thing Noelle wanted was to make Troy angry at her. "He's not so bad really. He just isn't very tactful."

"You're defending his behavior?" Roman asked incredulously.

"Troy doesn't mean anything by it," she explained carefully. "We all joke around a lot."

Roman's eyes narrowed as he gazed at her. "I'm beginning to understand. He has a nice little harem here."

"Your innuendo isn't any more acceptable than his," she flared.

"You're right, I shouldn't have said that, but what else am I to think? A disinterested party would be happy to see him get what he deserves."

"Thanks, but I can fight my own battles."

"If you happen to want to," he murmured sardonically.

Noelle gritted her teeth. "Enjoy your book, Mr. Widenthal." She marched away with her head held high.

Several men were riding stationary bicycles or working out on other equipment. Troy circulated among them, giving encouragement and adjusting the machines on request.

His eyes were wary when he turned and saw Roman, but he smiled and extended his hand. "I'm Troy Slattery, your fitness trainer. Glad to have you with us." He looked relieved when Roman didn't exhibit any hostility. "How can I help you today?"

"I'll just wander around and look things over. You have quite an impressive gym."

"All the latest equipment," Troy answered.

"Do women lift weights?" Roman indicated the barbells lying on the floor.

"The ones who want to develop their breasts." Troy gave him a lascivious smile. "I don't know if it does any good, but hey, I'm happy to be of assistance."

"The women who work here don't need any help in that department," Roman commented casually. "You're a lucky man."

Troy looked wary again. "I don't have an exclusive on them."

"Maybe not this week, but you must make out like a bandit when you're the only game in town."

Troy's face relaxed in a grin. "I can't complain."

Roman's eyes turned cold, but his manner remained pleasant. "Well, I'll see you around."

"Aren't you going to exercise?"

"No, I got what I came for."

Troy watched Roman leave. "Funny guy," he muttered. "I can't figure him."

Erica was the only person in the aerobics studio. "Where have you been?" she asked Noelle. "I've been waiting for you."

"Why? We obviously don't have a class."

"I know. I just wanted to hear how you made out with the handsome hunk."

"I didn't *make out*," Noelle answered testily.

"Too bad." Erica grinned. "But I suppose any man that gorgeous has an ego as large as he is."

"No, he's fairly pleasant." Noelle didn't want to discuss Roman. Not after his parting remark. "How was your group?"

"Just great!" Erica's face lit up. "Jeff and I talked about everything under the sun."

"How could you carry on a conversation while you were jogging?"

"We talked on the way back. The other two men quit after about a mile, but Jeff and I kept on. Then it got too hot to run, so we walked back. I found out all about him. You'll never guess what he does for a living." Without giving Noelle a chance to answer, she said, "He's a banker!"

Noelle smiled at the younger woman's enthusiasm. "What a disappointment. You thought he was a nuclear physicist."

"I knew it was something important."

"At his age, he must be just starting out."

"Not exactly. His family owns the bank."

"That's one way to get ahead," Noelle commented dryly.

"I'm sure he does a good job," Erica protested. "He's very nice and we really hit it off. Jeff asked me to go into the village for a drink tonight."

"That sounds promising. He's a fast worker."

"It's no big deal." Erica tried to hide her elation. "I don't expect anything to develop between Jeff and me. I simply enjoy his company."

"Then go and have a good time." Noelle smiled.

"I intend to. I'll tell you all about it tomorrow morning."

"I'll meet you at seven, but if only a handful of men show up, will you take the whole group? I sort of twisted my ankle today and I don't want to run on it if I don't have to."

"Sure, no problem. But what if Roman wants to hike again?"

"I'm quite certain he won't," Noelle answered evenly.

Chapter Three

A larger group of joggers showed up the next morning, but Roman wasn't among them. That was no surprise. He'd been thoroughly disgusted with her after she'd defended Troy, and she couldn't afford even to hint at her true feelings. It bothered her more than it should have, since she'd never see Roman again after this week. The only benefit was that now she'd have a chance to search Troy's room—if none of the guests preferred to hike.

Noelle held her breath when Erica mentioned the option, but they all chose the more strenuous exercise. Noelle waited impatiently for them to leave, because she had another tricky job ahead of her. Getting into Troy's room.

She'd considered concocting some story to tell the maid—they had keys to all the rooms. But that was too chancy. The woman might mention it to Troy.

Another set of duplicate keys was kept on a numbered Peg-Board in a small storeroom off Sybyll's office. That was a safer bet. The chance of anybody noticing one missing key was practically nil.

As soon as the men were safely on their way, Noelle walked over to the manager's office. Sybyll was working busily at her desk, something Noelle hadn't expected this early in the morning. She paused on the threshold in dismay.

The older woman glanced up. "Did you want something?"

"No, I, uh, I was just passing by and I... You're not usually here this early."

"The computer developed a glitch and erased heaven knows how many of our accounts receivable. It will take me days to track them down."

"Is there anything I can do to help?" Noelle asked tentatively.

"No, I'll just have to puzzle it out for myself."

"You look frazzled. Why don't you take a break and go have a cup of coffee?"

"Didn't you hear what I just told you?" Sybyll asked in exasperation. "I don't have time to waste."

"I just thought you needed a little break." Noelle looked longingly toward the back room.

"What I need is a new computer," the older woman muttered. "These gadgets are supposed to make life easier, not harder."

"Maybe I can help. Would you like me to tidy up the storeroom?"

"Don't touch a thing in there! I have everything laid out right where I want it."

"There must be *something* I can do," Noelle persisted.

"Why? Aren't you giving a class or something?"

"Nobody signed up. They're all out jogging with Erica and Troy." He'd joined them that morning, so Noelle's services really weren't required.

"Well, I suppose you can make yourself useful here." Sybyll rummaged around on her desk. "Take these menus and run them through the copy machine."

Noelle took as long as possible over the job, hoping Sybyll would leave the office for some reason. But the manager remained firmly planted at her desk.

"Is there anything else I can do?" Noelle asked, when she couldn't stall any longer.

"You can file those invoices." Without looking up, Sybyll indicated a stack of papers on the corner of the desk.

Noelle accepted the job gratefully, but her nerves were jangling like wind chimes in a gale. The minutes were ticking away and Troy would be returning soon. He *should* be busy for the rest of the morning, giving rubdowns and handing out towels in the locker room. But what if he stopped by his room for something first? Noelle had counted on a solid hour of uninterrupted time.

Just when it was beginning to look as if the plan would have to be scrubbed, Sybyll pushed back her chair and massaged her neck. "I have to take a break."

"That's a good idea," Noelle masked her eagerness under a casual tone.

"Will you stay and answer the phone while I'm gone?"

"Sure, no problem."

As soon as Sybyll left, Noelle went into the storeroom and pocketed Troy's key. It took only a moment, but then she had to wait for the manager to return. That meant a further delay. This day was turning into a disaster. Was it an omen?

Sybyll lingered over her coffee break for a full half hour, reducing Noelle to a jittery wreck. "Well, back to work," the older woman announced when she finally reappeared. "Were there any calls?"

"No, everything was quiet."

"Good, I hope it stays that way."

"I'll get out of here so you can get your work done," Noelle said. She left hurriedly before Sybyll could decide she was useful, after all.

Noelle's heart was thumping rapidly as she unlocked Troy's door and slipped inside quickly. *I'd never make it as a criminal,* she thought wryly.

The staff only got weekly cleaning service and the room was a mess. Troy's clothes littered the floor, drawers were half-open and the bed was unmade. Noelle glanced around in distaste. Troy was a slob in more ways than one. It worked to her advantage, though, since he'd never notice if anything was disarranged.

The idea of going through anyone's private belongings was repugnant, but Noelle forced herself to do it. She started with the dresser drawers. They held only what was to be expected, piles of socks, shorts and shirts.

The top drawer was a jumble of odds and ends—a pair of sunglasses, half-eaten packets of breath mints, scraps of paper. Just an ordinary collection of miscellaneous items.

When she was satisfied that the negatives weren't hidden in the dresser she moved to the nightstand. The drawers there were filled with girlie magazines and paperback books by authors who specialized in erotica. Every one of them had to be paged through, since they would be perfect hiding places for something small and flat.

Noelle hesitated. It was getting close to lunchtime and Troy might stop by his room first. She decided not to take any chances. There was always this afternoon and, if not then, tomorrow morning—although, she couldn't ask Erica to take over for her indefinitely.

Before leaving, Noelle peeked through the drapes to be sure nobody was around. The coast was clear, so she slipped outside with a sigh of relief.

In her haste to lock the door and get out of the vicinity, she fumbled with the key. The doors at the spa were the kind that had to be locked from the outside. This was to insure that guests didn't forget their keys and have to go to the bother of making a trip to the office.

Noelle jabbed at the lock with increasing frustration until it occurred to her that she might have the wrong key. She had put Troy's in her pocket along with her own. That proved to be the solution. The other key worked smoothly. As she turned away, a man's voice froze her in place.

"Aren't you getting a late start this morning?" Roman closed the short distance between them.

"I wasn't . . . I don't usually . . ." Noelle was almost incoherent after the fright he'd given her.

"Are you all right?" He looked at her closely. "You're shaking."

"No, I . . . You just surprised me, that's all. I didn't hear you coming."

He wasn't satisfied with that explanation, but he let it pass. "I haven't been in this area before. Are these the staff quarters?"

Noelle didn't want him to find out later that this was Troy's room. She could just imagine what Roman would deduce from that! "Well, we . . ." She paused awkwardly.

Roman's manner hadn't been overly warm to begin with. Now it cooled perceptibly. "You needn't worry about my knowing your room number, Noelle. I'm not going to come creeping over here in the middle of the night."

"I never thought you would." She took a deep breath to steady herself. "Not when you're going out of your way to avoid me."

"What gave you that impression?"

"You weren't among the joggers this morning, for one thing."

"I decided to sleep in."

"That's your privilege, of course," she said primly.

He could tell she didn't believe him. "Look, Noelle, I'm sorry about yesterday. I was way out of line. Your personal life is none of my business."

That was true, but for some reason she didn't want him to think she was having an affair with Troy. "It isn't what you think, honestly. Troy... has an inflated opinion of himself," she explained carefully. "Under different circumstances I might feel free to express myself, but I have to work with the man."

"You don't have to let him treat you like a sex object."

"It's just his way. We all laugh about him."

"You're remarkably tolerant," Roman answered grimly. "I'd put him out of commission for a few days."

"You're big enough to do it." Noelle smiled. "I'm not."

"I'd be glad to oblige."

"I'll keep that in mind." It suddenly occurred to her that this was no place for a chat. If Troy turned up, Roman would find out whose room this was. She started to move away. "Well, enjoy your day."

He walked alongside her. "What are you going to do this afternoon?"

"Probably help out around the office."

"How would you like to drive into Tucson with me? I'm interested in seeing the place. I hear it's a thriving little city."

"Are you getting cabin fever already?"

He smiled ruefully. "A vacation sounded great when I planned it, but I guess I don't have the temperament to sit and do nothing."

"That's why you're here—for rest and relaxation."

"I got a good night's sleep on Sunday when I arrived, and I laid around all day yesterday. How much rest does a person need?"

"We offer tennis and swimming."

"I might consider it if you'll join me."

"I don't play tennis, and we're not allowed to swim with the guests," she said regretfully.

"That doesn't make sense. If I needed a tennis partner, you could accommodate me, but you can't swim with me? What kind of reasoning is that?"

"A guest can't very well play tennis alone, but an employee's services aren't required in the swimming pool."

"You never get to use the pool?" Roman asked incredulously. "In this climate?"

Noelle grinned. "Don't tell anybody, but we sneak in sometimes when all the guests are asleep."

"That's the dumbest policy I ever heard of," he said with disgust.

"I don't make the rules, I merely follow them."

"You're not allowed to have any social contact with the guests?" Roman persisted.

"Not on company time."

"Okay, when do you get off work?"

"At the end of the day."

"Then how would you like to go out to dinner with me tonight?" he asked.

She hesitated. Fraternizing with the guests on one's own time wasn't strictly forbidden, but it wasn't encouraged, either. What concerned Noelle was Troy's reaction. His ego would be bruised, and she couldn't afford to offend him.

"Wouldn't you like to get away from this place for a while?" Roman coaxed.

"You're paying a fortune for your meals here. You should take advantage of them."

"All right, I get the message. I won't bother you anymore."

"It isn't anything personal." When he obviously didn't believe her, she said on impulse, "We could go into the village for a drink after dinner if you like." Troy didn't have to know.

Roman gave her a melting smile. "I'd like that very much."

The village pub was crowded when Noelle and Roman arrived that evening, but they found a table in the back. Most of the patrons wanted to be near the dance floor. Men in cowboy boots and jeans were enthusiastically twirling similarly dressed women, and everyone seemed to be having a good time.

"It isn't what you're used to, but it's fun," Noelle observed after they were seated.

"You and I come from the same place, more or less. Why do you assume I won't fit in?"

"Maybe because you're so sophisticated. I picture you at black-tie events, drinking champagne with glamorous women. You're the kind of man who flies the Concorde to Europe." When he looked uncomfortable, she exclaimed, "I knew it!"

"It was a business trip," he said. "I needed to get somewhere in a hurry."

"Don't apologize, I think it's great. It sure beats tourist class on the red-eye."

"I've done that, too. In fact, that was pure luxury compared to some of the forms of transportation I've used."

"Like what?" she asked curiously.

A curtain dropped behind his eyes. "I'll tell you about it some day. Right now we need a drink." He raised an arm to beckon the waitress.

After the woman had taken their order and left, Roman glanced at the wildly gyrating couples and remarked, "I'd ask you to dance, but there seems to be some weird kind of mating ritual taking place out there."

"Are you afraid you'll get carried away and commit yourself to something?" Noelle joked.

"No, I'm afraid we'll both get stomped by cowboy boots. Whatever happened to slow dancing?"

"You're too young to yearn for the good old days."

"And you're too young to know about them." He folded his arms on the table and gave her his full attention. "Tell me about yourself, Noelle. Why did you abandon your career?"

She evaded his penetrating gaze. "I haven't. I'll probably go back to New York some day."

"It's tough to get started in show business. Did you have any success at all?"

"It was difficult at first. The competition is tremendous. I went on dozens of tryouts before I finally landed a spot in the chorus of an off-Broadway show." Noelle smiled, lost in the memory of that glorious day. "You'd think I'd been picked for the lead in *My Fair Lady.*"

"It must have been a thrill," Roman said quietly.

"It was. Nothing has ever equaled it, even my first time on Broadway."

His eyes narrowed. "You made it to Broadway?"

Noelle was brought up short. Roman's interest had made her forget the need to be circumspect. She hastened to minimize the damage. "I was one of a dozen girls in the chorus, and the show closed after only a few performances."

"It was a start, though. The key to success is never give up. You have to keep storming the gates."

"*Now* you sound like an advertising man."

"It still happens to be good advice."

Noelle's smile faded as she remembered the hard climb up. "Obviously you've never faced rejection. You don't know what it feels like to stand center stage, give it your all and then hear someone say, 'Thanks. Don't call us, we'll call you. Next dancer, please!' "

"It must be very frustrating, but you can't let it get you down."

She examined his strong face. The square jaw and steely eyes belonged to a fighter. Had he ever had a moment of self-doubt? She couldn't imagine it. "You don't really know what I'm talking about."

"You think I've never been told I'm not good enough?" he demanded.

"I can't conceive of anyone telling you that to your face."

He smiled wryly. "Rejections aren't always delivered in person. Often they come in the mail."

"That might be better than being strung along with empty promises. Sometimes a producer will say, 'You're not right for this part, but call me next week. I might have something for you then.' "

Roman's lip curled. "It's contemptible to raise a person's hopes with no intention of delivering. Somebody like that doesn't deserve his own job."

"You're a very nice man," Noelle said softly. "I wish everyone was as straightforward and honest."

His expression changed and he sat back in his chair. "I'm afraid I sounded sanctimonious. It isn't up to me to judge anyone else. Lord knows I'm not perfect."

"You don't use people, though. That's a quality I respect."

He glanced across the room. "Would you like to dance? They're finally playing something I recognize."

Noelle thought his discomfort was endearing. Roman was an amazingly modest man, considering his many attributes. He was almost too good to be true.

He smiled as he took her into his arms. "I'm a little self-conscious. I've never danced with a professional before."

"I can't imagine you ever losing your cool."

"A lot of people would tell you differently. I have a towering temper."

"*That* I can believe. I wouldn't want to make you angry at me." She was very conscious of his hard frame and the whipcord muscles in his thighs.

"You have nothing to worry about. I try to be very gentle with women." His voice was like warm honey.

Noelle's active imagination supplied the details he hinted at. Roman would make love as he did everything else— masterfully. He would use that splendid body to arouse and tantalize his partner until she practically begged for fulfillment.

"How can I convince you?" he asked.

"What?" She stared up at him with dazzled eyes.

"That I'm harmless." His fingers trailed down her cheek to trace the shape of her lower lip.

Noelle took a deep breath to shake off his spell. "The last time I heard that line was from a producer who wanted me to spend the weekend with him."

Roman chuckled. "You can't blame a guy for asking."

"He was married," she answered crisply.

"But I'm not. What would your answer be if *I* asked you to spend the weekend with me?"

"I'd say yes, of course." As he looked at her with surprise and dawning excitement, she added, "All the employees are expected to work weekends."

"You set me up for that," he said reprovingly.

"It serves you right. We both know you weren't serious."

"You'd make a lousy gambler. Just say the word and I'll book a reservation at a hotel in Tucson."

She stared at him curiously. "Is Carefree Dunes that much of a disappointment? You're paying a fortune to stay there, but you don't seem interested in any of the attractions."

He ruffled her hair playfully. "I won't answer that, because I always try to avoid the obvious."

"I'm serious, Roman. What are you doing here?"

"It seemed like a good idea at the time. I'd been working hard and I decided I needed a vacation. A little of that goes a long way, though. I discovered I'm not cut out for a life of leisure."

"You've only been here three days."

"What can I tell you?" He grinned. "I unwind faster than most men."

"Will you make it to the end of the week?"

"With a little help from my friends. How would you like to go horseback riding tomorrow? It says in the brochure there are stables nearby. We can ride in the morning and then have lunch somewhere."

"I can't." She refused with regret. "I explained the rules to you."

"You said the swimming pool was off-limits, but surely it isn't company policy to allow a guest to go horseback riding alone. What if I got lost in the desert?"

She couldn't help smiling at the notion. Roman was the most competent man she'd ever met. "This isn't exactly the Wild West."

"It could happen, though. You'd have to live with the guilt if I wandered around for days, half-crazed by thirst."

"All you have to do is give the horse his head. He'll find his way back to the stable."

"What if I get a horse with a lousy sense of direction? I could wind up in Phoenix."

The music changed to hard rock and the couples around them were galvanized. Roman made a face and led Noelle back to their table.

The interruption didn't deter him, however. He picked up the subject where he left off. "Do we have a date tomorrow?"

She hesitated. "The only way I can go is if I ask the other guests if they'd like to join us."

"Some of them sleep in. I don't think they'd appreciate being awakened."

"I meant the early-morning joggers. I have to ask them." She expected him to object, but Roman was surprisingly agreeable.

"Fair enough," he said.

The evening passed quickly. They talked and joked together like old friends. Noelle hadn't found a man this stimulating in a long time, and never one who combined wit, intelligence and an awesome physical attraction. She didn't realize how late it had gotten until Roman glanced at his watch.

"Let's get out of here and take a little ride," he suggested.

"I guess we really should start back," she said without conviction.

"We'll head in that direction."

Roman had rented a convertible at the airport when he arrived. The top was down, allowing them to see the night sky, spangled with stars. Halfway back to the spa he pulled over to the side of the road and cut the engine. Noelle glanced at him warily, but he merely slumped down in the seat and put his head back.

"Listen," he said. "Isn't it great?"

"I don't hear anything at all."

"That's what I mean. I've never heard complete silence before."

"Are you becoming a convert?" she teased.

"A night like this could do it." He turned his head to gaze at her. "I had a very good time."

"I did, too," she answered softly.

He straightened and turned toward her, resting an elbow on the seat back and propping his head on one hand. "Your hair is silver in the moonlight. You look like one of those angels people put on the top of a Christmas tree."

"That's a nice compliment. I remember the one we had when I was a little girl. My parents let me help trim the tree, but I was never allowed to touch the angel."

Roman smiled. "Are you trying to tell me something?"

"Would it do any good?" she asked lightly.

"I've never imposed my will on a woman, but you must know I want to kiss you." He moved closer and lifted her chin in his palm.

Excitement raced through Noelle as she gazed into his brilliant eyes. She was very conscious of Roman's firm mouth only inches from hers. It was tempting—*too* tempting. The attraction between them had the potential to turn into an avalanche, carrying her away. But she couldn't afford to get involved. Not when it might scuttle her mission.

Giving a shaky laugh, she said, "I never kiss good-night on a first date."

"Fortunately I don't have the same reservations." He cradled her in his arms and slid her close. Stringing a line of kisses down her cheek, he asked, "Do you mind if *I* kiss *you?*"

"You already are," she answered faintly.

"Not the way I'd like to." With his mouth poised over hers, he paused.

Noelle knew she could draw back and Roman wouldn't stop her. But the seduction of his mouth was too powerful. With a sigh of surrender, she twined her arms around his neck.

Roman gathered her close and parted her lips for a kiss that sent excitement surging through her. While his tongue probed deeply, his arms wrapped her in a tight embrace that made her burningly aware of his strong, muscular body. When he finally dragged his mouth away, they were both breathing rapidly.

"Beautiful Noelle," he sighed, kissing her closed eyelids. "You're utterly bewitching. I want you so much."

Her lashes fluttered open. "Roman, I—"

"Not here, darling." He chuckled. "Somewhere private where I can undress you slowly and kiss every inch of your delicious body. You're so exquisite. I want to make love to you for hours. I want to see your eyes glow with passion when I bring you as much pleasure as a man can give a woman."

Noelle's body eagerly agreed, but she forced back her desire and moved out of his embrace. "You're presuming a lot from one kiss."

"Are you telling me you don't feel the magic between us?"

"It's called sexual attraction, and I'm not denying it. You're a very attractive man, but I don't indulge in casual affairs," she explained carefully.

He reached out and rubbed his knuckles across her flushed cheek. "I don't think it would be casual."

"How could it be anything else? You'll be gone in a few days and we'll never see each other again."

"I'd be very sad if that happened."

"It will, though. You know it as well as I do. People on vacation always promise to keep in touch, but they never do."

"Come back to New York with me, Noelle," he said impulsively. "I know a lot of people. I can help you."

"I thought you lived in Chicago."

His pause was imperceptible. "I do, but I have connections in New York."

"Even if I took you up on your offer, we'd still be living in different cities," she pointed out.

"I told you, I go to New York often."

Noelle was silent, trying to figure him out. Had Roman told her the truth about himself? She had the uneasy feeling he was hiding something. What if he wasn't Mr. Nice Guy? Suppose that was just the role he played to get women into bed? The possibility disturbed her more than it should have.

"Think about it, anyway." He started the engine. "You don't have to make up your mind this minute. I'll be around till the end of the week."

The subject was dropped, but it had cooled their ardor. Both were a little distracted for the rest of the drive.

Noelle said a formal good-night in the parking lot. "Thank you for a fun evening, Roman."

"I'll walk you to your room."

"That isn't necessary," she answered quickly.

"I was taught that a gentleman sees a lady to her door."

"There aren't any shady characters lurking around the spa. I'll be fine."

Roman frowned. "I have no intention of forcing my way into your room, if that's what's bothering you."

"It isn't." The problem was having him remember she'd come out of a different room earlier. "I'd just rather no one saw us together this late. They might get the wrong idea."

"If they saw us saying good-night at your door?"

"They might think you were coming out."

His stern face relaxed in a smile. "I only wish they were right."

"Yes, well, I'd better go," she mumbled.

Roman framed her face in his palms and kissed her sweetly. "It's going to happen some day, honey. You know that, don't you?"

"I..." She stared into his eyes, wanting to believe in him.

He hugged her briefly, then released her. "Go to bed, angel face. I'll see you in the morning."

Noelle walked back to her room, savoring the memory of his lithe body pressed against hers.

Erica knocked on Noelle's door early the next morning. "Where were you last night?" she asked. "I stopped by to talk, but you weren't here."

"I went to the pub with Roman."

"Fantastic! I'll bet you had a great time."

"It was nice." Noelle was reluctant to make too much of her relationship with Roman. He'd troubled her sleep most of the night.

"Come on! He's special even by New York standards. Jeff thinks he's great."

"What does Jeff say about him?"

"I just told you. He likes him a lot."

"I meant, does Roman talk about himself much?" Noelle asked hesitantly. "Like where he lives and what he does for a living?"

"Surely Roman told you those things himself. What do you two talk about all those hours you're together?"

"Oh, various things," Noelle answered vaguely.

"What's wrong, Noelle? Something's bothering you. Did he make a pass and you're afraid he's married?"

"No, I don't think he'd lie about a thing like that."

"Then what do you suspect him of?"

"Nothing really." Noelle couldn't tell her she wondered if Roman was a private detective. "A couple of things he said just didn't ring true."

"Guys brag to impress women, but Roman doesn't strike me as a phony."

"You're probably right."

"If it will make you feel better, I'll ask Jeff to see what he can find out about him."

"You two sound as if you've gotten pretty chummy," Noelle remarked.

Erica's face turned dreamy. "I know you'll tell me I'm crazy, but I think I'm falling in love."

"Jeff seems very nice, but you've only known him a few days," Noelle felt compelled to point out.

"I knew he was special the minute I saw him, and we've gotten to know each other really well. I was out with him again last night. We went for a long walk and talked for hours. He told me all about his family and his work. Jeff's father died recently and he had to take over at the bank. Of course he has advisers, and his mother has a lot to say about what goes on. She's a major stockholder. But Jeff has loads of responsibility."

"I'm sure he does." Noelle smiled at the younger woman's enthusiasm.

"He invited me to come to New York for a visit."

"That sounds promising."

"I'm sure he likes *me* a lot, too." Erica was slightly defensive.

Which one of them was she trying to convince? Noelle wondered. "I don't doubt for a minute that he likes you. He'd be crazy if he didn't." She paused to choose her words carefully. "Carefree Dunes is a different world, though. Men come here for a week of fun and games, and then they go home to their normal lives."

Erica's animation died. "You don't think he could fall in love with me." It was a statement, not a question.

"I didn't say that," Noelle replied swiftly. "You'd be the best thing that ever happened to him, but sometimes men don't realize how lucky they are."

"No, you're right. How could he be seriously interested in me? I haven't had any of his advantages—not to mention schooling. Jeff went to prep school and then to Harvard."

"Big deal! I'll bet you're every bit as informed as he is. Don't ever put yourself down."

Erica summoned a smile. "I wish I could figure out which side you're on. First you warn me not to fall in love with Jeff, and then you tell me how terrific I am."

"You are. I just don't want to see you get hurt," Noelle answered gently. "Why don't you simply enjoy his company and see what develops?"

Erica brightened. "You're right. I still have almost five days. Who knows what could happen?"

"That's the spirit." Noelle picked up her key. "Come on, it's time to act charming. Although how anyone can manage that at seven in the morning beats me."

"You succeeded in fooling Roman," Erica teased.

I only hope he isn't doing the same to me, Noelle thought.

Roman and Jeff were among the small knot of men warming up by the swimming pool. They walked over to meet the two women as soon as they saw them approaching. Troy watched with annoyance, but he vented his displeasure mostly on Noelle.

"Nice of you girls to show up," he remarked sarcastically. "I thought you were going to goof off again today, Noelle."

"No, I'm ready to go." She ignored his tone.

"Noelle and I are going horseback riding today," Roman announced.

She smothered a groan at the sullen look on Troy's face. In an attempt to contain the damage, she quickly asked, "Who else would like to go? The stables are close by and we'll be back for lunch."

Two of the men accepted her invitation. "Count me in," Ed Moroni said. "I'll let the horse do my running for me this morning."

"Sounds good to me, too," George Selby agreed.

"Anybody else?" Noelle asked brightly. "No? Then we can all go in one car." She avoided looking at Roman.

He didn't seem annoyed as she had feared. In fact, he was smiling. "We can take my car. I brought the keys. You'd better get a scarf for your hair, Noelle. I have a convertible."

She'd found that out last night, but she couldn't very well say so. What was Roman up to? "I don't care what happens to my hair," she assured him.

"You'll be uncomfortable when it starts whipping around your face. At least get a ribbon to tie it back. We'll meet you in the parking lot," he said before she could offer any more objections.

Noelle was slightly puzzled by his insistence, but it wasn't worth arguing about.

Roman waited until she was out of hearing to ask Troy, "Do they have a snake-bite kit at the stable?"

"I don't know," Troy answered in surprise.

"Then we'd better take a sharp knife just to be on the safe side. In case of snake bite, you're supposed to slash the fang wound to let the poison drain out before you head for the nearest emergency hospital."

"Hold on a minute!" George looked alarmed. "Are there any snakes out there?"

Roman shrugged. "This is rattlesnake country."

"Only in the uninhabited part of the desert," Troy said reassuringly. "You'll be riding along established trails."

"I've read about people finding snakes in their gardens," Roman commented.

"Well, of course it *has* happened, but it's fairly rare," Troy answered.

"*Fairly* rare!" George exclaimed. "I don't like the odds. I'm going to pass."

"Me, too," Ed said. "Jogging's suddenly gotten more appealing."

Roman was waiting beside the car when Noelle arrived. She glanced around. "Where are the others?"

He smiled. "They had a change of heart."

"You wouldn't happen to know why?" she asked suspiciously.

"It beats me. Some men can't seem to decide *what* they want."

"Nobody could ever accuse *you* of that failing." She knew he'd arranged for them to be alone, even though she didn't know how. "I'm beginning to think you're a very devious man."

"Hardly." He chuckled. "I haven't made any secret of my intentions." When she slanted a glance at him, he said blandly, "I always intended to go riding this morning. Let's get started." Putting an arm around her shoulders, he walked her to the passenger side of the car.

Chapter Four

Noelle forgot her suspicions of Roman as they rode through the picturesque countryside. The trail led through tree-lined lanes so it was pleasantly cool, even when the sun climbed in the sky. After about an hour they dismounted, tied up the horses and sat under a large tree.

"Isn't this lovely?" Noelle sighed happily. "I'm going to hate to see this week end."

"It doesn't have to." He reached over and took her hand. "It can be a beginning if you say the word."

"What I meant was, I feel as if I'm on vacation, too," she explained carefully.

He looked at her dispassionately. "Has anyone ever told you you're a tease?"

"Not so! I can't help it if you leap to conclusions."

"Are you telling me that I'm merely a pleasant way to pass the time, but any of the other men here would just as easily do?"

"You're putting words in my mouth," she protested.

"The question is, are they true?" He tipped her chin up. "Will you give me a second thought after I leave?"

"Probably a third and fourth." She smiled.

"I'd like to believe that." He cupped her cheek in his palm and gazed deeply into her eyes. "I don't know how to explain it, but something happened the first time we met."

Her quickened pulse told Noelle it was time to head him off. "You bring that up at least once a day," she said lightly.

He looked blank for a moment, then he chuckled. "I wasn't talking about the circumstances. *You're* the one who brought up the incident this time."

She was relieved when he settled back against the tree trunk. The sexual tension between them was defused, for the moment at least.

"Let's make a pact that *neither* of us mentions it again," she said. "Sybyll would have a heart attack if she ever found out."

"Your brochure does say you offer everything for the stressed-out businessman," he teased.

"I can't speak for all the men here, but I'm sure that's not what *you* came for."

Roman's expression changed. "That's true. It's nice to know I provided you with a vacation, anyway. Are the women guests very difficult?"

"I didn't mean to give that impression. They're just more . . . dedicated. They come here to lose weight."

"That must make them good and cranky."

Noelle laughed, then looked guilty. "I wouldn't say that."

"You don't have to. Your face is very expressive. A bunch of rich, pampered women would be hard to deal with, even under ideal circumstances. I don't envy you your job."

"It isn't so bad. Some of them are very nice."

"You don't have to be diplomatic with me."

"No, honestly. They can be a lot of fun. We had three ladies from Texas who'd never been to a reducing spa before. They were really hungry when they came into dinner the first night." Noelle smiled reminiscently. "There was a plate on the table with three small crackers that they polished off immediately. While they were looking at the menu, one of them called the waitress over and told her to bring more crackers. When the girl explained they were only permitted one cracker apiece and they'd just eaten it, they went into shock. One of them said, 'Honey, in Texas we call those little bitty things crumbs!' "

Roman shook his head in amused disbelief. "What kind of women would put themselves through such misery? Are they that vain?"

"It isn't always a question of vanity. Thin is healthier than fat."

"I suppose you're right. Do they all work out in the gym?"

"It isn't obligatory. Some women use the equipment, but others prefer aerobics or walking. A few just rely on massages to tone up."

"Those aren't included in the weekly rate, are they?"

Noelle stared at him. "For a man who isn't wildly impressed with Carefree Dunes, you're showing a lot of interest in the women who come here."

"I'm attempting to understand the female thought processes—an age-old mystery to men," he answered lightly.

"That's an innovative excuse, anyway."

"You don't believe me?"

"I don't know what to believe," she answered frankly. "You don't talk much about yourself."

"You're a far more interesting subject." He gave her a melting smile. "I could spend an hour describing the different shades of gold in your hair. It's absolutely glorious. You could model for a shampoo ad."

Noelle wasn't diverted. "You see? You're changing the subject again, the way you always do."

"Not intentionally. What is it you're burning to know?"

"Something more than your profession and where you live."

"Okay, you asked for it. I'm told I was a beautiful baby. My mother still displays a picture of me lying nude on a blanket." Roman's eyes brimmed with devilry. "I must admit I had a cute little bottom. You only got a frontal view, so you missed that."

Noelle rewarded him with a stony stare. "That wasn't the information I had in mind."

His laughter faded. "Why is it important to you, Noelle? What are you trying to find out?"

She decided to be direct. No other approach had worked. "Are you a private detective?"

He stared at her in amazement. "You must be joking! Where on earth did you get an idea like that?"

His complete incredulity convinced her. It was a spontaneous reaction, not a feigned one. But now she was left with the problem of explaining why she'd suspected him.

"Is there something shady going on at the spa?" he asked.

"No, of course not! It's just that you asked so many questions. And you're not crazy about it here. I couldn't help wondering if you had some ulterior motive for coming."

Roman gazed directly at her. "I didn't lie when I told you I was tired. I'd just come off a big project and I was suffering burnout. Since I'm a workaholic, however, I brought some work with me. Tonight I intend to get around to doing it. If you hear my typewriter clattering late into the night, it's nothing more sinister than that."

"I'm sorry, Roman. I guess I simply let my imagination run away with me."

He continued to look at her thoughtfully for a moment, then his amusement returned. "I'm willing to kiss and make up."

"That's very magnanimous of you," she commented lightly.

He put an arm around her waist and turned her to face him. "Didn't Alexander Pope say, 'To err is human, to forgive divine'?"

"I never knew who said it," she murmured, feeling the pull of his magnetism.

Roman lowered his head until his mouth was only inches from hers. "I believe it was also attributed to Plutarch."

"You're very well-informed," she whispered.

"I'll be happy to teach you everything I know."

His lips brushed hers softly, a tantalizing caress that only whetted her appetite. A thrill of desire raced through her, demanding more. When the tip of his tongue lingered enticingly between her parted lips, she cupped the back of his head and increased the pressure.

Roman's arms tightened and he lowered them both to the soft grass. One leg twined around both of hers, molding their bodies tightly together.

"Sweet, sweet Noelle," he muttered, trailing kisses over her face. "You're driving me a little crazy. I've never wanted any woman this much."

Elation filled her. "Tell me how much."

"Does this give you some idea?"

His passion was unleashed in a kiss that brought a response from her entire body. She trembled as he unbuttoned her blouse and slipped his hand inside to caress her breast. The sensitive tip firmed like a rosebud under his circling thumb. Noelle's indrawn breath mingled with his, making him a part of her.

"I've dreamed about touching you like this." He widened the opening of her blouse and slid his mouth across the lace edging of her bra, trailing a path of fire.

She gasped as his lips closed around her nipple and his tongue tasted her through the fragile covering. The sensation was so inflaming that she arched her body into his and murmured his name over and over again.

"My beautiful, passionate Noelle." He kissed the pulse that thundered in the hollow of her throat. "I want to make love to you for hours. You're so utterly perfect. I want to know every exquisite inch of you."

She already knew *he* was perfection. Sliding her hands under the waistband of his low-slung jeans, she kneaded his rigid buttocks.

Roman reacted with a groan of pleasure. "Are you trying to destroy what little self-control I have left?" he demanded.

"Yes!" she said exultantly. "I want you completely in my power." It was a heady thought.

"I'm yours to command," he answered deeply, capturing her mouth.

They were so lost in the wonder of each other that the voices in the distance didn't register immediately. Then a loud cowboy whoop shattered the mood like a nail on a blackboard. They looked at each other in confused protest for a moment.

Roman was the first to recover. He sat up and gently pulled Noelle's blouse together. After a stunned instant, sanity returned and she was appalled at herself for letting this happen. Turning her back, she hastily buttoned her blouse. By the time the riders appeared she was presentable, although her emotions were still in turmoil.

Two couples rode into view, obviously tourists, judging from their brand-new Western getups. The men were enthusiastic, if inept, horsemen. They reined in their mounts too sharply and one of the horses reared. The female members of the group, two women in their late forties, looked alarmed.

"Will you stop showing off, Charlie?" one of them called. "You're going to break your neck."

"Shucks, Helen, this little ole filly is just a mite skittish." The man nodded at Roman and Noelle. "Howdy, pardners. Fine day, isn't it?"

"You'll have to excuse my husband," his wife told them. "We've been here three days and all of a sudden he thinks he's Wyatt Earp. I don't know why, since we're from Cleveland."

"Well, that's the West, isn't it?" Charlie demanded.

Roman smiled. "The Midwest, anyway."

"Are you visiting here, too?" the other man asked.

"No, the wife and I have a cattle ranch a few miles from here." Roman put an arm around Noelle's shoulders. "Just a small spread. We only run about a thousand head."

"A real cowboy," Charlie breathed.

Roman got to his feet and hooked his thumbs in his waistband, resting his weight on one hip. "Yep, the gen-u-wine article," he drawled.

Charlie's dazzled eyes traveled up Roman's lean length. "Gee, maybe we could ride over and see your spread one day. We'll be here till the end of the week."

"I'd sure like that, but we're driving the herd to market," Roman answered. "Enjoy your stay, though."

"We'll do that. It was nice meeting you." Charlie reluctantly led his group away.

Noelle knew why Roman had struck up a conversation with the strangers. He realized she was upset, and he wanted to give her time to get her emotions under control. She couldn't have faced him immediately. It was a thoughtful thing to do, since he couldn't have felt like making small talk, either.

When they were alone again, she smiled tentatively at him. "You made their day, pardner."

Roman chuckled. "I *was* pretty convincing, wasn't I?"

"Why not? You look the part." Noelle glanced at him, then looked away quickly. The lithe body under those tight jeans was already etched in her memory. "Shall we continue our ride?"

"Not until we talk." He put his hands on her shoulders and turned her to face him. "You can't just pretend nothing happened between us."

"I'd prefer not to talk about it."

"Why? It was a lovely, spontaneous moment."

"It was a lot more than that! If those people hadn't come along..."

"I'm glad they did." He smoothed her hair tenderly. "The chemistry between us is awesome, but I don't want to make love to you in a hurry. I want our first time to be something special."

Noelle took a deep breath. "You're right, Roman, we have to talk. What happened between us was a mistake."

"You don't mean that."

His husky voice vibrated in her midsection like a tuning fork, but she forced herself to ignore it. "Yes, I do. It was my fault as much as yours, but it mustn't happen again."

"Why, when our feelings are mutual? Is there something you haven't told me?" He watched her face closely. "Are you involved with someone else?"

Noelle was tempted to say yes, but Roman would know she was lying. How could she have responded to him so totally? "It has nothing to do with other people. I explained how I felt about brief affairs."

"You don't think it's going to end here. Not now."

"I don't know." The thought was painful. "I hope not, but I need a little more time. Maybe I could meet you in New York in a week or two."

"That would be wonderful, but why do we have to wait until then?"

"Because..." She searched frantically, but no excuse came to mind. "You'll just have to take my word for it."

His manner cooled and he looked at her dispassionately. "It's your decision, of course. I won't try to talk you into something you'd regret."

He must know better. But she couldn't tell him why it was too risky here. Once they made love, Roman would want to be with her constantly. She'd never be able to hide their relationship from Troy.

Roman swung himself onto his horse. "Perhaps we'd better head back to the stable," he said evenly.

"Yes, I guess that's a good idea." She mounted and followed him with a heavy heart.

Noelle found a slip of paper under her door when she returned to the spa. It was a message from Diane, asking her to call.

Diane sounded frantic again. "I haven't heard from you in days! How can you leave me hanging like this?"

"Try to calm down," Noelle urged. "I told you it would take time."

"I don't know how much time I have left."

"Has Troy been pressuring you?"

"No, I was able to hold him off, but Drew's lawyer called me. Drew is having an attack of conscience."

"He wants to get back together?"

"No, he wants joint custody of Christine."

"Well, he *is* her father. I guess it's natural that he'd want to see her on weekends."

"You didn't hear me. I said *joint* custody, meaning every other month. Who would take care of her when Drew is at the office? Certainly not that trophy wife of his!" Diane's voice was shrill with outrage and panic.

"That's contemptible!" Noelle exclaimed. "You can't bounce a six-year-old back and forth every month like a Ping-Pong ball. The court would never allow it."

"I can't be certain. Drew has a lot of influence. But that's only *one* of my worries. If he ever found out about Troy, he could take Christine away from me entirely!"

"Don't borrow trouble." Noelle tried not to betray her own misgivings.

Diane was right on target. Divorce might make Drew do ugly things—especially when he was already suffering from guilt. Diane's indiscretion would give him a chance to justify his own behavior.

"I won't let him take her, no matter what I have to do!" Diane was on the edge of hysteria. "I'll take Chris and run away. We'll go to Europe and change our names. Drew will never find us."

"Don't talk nonsense," Noelle ordered. "You're going to sit tight and wait. I'll get those negatives. It'll take a little time, but I'll manage somehow. Nothing is going to change, do you hear me? You and Chrissie will be all right.''

''I don't know what I'd do without you, Noelle. I've been absolutely frantic.'' Diane started to cry.

''I know it's hard, but you have to pull yourself together. You don't want your daughter to see you like this, do you?''

After a few more minutes of reassurance, Noelle hung up with a sober face. How was she going to make good on her promise? She was far less confident than she sounded. What if she failed? More than Diane's reputation was at stake now.

Noelle set her jaw grimly. She *couldn't* fail. Every waking moment had to be devoted to finding those negatives. The rift with Roman was just as well, she reflected forlornly. Diane and Chrissie had to come first.

Erica was coming down the path when Noelle started back to her room.

''What are you doing here?'' she called to Noelle. ''I thought you and Roman would stay out for lunch.''

''No, he, uh . . . he had some work to do.''

''He's supposed to be on vacation.''

''Yes, well, executives are like that.''

''Not Jeff. He doesn't ever want to go home.''

''He must not enjoy his work,'' Noelle remarked abstractedly.

''Thanks a lot!'' Erica answered indignantly. ''I suppose it never occurred to you that *I* might be the attraction.''

''I'm sorry, Erica. My mind was on something else. How's the romance coming?''

''So great I'm almost afraid to believe it! I know you advised me to go slow, but we're so perfect together. We agree on just about everything." Erica's young face was radiant with happiness. "We're together all the time, and we never get tired of each other's company. I know it's not going to end when Jeff goes home."

"I'm really happy for you," Noelle said gently.

"To show you the depths of his devotion, he's coming to aerobics class today. If that isn't love, what is?" Erica laughed.

"We'll have a class this afternoon?" Noelle asked in dismay.

"I wouldn't exactly call it a class. Jeff said he'd ask some of the other men to come, but I know they won't." Erica grinned. "Just between you and me, I don't think he intends to try too hard to persuade them."

Noelle breathed a sigh of relief. "Then you won't need me. Two teachers for one person would be overkill."

"You're right." Erica beamed. "I can handle this one all by myself. Come on, let's go to lunch."

"I'm not really hungry." Noelle hesitated. "Troy hasn't joined us for meals lately. Where does he eat lunch?"

"Don't worry, he won't be there. He grabs a sandwich in the gym when he has a chance. The men really keep him hopping. They're more demanding than the women. In different ways, of course."

"Of course." Noelle forced a smile.

Erica looked at her watch. "Let's go. I'm meeting Jeff in forty-five minutes."

"Go ahead, then. I think I'll skip lunch today. I have a couple of things to do," Noelle said vaguely.

Roman was in a foul mood when he stalked into the dining room. Like Noelle, he'd considered skipping lunch, but he didn't have anything else to do. He was scowling at the menu when Jeff sat down opposite him.

"How was your horseback ride?" the younger man asked.

"Fine," Roman answered curtly, hoping to head off further questions.

"Did you see any snakes?"

"No."

Jeff slanted a knowing look at him. "I didn't think so. It was pretty neat the way you got rid of those other guys."

"It was a sophomoric prank that backfired," Roman growled. He glanced back at the menu. "What are you going to eat?"

Jeff raised his eyebrows, but refrained from commenting. They both concentrated on making their selections.

After the waitress had taken their orders and departed, Jeff's irrepressible good spirits overcame his caution. "Isn't this place fantastic? I can't believe I had to be talked into coming."

"That's why I'm here, too, but I don't share your enthusiasm," Roman said sourly. "If God had meant man to vegetate, he would have created him in the form of a plant."

"There's plenty to do here. You look like an athletic guy. Why don't you go swimming or play tennis?"

"I haven't gotten around to it," Roman muttered.

"You should. Carefree Dunes has everything anybody could want."

Roman smiled sardonically. "Just like summer camp at Lake Winnetonka? I didn't realize you were that young."

Jeff laughed self-consciously. "Okay, so it doesn't have *everything*. But that's not what you come here for."

Roman couldn't help being amused. "I believe your purpose was to network with mature males. It's nice that you're enjoying it so much."

Jeff grinned. "You know I've been spending all my time with Erica, don't you?"

"It occurred to me that she might have something to do with your rosy view of the place."

"She's wonderful, Rome. Erica is not only beautiful, she's intelligent. We discuss everything from politics to poetry."

"Is that what you do on those long walks you take together?"

"I'm serious," Jeff insisted. "She makes the girls I know back home seem like cardboard cutouts. All they're interested in are the latest fashions and the next big social event. They're so superficial. Erica isn't like that. She couldn't care less if she never went to a charity ball."

"You told her about the kind of life you lead?"

"We've found out everything about each other. She knows more about the real me than my own family." Jeff's face filled with wonder. "I don't know how it happened so fast, but I'm in love."

"You've really had a successful vacation," Roman remarked ironically.

"You think this is some passing fling? No way! I'm going to ask Erica to marry me."

"Don't you think you're being a little hasty? She's lovely, but . . . well, you *are* a very eligible young man."

"Erica isn't interested in my money."

"I'm sure she shares your affection, but it's something to consider. You don't have to commit yourself right now."

"What's there to wait for? My feelings won't change. If you've ever been in love, you'll know what I'm talking about. I get up happy every morning because I'm going to see her. I resent all the rules and regulations that keep us apart. If it weren't for Erica, I'd feel the same way you do about this place."

Roman smiled wryly. "I guess I'll survive."

"It's too bad things didn't work out with you and Noelle. She's a real knockout."

"Noelle is quite charming, but I don't like women who play games," Roman answered coolly.

"Oh, one of those. They're the only kind I know back home. You're better off working out at the gym." Jeff laughed.

"What do you know about that overgrown beachboy they call a fitness trainer?" Roman asked abruptly.

"Not much. Erica says he's a jerk. He's always hitting on the girls who work here." Jeff scowled. "I'd better not hear of him trying anything with Erica."

"Maybe some of the women like it," Roman remarked casually.

"I suppose so. There's no accounting for tastes." Jeff looked at his watch. "I have to run. I was going to ask if you wanted to take an aerobics class with me, but I guess you're not interested."

"No thanks, I'm going to do some work."

Roman's intentions were good, but he couldn't concentrate. Jeff's adolescent prattling about love kept coming back to him. The kid needed to grow up. Wanting to be with someone all the time wasn't love. It was more apt to be a mixture of sexual attraction and boredom.

Roman jammed his hands into his pockets and wandered around the room, remembering how Noelle had felt in his arms, the fragrance of her skin and the way her body conformed to his. The vivid recollection made his groin ache. If she'd played straight with him, who knows what might have developed between them? He'd never felt so drawn to a woman.

Were you completely honest with *her?* a small voice asked. That was different, though. This job had nothing to do with her. A woman who got her kicks by playing sexual games wasn't worth a second thought. He'd forget about her in a minute once he got away from this over-priced playpen.

Roman sat down and rolled a sheet of paper into his portable typewriter. After staring at it for about twenty minutes, he shoved back his chair in disgust and slammed out of the room.

Noelle entered Troy's room with grim determination. There were only just so many hiding places in this small area. Today she was going to uncover Troy's.

After emptying the top drawer of the nightstand, Noelle sat cross-legged on the floor. His unmade bed repulsed her—along with his reading matter. The men's magazines were the raunchiest kind. Noelle was no prude, but the poses of the nude women were degrading, and the printed material made her mouth drop open. She concentrated on turning the pages rapidly.

It was a waste of time; nothing was hidden in the magazines. She pushed them aside and started on the paperback books. Initially a thrill raced through her when she noticed that some of the pages were dog-eared. Her excitement faded when she realized Troy had merely marked the more lurid passages for future reference.

She lost all sense of time. Her legs were cramped and her back ached from sitting hunched on the floor for so long, but she didn't even notice. The sound of a key in the lock shocked her back into awareness. She glanced at her watch and realized it was after five o'clock! Troy must be through for the day.

After an immobilizing instant of panic, Noelle took the only course open. She wriggled under the bed, sweeping all the reading material with her, praying she wasn't visible. With any luck, the trailing covers from the unmade bed would block Troy's view.

Her heart started to beat again when he flopped down on the bed with a loud groan. She was safe temporarily, and Troy should go to dinner soon. She might even have a chance to sneak out while he was in the bathroom—unless he'd showered at the gym.

The minutes dragged by as Noelle's tension built. Another hazard had occurred to her. What if Troy decided to read for a while? That worry faded when he began to snore. Did she dare try to slip out of the room? No, it was too chancy. He might be a light sleeper.

Just when she thought the nightmare would never end, there was a knock at the door. Troy awoke with a grunt. Muttering something unintelligible, he turned over.

When the knock came again, he snarled, "Go away."

Erica's voice sounded through the panel. "Troy! Mr. Moroni wants to see you."

"Tell him to..." Troy's suggestion was anatomically impossible, as well as vulgar.

"He's waiting in the gym," Erica answered imperturbably. "You'd better get over there on the double."

"The hell I will! Tell him to forget it. I'm beat."

"Tell him yourself. I'm not your errand boy."

"He can sit there and play with his toes for all I care."

"It's okay with me. You're the one who will have to answer to Sybyll if Moroni complains." Erica's footsteps receded down the corridor.

Uttering a stream of profanity, Troy hauled himself off the bed. The entire room shook as he slammed the door on his way out.

With a silent prayer of thanks, Noelle wriggled out from under the bed and raced to the door. She had almost reached freedom when she remembered the books and magazines. It was torture to remain there a second longer, but she ran back and gathered them up frantically. Without trying to remember how they'd been arranged, she threw everything into the drawer and dashed out of the room.

The close call left Noelle shaken. Making conversation with Troy would be especially difficult. But since she'd skipped lunch, her absence at dinner would be noticed and commented on—the last thing she wanted. Fortunately Troy gulped down his food and left, muttering something about hitting the sack.

Erica chuckled. "That's the first time Troy was ever in such a hurry to go to bed alone."

"It really warms my heart to see him worked like a pack mule," Mitzi remarked. "I'll be sorry to see the men leave."

Noelle was abruptly reminded of Roman. She hadn't thought about him for hours. That was the only good thing to come out of her traumatic experience.

He continued to fill her mind during the rest of an endless evening, making her even more miserable. Anything that might have been was over between them. Roman thought she was a tease. Noelle paced the floor, wondering why his opinion bothered her so much.

It wasn't as though she was in love with him. There must be thousands of handsome men with Roman's charm, intelligence and awesome sex appeal. Too bad she'd never found one till now, she thought ironically.

To escape her unsolvable problems, Noelle went to bed early, but the oblivion of sleep refused to come. At midnight she gave up and decided to go for a swim. That usually relaxed her.

The swimming pool was dark and deserted at this hour. A quarter moon didn't cast much light. The surface of the water looked like a dark mirror in a frame of pale concrete.

Noelle tossed her towel onto a chair and walked down the steps at the shallow end. Striking out strongly, she swam the length of the pool. When she reached the deep end and turned to start back, something startled her. A pale oval glimmered in the shadow cast by the diving board. Someone was in the pool with her!

"Who's there?" she called sharply.

"I didn't mean to frighten you." Roman glided out of the shadows and swam over to her.

Noelle drew a shaky breath. "I couldn't see you in the dark. I thought I was alone."

"I was admiring what I could see of you. Are you wearing a bathing suit?"

"Of course! Aren't you?"

Roman's white teeth gleamed in the muted light. "No. Does it make a difference?"

"Not to me," she lied. The vivid picture was mind-boggling.

They were both holding on to the coping with one hand while treading water. Noelle slid her hand along the tile and backpedaled, putting more distance between them.

"I forgot." His grin disappeared. "You're the lady who doesn't want to get involved."

"What are you doing here, anyway?" she asked crossly. Roman had destroyed any relaxation she might have achieved. "You don't even use the pool in the daytime."

He shrugged. "Maybe I prefer it at night."

"I'm glad you found *something* you like."

"It's good of you to care."

"*I* thought so," she flared, stung by his heavy sarcasm. "I'm not paid to be polite at this hour."

She started to swim away, but Roman caught her arm and hauled her back. "So you're finally being honest with me. The time we spent together was a paid performance on your part."

"I didn't say that!"

"You said more than you meant to," he replied grimly. "I see where I made my mistake. The only way to get the truth out of you is to make you angry."

"You're acting like a spoiled child." She tried to pull away, but his grip tightened. "It's time you learned you can't have everything you want in life," she stated.

"You can at Carefree Dunes," he answered mockingly. "It's after midnight, so consider this today's performance."

Before she could react, Roman snaked an arm around her waist and jerked her body against his. When she tried to protest, his mouth closed over hers in a punishing kiss that held all his pent-up anger. She pounded on his shoulders, but he only held her tighter, winding his legs around both of hers so their bodies were welded together.

Noelle's struggles became weaker as the heat of his body penetrated hers. She felt lighter than air, cradled by the water and Roman's arms. Her fists uncurled and she touched his smooth skin, tentatively at first. Almost without realizing it, the timid strokes turned into caresses as her hands moved over his powerful shoulders. Finally she twined her arms around his neck.

His mouth softened and he kissed her tenderly now. "I'm sorry, angel. Why do I say things like that to you?"

"Because you believe them," she answered sadly.

"I don't know what I believe anymore," he muttered, cupping her bottom and fitting her more closely to the juncture of his thighs. "I've never refused to take no for an answer before, but I can't leave you alone."

Noelle didn't want him to. Her body was tense with desire. Pulling his head down, she reached for his mouth.

Roman's kiss was scorching in its intensity. Their passion soared, fed by the lapping water and their urgent need. But when he slipped the straps of her bathing suit down and whispered in her ear, Noelle returned to the real world.

"Don't do this to me again," Roman said urgently as she drew away. "I know you want me, too. What's keeping us apart, Noelle? You have to tell me."

"I can't," she whispered.

"You said there's nobody else. What other reason could there be?"

"I didn't want this to happen. Please believe me."

After gazing for a long moment at her stricken face, he said, "I do, darling. But if you'd just tell me what's wrong, maybe I can do something about it."

She shook her head sadly. "Nobody can help. All you can do is trust me. I know that's a lot to ask, but I hope I'll be able to explain everything soon."

He frowned. "Are you in some kind of trouble, Noelle?"

"Don't ask me any more questions. I'd better go."

Roman didn't try to stop her as she swam over to the ladder and hoisted herself out of the pool. Noelle didn't look back, but she was conscious of his eyes following her till she blended into the shadows.

Chapter Five

Noelle reluctantly dragged herself out of bed at six-thirty the next morning, dreading what she had to do. The thought of going into Troy's room again made her faintly ill. But she only had three more days of comparative safety. Luckily her mornings would be free, since she wouldn't be spending them with Roman.

Noelle didn't have to show up that early. The joggers were accustomed by now to running with Erica and Troy. But she wanted to see them safely away.

Erica and the men were doing warm-up exercises in the pool area, which looked completely different in the sunshine. No shadows turned the water to a sensuous trysting place.

Noelle bit her lip and looked away—straight into Roman's eyes. "I didn't expect to see you here this morning," she faltered.

"Ever since I met you, I've felt the need for physical exercise—and a lot of cold showers," he answered dryly.

Her cheeks reddened and she looked away. "I'll tell Erica you'll be joining her group."

"I don't want to jog. I want to walk—with you."

Noelle's nerves were already wound tightly. She couldn't take another barrage of accusations. "When are you going to get through punishing me for my supposed sins?" she asked in a taut voice.

His jaw set grimly. "Is my company so disagreeable?"

"You can't enjoy our flare-ups any more than I do. Go with the joggers," she pleaded.

He looked at her more closely. "Are you all right? You look terrible."

"Thanks! I really needed to hear that."

"I meant, you have dark circles under your eyes."

"I didn't get much sleep last night," she answered wearily.

"Join the group." His voice held irony. "I can't say I've gotten a lot of rest here."

"Then why don't you go take a nap? We'll both benefit from it."

"I know something you need more." Roman took her arm. "Come with me."

"Where to?" Noelle asked as the others jogged by with cheery waves.

"You're tied up in knots. That's what's making you so cranky."

"I am *not* cranky," she stated through gritted teeth. "You're the one who's being difficult. If you'd just go on about your business, I'd be fine!"

"Trust me. I promise you won't be sorry."

His soothing tone had the opposite effect. She tried to pull away, but he had a firm grip on her arm.

"Will you at least tell me where you're taking me?" she demanded.

"We're here." They'd arrived at the goldfish pool. He sat her down on a flat-topped rock. "It would be more convenient in my room or yours, but we'll have to settle for this."

"What do you think you're going to do?" she asked, starting to rise.

"This." He put his hands on her shoulders and started to massage them. "You need to relax."

Did he think this was going to help? "Tell me something I *don't* know," she muttered.

He moved in back of her and kneaded her tense neck muscles. "Close your eyes and imagine you're floating through the air like a butterfly. You haven't a care in the world."

"Don't I wish!"

"Shh, butterflies can't talk. They just fly around and smell the roses all day."

"Do butterflies have a sense of smell?"

"Why else would they hang around gardens? You hardly ever see them in department stores."

Roman's strong hands moved over her back with firm strokes. The hypnotic rhythm was accomplishing its purpose. Noelle could feel herself unwinding.

"I think they're attracted to bright colors," she said languidly.

"Okay, I'll buy that. Whatever turns you on." His hands became subtly caressing for a moment, then resumed their steady massaging. "Doesn't that feel good?"

"Mmm, fabulous." She swept her long hair up and leaned forward to rest her forehead on her knees. "Do my neck some more. You're fantastic."

"I've been trying to convince you of that for days."

She sat up and turned her head to look at him. "Why are you being so nice to me, Roman?"

"Is there any reason I shouldn't be?"

"I thought after last night..." She looked away.

Roman cupped her chin in his palm and gently turned her face toward him. "I'll admit I've been annoyed with you on occasion because I thought...well, let's say I didn't realize you had something quite different on your mind."

"It doesn't have anything to do with you," she said earnestly.

"It does if it comes between us. Wouldn't you feel better if you told me about it?" he coaxed.

Her lashes drooped. "I can't."

Roman stared at her for a long moment. Then he said, "All right, angel. I don't want to add to your troubles."

"I'm glad you're not angry," she murmured.

He lowered himself to the ground and sat cross-legged at her feet. "I can take rejection. It's happened to me before."

Noelle gazed at his handsome, smiling face and lean length. "She must have been crazy."

"That's what I thought." He grinned. "You have three more days to change your mind."

"I guess you'll be out of here first thing Sunday morning." She tried to match his light tone, but her heart wasn't in it. Roman wouldn't be soon forgotten.

"I might hang around for another few days," he remarked casually.

"You can't. The women start arriving Sunday night."

"Maybe I'll go into Tucson for a little while."

"I thought you were anxious to get back to work."

He gave her a melting smile. "I've decided I want to see more of Arizona."

A bubble of happiness rose in Noelle. Would Roman really stay on just to be near her? Once he was away from Carefree Dunes, everything could be different between them.

"That would be great!" she said breathlessly. "Perhaps I could meet you there for dinner one night. If you want me to, that is," she finished uncertainly. He was staring at her with a puzzled frown.

"You're willing to have dinner with me after I leave here, but not before, is that it?" he asked slowly.

"I explained about the rules," she answered quickly.

"Not to my complete satisfaction."

Noelle sighed. "I might have known our detente wouldn't last." She rose.

Roman got to his feet, also. "There's always a certain amount of wrangling at the peace table. You can't walk out over the first setback."

She gave him a wan smile. "Do you think we'll ever agree on a ceasefire?"

"The important thing is to keep talking." He put an arm around her shoulders. "Let's take a walk."

Roman did his best to keep the conversation uncontroversial as they strolled around the grounds. They discussed movies they'd seen and books they'd read. Roman mentioned a bestseller he wanted to read.

"I'll give you my copy," Noelle offered. "It's so exciting you won't be able to put it down. I stayed up all night finishing it."

"That's one way to get some excitement in my life." When she glanced at him warily, he laughed. "I should be entitled to pout a little at not getting my way at the bargaining table."

"At least you didn't walk out," she said lightly.

"Not a chance. I don't quit till I've won the war." He turned his head to look at her consideringly. "It would be nice to know who I'm fighting, however."

Her face was wistful as she looked back at him. "I'm not your adversary."

He swore softly. "How do you manage to look so sexy in a baggy warm-up suit? All it does is make me visualize what's underneath."

"What more can I do?" She smiled. "I'm not even wearing any makeup."

"You don't need any. You're like an exquisite flower." His voice was husky as he stroked her cheek with his fingertips. "I'm drawn to your mouth like a bee to honey."

Her lips parted as his head dipped slowly toward hers. They moved together as though caught in an irresistible tide. When Roman's mouth covered hers, Noelle wrapped her arms around his waist with a tiny sound of contentment. She was familiar now with every angle of his hard frame, and it was becoming more and more difficult to deny them both.

After a stirring moment, she drew away. "It won't work, Roman. I know this isn't what you intended, but it happens every time we're alone together."

He released her reluctantly. "Doesn't that tell you something?"

"It tells me I have to stay away from you. I don't want you to wind up hating me."

"I can't conceive of that ever happening," he answered tenderly. "But you're right. I broke the rules. If countries have this much trouble respecting each other's boundaries, I can understand why there's so much tension in the world."

"They always promise not to do it again, but both sides know they will," she said soberly.

"I never break a promise, so I'm not going to make one. But I will try to restrain myself." He stuck his hands in his pockets. "See? No touching."

"Maybe if we talked about something else. Tell me about the advertising business. Do you write those little jingles for television?"

"I tried my hand at it a long time ago, but now I work at a desk—at least, part of the time."

She looked at him appraisingly. Roman had all the leashed energy of a thoroughbred horse. "It's hard to imagine you at a desk job."

"Most of the men here at the spa work in an office of some sort, even the movie mogul. How about the women guests? Do they have careers or simply a lot of time on their hands?"

"Some do, but we get a lot of career women who come for the same reason you did—to unwind. Although they often want to lose weight, too."

"Are they satisfied with the results?"

"They must be. Many of them have standing reservations, twice a year in some cases. Sybyll knocks herself out to keep them happy. One time she even—" Noelle checked herself. "I'm telling you more than you really want to know."

"No, you aren't. Go on."

She frowned slightly. "Why? You can't possibly be interested."

He gave her a winning smile. "We've finally found a subject that keeps us out of trouble. Tell me more about the sow's ears you make into swans."

Noelle laughed. "I think you have your metaphors mixed."

The morning passed without any further incidents between Noelle and Roman. She was feeling happy and relaxed until he asked about her plans for the afternoon, bringing her abruptly down to earth.

"Drive into Tucson with me after lunch," he said. "You can help me pick out a hotel."

"I can't go with you, but I'll give you the names of several good ones."

"Why can't you go with me?"

Noelle sighed. "You know why, Roman."

"I have trouble understanding such an arbitrary rule. If you don't have a class, why do you have to hang around all afternoon?"

"I, uh, have various things to do."

"Such as?"

"Well, I help out in the office. The computer broke down and Sybyll is swamped with work. She needs me."

"I need you, too, and I'm a paying guest. I think I'll tell her so."

"Don't do that!"

"I was only joking, honey." He shook his head in disbelief. "I don't know why this job means so much to you."

"I'll lend you the book I promised," she said hastily. "I guarantee you won't know where the afternoon went."

"Okay, angel, we'll do it your way. I'll walk over with you and get it."

"I have to stop at the office first. I'll drop it off at your room." She smiled determinedly. "Don't start it before lunch or you'll never make it to the dining room."

Noelle didn't like the thoughtful way he looked at her. Roman was entirely too perceptive. But at least he didn't raise any more objections.

Noelle was a bundle of nerves when she let herself into Troy's room after lunch. Every distant footstep outside sent her flying to the window to peek out. She wasn't going to chance another nasty surprise.

The constant need to be on guard played havoc with her concentration. Everything took longer than it should have. Not that she could think of any more places to look.

After the books and magazines had failed to yield anything, Noelle stood on a chair and felt in the back of the drapes for something pinned to them. She tugged the chest away from the wall to see if anything was taped to the back. She even crawled around the floor on her hands and knees, searching for signs that the carpeting had been pulled back and then replaced.

When none of her efforts produced results, Noelle was despondent. That left only the bathroom, not a very promising place to conceal anything. It would have to wait until tomorrow, though. Her time today had run out.

As Noelle was unlocking her door, Erica popped out of the room next door. "I've been looking everywhere for you!" she exclaimed. "Where do you disappear to every afternoon?"

"Well, I..." Noelle was too weary to think up an excuse.

She needn't have bothered because Erica wasn't listening. "I have the most fantastic news! Jeff and I are engaged."

"Erica, that's wonderful! When did it happen?"

"This morning. At first I thought he was joking."

"Men seldom consider marriage a laughing matter," Noelle remarked dryly.

Nothing could dampen Erica's mood. "He said he'd been looking for a girl like me all of his life."

Which wasn't very long, Noelle reflected, but she refrained from saying so. "Have you made any plans? What happens when Jeff leaves on Sunday? He can't stay on here.''

"We're going to be married as soon as possible. He just has to go home and tell his mother. Jeff says she'll probably insist on a big church wedding with lots of bridesmaids and hundreds of guests. I have to admit the idea scares me. I won't know any of those people. But Jeff says we should humor her. He's all she has, and this is the only wedding she'll ever get to plan.''

"It sounds very exciting.''

"I guess it will be if I don't die of stage fright. All the girls Jeff has dated are debutantes. I just know they'll be looking down their noses at me.''

"Bloodlines only count in racehorses and show dogs. *You're* the one he wants to marry.''

"That's true." Erica brightened. "I'll have to tell Sybyll I'm leaving.''

"There isn't any rush. You don't know exactly when that will be.''

Erica looked at her soberly. "You don't believe Jeff is serious about wanting to marry me, do you?''

"Of course I do!'' But Noelle did have some private doubts. Once Jeff was back in his own environment, Erica's allure might fade.

"You can be honest about it. I had my own doubts at first. I even told Jeff there were too many differences in our backgrounds. But he pointed out the one thing that made all the others unimportant. We love each other.''

Noelle was impressed by the young woman's calm conviction. "Then go for it. Jeff is right. When two people are in love, everything else is incidental.''

"I only hope you can find somebody like him some day.''

"I do, too.'' Noelle smiled wistfully.

"You will. With your looks and personality, you can't miss," Erica said fondly.

"Thanks, but I haven't had much luck so far. I'm not sure I even know what love is."

"One way is to ask yourself how much it would hurt if you never saw that person again."

Noelle flashed back to her feelings when Roman said he was going to stay on. It was a gift from above. The chance to be with him, away from Troy and Carefree Dunes, was like an impossible dream come true. She was admittedly attracted to him, but was it more than that? Noelle's heart started to pound as she faced the realization that she'd fallen in love with Roman.

"Just use that test when you do meet someone special," Erica said.

"What?" Noelle stared at her blankly, still lost in the wondrous revelation. "Oh. Yes, I will."

"Good. Then let's go to dinner. I can't wait to tell the others."

Jeff was as euphoric as Erica. At dinner that night he said to Roman, "I did it! I asked Erica to marry me, and she said yes."

"Congratulations," Roman said. "I hope you'll both be very happy."

"We will be," Jeff answered confidently. "Nothing could possibly change our feelings for each other. I'll love her just as much twenty years from now."

"When you're a middle-aged man of forty five?" Roman joked.

"I know we're both young, but when you've found the person you want to spend your life with, you don't let her slip through your fingers."

Roman's face sobered. "Have you set a date yet?"

"No, I have to go home and make arrangements first. My mother will probably want a big fancy wedding, but Erica and I want to get married immediately."

"Then do it. It's your wedding."

"I know, but if it means that much to Mother, I don't have the heart to refuse," Jeff said hesitantly.

"Keep a good thought. Maybe you can sell her on the idea of a small, intimate gathering."

"That's what I'm hoping." Jeff's face brightened. "Erica and I plan to celebrate our engagement tonight. Do you know where I can buy a cigar?"

"Aren't you being a trifle premature? You hand out cigars to announce the birth of a baby."

Jeff laughed. "I only want the band from the cigar. I'm going to buy her the biggest diamond ring in New York City, but I want something to put on her finger tonight."

"I'm sure one of the men here must have a cigar," Roman said gently.

"Would you like to join us? We're going to the pub in the village."

"Thanks, but you don't need company."

"Sure we do. What's an engagement without a party?"

"Well, if you're not just being polite, I'll ask Noelle."

"Did you change your mind about her?"

"On a regular basis," Roman answered dryly.

Noelle was less than delighted when Troy joined them at the table. He was never a joy, and that night he seemed more obnoxious than ever. Perhaps because she was beginning to realize she'd never find the negatives on her own. That meant playing up to Troy, a prospect that turned her stomach.

"What's all the excitement? You sound like a bunch of cackling hens," he said, pulling out a chair. "Settle down, chicks, the rooster is here."

"Where? All I see is a jackass," Mitzi remarked.

As his face darkened, Noelle said hurriedly, "We were congratulating Erica. She's engaged."

"To Jeff Mainwaring," Erica added.

"The tall skinny kid?" Troy looked at her with a raised eyebrow. "You must be smarter than I gave you credit for. He may not be long on looks, but he's loaded."

"You only wish you were as handsome," Erica replied angrily.

"Jeff has plenty of muscles, too," Mitzi chimed in. "Only they aren't between his ears like yours."

Troy was getting surly, the last thing Noelle wanted, so she changed the subject. "I'll bet you'll be glad when this week is over," she told him. "Those guys have really kept you on the go."

"They think they're hotshots just because they have money," he said resentfully. "Big deal! I can make more money than they do without working for it."

"Do you have some secret you haven't shared with us?" Thelma asked.

"You think I tell you everything?" His smug expression made Noelle want to slap him.

"First you have to *know* something," Mitzi said.

"You'd be surprised at some of the things I know about people," he answered.

"It's amazing the personal details people will tell a complete stranger," Noelle remarked casually.

"I can vouch for that," Thelma agreed. "When I'm giving a massage and they're supposed to be relaxing, they talk a blue streak."

"Share it with us if you get any good tips on the market," Mitzi joked.

"I was referring to the women guests," Thelma said. "Mostly they talk about their husbands or boyfriends. I hear things that would make your hair curl."

"Too bad you miss out on all the gossip," Noelle told Troy.

"Don't you believe it. Those broads spill their guts to me."

"You have such a wonderful command of the English language," Erica said disdainfully.

"Troy's just trying to get a rise out of you," Noelle said. "He's very polite to the guests."

"Somebody's gotta keep the old bags happy." He grinned. "They sleep with my picture under their pillows."

"Where do they get it? Off a 'wanted' poster in the post office?" Thelma shot back.

This was the opportunity Noelle had been angling for and she wasn't going to let their baiting ruin it. "Are you a good photographer?" she asked him innocently. "I can never take decent snapshots."

"Me, either. I specialize in *in*decent ones," he answered with a nasty laugh.

At last Noelle had her opening. She gazed at him archly. "I'd have to hide those, and there's no place in my room."

"Why hide them?" he asked. "Erotic art is the in thing."

"You mean, you keep yours out in plain sight?" she persisted.

He smiled broadly. "Well, maybe not all of it."

"For heaven's sake, don't encourage him," Erica said in disgust. "Surely you don't believe his tall stories?"

"He was just clowning around," Noelle replied. "I'll bet Troy could teach me a lot about photography."

"And a few other things," he murmured meaningfully.

"Like how to be obnoxious?" Mitzi asked. "What kind of camera do you have?" she asked Noelle. "I know a little about photography. Maybe I can help you."

"I, uh…it's just an inexpensive camera. Perhaps that's my trouble."

"It could be," Erica said. "All my snaps used to be fuzzy. I thought it was my fault, but the man at the camera shop said those cheap models won't give you sharp pictures."

"Are you going to have your wedding videotaped?" Mitzi asked. "My sister had that done and it was really neat. You can play it years from now to remind you of all the excitement."

"Are you planning on a big wedding or a small one?" Thelma asked.

"I don't care what size it is," Erica answered softly. "I just want to be Jeff's wife."

"That does it." Troy shoved his chair back. "I'm outta here."

Noelle rose, also. "I'll walk back with you."

He looked at her in pleased surprise while the others registered incredulity. "I knew it was only a matter of time until you thawed out," he said smugly.

Noelle waited until they were out of earshot before asking, "What gave you the idea I was cold?"

"You never gave me a tumble before."

"Maybe I don't like to be rushed."

He frowned. "You didn't seem to mind when Widenthal was playing touchy-feely."

"If you mean that day at the pond, Roman explained that. I twisted my ankle and he was helping me stand up."

"Sure he was! How about all the mornings you've been spending with him? What was he helping you do then?"

"Most of the time he was droning on about the advertising business. The man is a crashing bore."

"You mean he never tried to hit on you?" Troy asked suspiciously.

Noelle shrugged. "I set him straight the first day. He keeps hanging around hoping I'll change my mind, but he's not my type."

Troy showed a lot of white teeth. "You prefer blondes?"

"You might say that," she answered lightly.

"We have a lot in common. I like blondes, too. Are you a natural blonde?" His tone was suggestive.

A ripple of distaste shivered through her, but she forced herself to keep smiling. "Does it matter?"

"Not to me, but I'll be interested in finding out. Shall we discuss it at your place or mine?"

Noelle had to cool him down and steer the conversation around to where people hide things. "What I really want to talk about is photography. I wasn't kidding back there."

"Did anyone ever tell you you've got lousy timing?" he asked.

"Were you just bragging about being an expert?"

They had reached Troy's room. He took out his key and gave her a sensuous smile. "Would you like a demonstration?"

"I'll bet you don't know one end of a camera from another," she challenged.

"Come inside and I'll show you some pictures."

Noelle had a good idea of what kind. She knew there were no snapshots in his room, but she had to go along with him.

"We'll have a drink and see what develops." He opened the door, looking pleased at his own cleverness.

The room was in its usual disorder. "Don't you ever make your bed?" She caught her breath at the slip, but he didn't seem to notice.

"What's the point? It just gets messed up again." He pulled the covers haphazardly over the rumpled sheet. "Make yourself comfortable."

He smirked when she selected the chair, instead of the bed. "What will you have to drink? I have scotch or scotch."

"That's fine—with lots of water."

"Are you afraid you'll get drunk and lose your inhibitions?"

"Yes, but not the way you think. I get talkative. How about you?" she asked casually.

"Not me. I believe actions speak louder than words."

"Then how can I get you to tell me your secrets?" she asked coquettishly.

"Blow in my ear and I'll tell you anything." He handed her a glass filled mostly with scotch. "Drink up."

She took a tiny sip and glanced around. "I don't see any snapshots. Where do you hide them?"

A look of annoyance crossed his face. "Will you forget about those damn things?"

"I was right, wasn't I? You *were* bluffing."

"You want to see pictures? Okay, I'll show you some sizzlers. Come sit over here." He sat on the side of the bed and patted the place next to him. "Maybe these will get things going."

"You can hand them to me."

"I want to point out the camera angles."

Noelle joined him reluctantly because there was no alternative. She had to play along with him, no matter how disgusting it was. Otherwise she'd never get him to talk.

As Troy opened the bedside-table drawer, a knock sounded at the door. He swore pungently. "Can't those rich jerks do anything without me? I'm damned if I'm going to let them pull my string tonight."

"You'd better find out who it is," Noelle advised. "He can tell by our voices that you're in here."

Troy stalked to the door and threw it open wide. His expression darkened when he saw Roman—whose face became equally forbidding when he saw Noelle.

She was speechless with surprise and horror, knowing exactly what was going through Roman's mind. The situation couldn't have looked more compromising. Anyone who saw her sitting on a rumpled bed with a glass in her hand would have thought the same thing.

Troy's resentment changed to sly satisfaction as he witnessed Roman's displeasure. "What can I do for you?" he asked blandly.

"I was looking for Noelle, but it isn't important. I don't want to disturb you." Roman's face was austere.

Troy smiled broadly. "We were having a little drink. Would you care to join us?"

"No thanks," Roman answered curtly, turning away.

"Stop by anytime," Troy called. "When Noelle isn't in her own room, she's usually here with me."

Roman turned back to stare at him. "Isn't this her room?" He glanced over at Noelle. "But I saw you coming out of—"

She stood hurriedly. "I'm afraid there's been a little misunderstanding."

"There certainly has." He looked at her contemptuously. "And I'm the one who made it."

"I'll explain everything to you tomorrow morning." Noelle was desperate to get rid of him before he ruined everything.

"Don't bother." Roman's voice was icy. "I don't need an explanation."

"You're a good loser," Troy drawled. "Better luck next time."

"The same to you." Roman turned on his heel and strode away.

"He won't be hanging around you anymore," Troy remarked with satisfaction, closing the door.

"How could you give him the impression we're having an affair?" Noelle asked distractedly.

"We both know it's only a matter of time, baby. Drink up and let's take up where we left off."

"Some other time." She started for the door, too upset to continue the charade with Troy.

He caught her arm in a strong grip. "What's wrong with right now?"

"I just remembered I have to give Sybyll a message," she mumbled.

"Don't hand me that! You were coming on strong to me before your rich boyfriend showed up. Now you want to hotfoot it over to his place and try to convince him you weren't two-timing him with me. I know the games you women play!"

"You're wrong. I really did forget to tell Sybyll something important. Maybe we can get together later." She forced herself to make the offer, hoping to salvage the situation when she was calmer.

"Forget it! I don't play second fiddle for any broad."

Troy's mood made it impossible to placate him just then—if ever. Noelle's spirits were at their lowest ebb as she walked out into the balmy night.

Troy would be even harder to approach now, and Roman would avoid her like the plague. Both men were con-

vinced she was a liar and a cheat, but Roman's opinion was
the only one that mattered.

She couldn't bear to let him think those things about
her. He wouldn't be any more receptive at the moment
than Troy, but she had to try to explain—a daunting prospect since she couldn't tell him the truth. After hesitating
irresolutely for a minute, Noelle squared her shoulders and
started toward his room, half hoping he wouldn't be there.

Roman's stormy expression intensified when he flung
open the door in answer to Noelle's tentative knock.
"What are you doing *here?* Couldn't you and Neander-
thal man recapture the mood?"

"There's nothing romantic going on between Troy and
me," she answered quietly.

"I didn't suppose there was much romance involved,"
Roman drawled.

Noelle's nails bit into her palms. "We were only having
a drink. That's no reason to leap to a lurid conclusion."

"It enters my mind when I also see drawn drapes and a
rumpled bed."

"Troy's bed is always—" She stopped in dismay at
having made matters worse.

"Please, spare me the sordid details."

"It wasn't what it looked like," she insisted.

"Just answer me one question. Do you or do you not
have a key to his room?" The look on Noelle's face gave
her away. Roman's jaw set. "Never mind, I get the picture."

"I guess I can't blame you for jumping to conclusions." Her shoulders slumped. "I just hoped you'd give
me the benefit of the doubt."

"I wish I had one." He stared at her searchingly. "I really thought you were different, that something special was developing between us."

"I felt it, too," she whispered.

Skepticism fought a battle with Roman's desire to believe her. "I saw you coming out of Slattery's room," he said slowly. "You locked it with his key. You let me think it was *your* room."

"I didn't mislead you intentionally," she lied, having no other recourse.

"Didn't you? Then why wouldn't you let me walk you to your door the night we were out together? Why didn't you want me to come to your room to get the book you lent me?"

"I explained all the reasons." Her eyes shifted away from his penetrating gaze.

"Yes, you're very inventive, and I'm very gullible." Roman's face hardened as the weight of evidence stacked up against Noelle. "I should have known the score when you refused my offer to rearrange your boyfriend's features, but I guess I wanted to be fooled."

Noelle's heart was breaking into a million pieces and she was powerless to stop the pain. Only the truth could do that, and she wasn't at liberty to reveal it. There was no use in prolonging this agony.

"I'm sorry," she said soberly.

"You admit you've been putting on a good act all week? I'll bet you and Slattery got a big laugh out of it. Did you tell him how you pretended to respond when I kissed you?"

Noelle couldn't bear the blazing contempt in his eyes. "Don't make it any worse," she pleaded, turning away.

He jerked her back to face him. "Do I detect a trace of remorse? I'd be more impressed if I knew what you're ashamed of—your behavior, or getting found out?"

"I regret hurting your pride," she said in a low voice. "You're lucky that's all it was."

His anger died as he stared at her quivering mouth. His punishing grip loosened and he removed his hand reluctantly. "Why don't I feel lucky?"

"You will when you take time to think about it." Noelle hesitated, hating what she had to say. He would see it as the final proof her guilt. "I'd appreciate it if you didn't tell anyone I have a key to Troy's room."

Roman's momentary softening vanished. "Doesn't everybody know about your affair already? Slattery strikes me as the kind of guy who would tell anyone who'd listen. You've got a real winner there."

Noelle took a deep breath and lifted her chin. "You have no reason to do me a favor, but I'd appreciate it."

He stared at her with a mixture of emotions—anger, regret, frustration and something more. "Sure, why not? That's just one of the things I'd like to forget."

"Thank you." Noelle turned and walked away, keeping her head high.

Roman remained in the doorway, watching until she was out of sight.

Chapter Six

Roman crossed the room in two giant strides when a knock sounded at his door a short time later. His expression changed when he saw who was there.

"Are you ready to go?" Jeff asked. "We'll swing by and pick up Erica and Noelle."

"Noelle can't make it," Roman said curtly.

"Too bad. Maybe you can find somebody in the tavern to take her place."

"Thanks, but you two go ahead without me. I'm not really in a mood to celebrate."

"I gather Noelle threw you another curve. What you need is a change of scenery. We'll go into town and have a few laughs. By the end of the evening you'll regain your faith in women."

Roman smiled mirthlessly. "I'll bet you still believe in the tooth fairy, too."

"Don't be such a cynic, Rome. Come on, Erica and I are celebrating our engagement."

"And I don't want to put a damper on the party. Have a round of drinks on me."

Jeff finally had to accept defeat. After he left, Roman wandered outside, wondering how to get through the evening.

He eventually wound up at the bar, which was deserted at this hour. The room served as a lounge during the rest of the year. For the benefit of the men, a self-service bar had been set up in one corner. Guests helped themselves and signed a chit.

Roman splashed a generous amount of bourbon into a glass, added ice cubes from an insulated ice bucket and bypassed the array of mixers. He took his drink to a window with a view of the pool and tennis courts in the distance.

The tranquil scene did nothing to calm his smoldering anger. How could he have been so wrong about a woman? he asked himself. Not only had Noelle fooled him completely, the man she was involved with had the IQ of a turnip!

"So you made a mistake," he muttered. "It isn't the first, and it won't be the last."

That was cold comfort right now. He wanted to shake some sense into Noelle. Couldn't she see what a dirt bag Slattery was? Roman's hand tightened around his glass as the object of his wrath appeared on the path outside. Troy was heading for the tennis court, carrying a racket.

Roman's first impulse was to go after him and wipe the self-satisfied smirk off his face. On second thought, he left the lounge and went in the opposite direction.

* * *

Most of the employees' rooms were dark, but a light shone through the drapes of a room several doors down from Troy's. Roman banged on that one first, fully prepared to try every room along the corridor until he found Noelle's.

She opened the door wearing a short cotton robe printed with violets. Her long hair was tied with a purple ribbon and fastened to her crown, but little golden tendrils escaped and curled around her delicate face. Roman stared at her in bemusement, momentarily forgetting why he'd come.

Noelle clutched her robe nervously. "I thought we'd said everything there was to say."

His scowl reappeared. "I haven't even scratched the surface."

"That's too bad, because I have things to do."

His eyes roamed over her body. It was obvious she was nude under the thin robe. "You're due for a long wait," he drawled. "I just saw lover boy on his way to play tennis."

"Go away, Roman." She tried to close the door, but he pushed his way inside and slammed it behind him.

"Not until I talk to you," he said, glowering.

"About what? You've already expressed your opinion of me. That should have made you feel better."

He barely heard her. "I can't believe it was all an act. Not that day by the bridle path, and certainly not last night in the pool. Look me straight in the eye and tell me our feelings weren't mutual."

"The situation was provocative," she explained carefully. "What happened was unfortunate."

"Your response was due purely to circumstances?"

"Yes."

"You would have reacted the same way toward any, not too repugnant male?" he prodded relentlessly.

Noelle bit her lip. "I didn't say that. You must know you're a very attractive man."

"Then you're agreeing that the feeling *was* mutual. Doesn't that make you wonder if it isn't time to break it off with Slattery?"

"You just don't understand," she said hopelessly.

"I'm trying to. Tell me what you see in him. He's a coarse, insensitive chauvinist." Roman clasped her shoulders. "Maybe you and I aren't right for each other—although I'm not convinced of that—but you deserve better than a jerk like Slattery."

Noelle gazed up at the man she loved, drowning in the misery of denial. "Why do you care?" she whispered.

His hands tightened on her shoulders. "I'm damned if I can answer that. I only know the thought of him touching you makes me see red."

"It bruises your ego to think he succeeded where you failed," she said sadly.

"I wish that's all it was." He wound a soft tendril around his finger. "I really care what happens to you, Noelle. I can't stand to see you throw yourself away on a guy like that."

"I wish I could convince you that things aren't the way they seem."

He stared into her shadowed blue eyes for an interminable moment. "I'm probably the biggest damn fool west of the Rockies, but I believe you. I'm not wrong about the chemistry between us. You want me right this minute every bit as much as I want you."

"Please, Roman. We've been through this before, and it always ends in recriminations." She tried to pull away, but he wouldn't release her.

"It was my fault for losing my temper and letting you get away with it. This time you're going to tell me what it is you're holding back."

"If you'll just wait a few days," she pleaded.

He drew her close and stroked her cheek gently. "I feel as though I've waited for you all my life. If you really want me to leave you alone, tell me I don't mean anything to you."

Noelle felt her willpower slipping away as she gazed into his compelling eyes. Every inch of her body yearned for him. How could she end everything between them?

"You can't say it!" Roman exclaimed triumphantly.

His mouth covered hers in a kiss that left her clinging to him. Liquid fire raced through her veins as he wrapped his arms around her, welding their bodies together while his hands roamed restlessly over her back.

"Sweet, wonderful Noelle," he groaned. "Why did you try to make things so difficult for us?"

"I don't know." At that moment she truly didn't. All that mattered was having him back.

He slipped his hand inside her robe to cup her breast. "This is the way I want to make love to you, slowly, with infinite time to discover how beautiful you really are."

"I shouldn't," she murmured.

"Do you want me to stop?"

How could she say yes when his thumb was circling her nipple, sending shock waves throughout her entire body? She clamped her hand over his, but the sensation only intensified.

"Don't fight it, darling," he crooned, kissing the valley between her breasts.

Noelle couldn't. Her hand fell away, allowing him to part her robe. When his tongue curled around her hardened peak, she reached the point of no return.

"Don't stop," she gasped. "Don't ever stop!"

"That's a promise."

He untied her belt and gazed at her body with a molten expression. Noelle quivered as he caressed her stomach and hips. But when his hand glided between her legs to caress the soft skin of her inner thigh, she was shocked into an awareness of the consequences that would follow. She couldn't afford this indulgence.

Bracing her palms against his chest, she said, "We can't do this. I know all the terrible names you're going to call me, but it would be a dreadful mistake."

Roman didn't get angry, as she'd feared. Worse than that, he stroked her even more intimately. "Convince me," he said softly. "Tell me this isn't what you want."

"I can't *do* what I want." She moaned as he continued his sensuous exploration, in spite of her efforts to stop him.

"I intend to prove you're wrong." Scooping her into his arms, he carried her to the bed.

Noelle had never gone through such torment. Roman was laying siege to her body with his hands and mouth. The arousing kisses on her most vulnerable points were destroying her will to resist.

In an effort to fight his seduction, she squeezed her eyes shut and reminded herself of how much was at stake. "If Troy finds out, it'll all be over," she muttered.

Roman raised his head. Fury blazed in his eyes as he glared down at her. "I don't know which one of us is the bigger fool. Slattery owns you body and soul, doesn't he?"

Noelle shrank back from the primitive emotion on his face. "Roman, I—"

He was beyond listening. "The guy must be really terrific in bed. Too bad you didn't do a little comparison shopping, though. I might have given him a run for his money." Roman's tone was meant to be insulting.

She pulled her robe together and huddled against the headboard. "I'd like you to leave."

"Don't worry, I'm going—and this time I won't be back." He leaned forward and gripped her chin hard. "But first, how about something to remember me by?"

Noelle tried to twist her head away. She couldn't bear to have him kiss her in anger and contempt. But Roman was too strong for her. His mouth ground into hers with punishing force. This was the final indignity. Her eyes filled with tears and she uttered a tiny, involuntary whimper.

The pressure of his mouth eased instantly and he cradled her face gently between his palms. "I'm sorry...so sorry."

"I am, too," she whispered.

Roman groaned as he gazed at her wet lashes and trembling lips. "What hold does that devil have over you?"

"He's a blackmailer." All of Noelle's defenses were down and she couldn't hold it in any longer.

"*What?*" His first reaction was incredulity. It was followed by relief and dawning excitement. "*That's* why you let him treat you the way he does?"

"Yes," she answered simply.

"But why didn't you tell me? How could you let me accuse you of all those rotten things without saying a word to defend yourself?"

"I couldn't tell you the truth—and you have to keep quiet, too." Belated alarm gripped her. "I never should have told you. Promise you'll keep it a secret."

"And let that piece of garbage get away with it?" Roman asked in outrage.

"There's no other way. He has the power to ruin a lot of innocent lives."

"What could he have on you that's so terrible?"

"Not me. He's blackmailing a dear friend of mine."
Now that the damage was done, it was a relief to get the
whole sordid story off her chest. "So you see why it's vi-
tal that nobody finds out," Noelle concluded. "It would
be a real tragedy for Diane and Chrissie."

"You've gone through all this grief for a friend?"

"I was afraid of what she'd do if I didn't. Diane is really desperate. The loss of her husband was devastating
enough. She couldn't survive losing her child, too."

Roman smoothed her hair. "I always knew you were one
of a kind."

"Unfortunately I haven't been able to find the negatives. I'd hoped this miserable business would be all over
by now, but I've searched Troy's room from top to bottom. If they're hidden there, I don't know where."

Roman frowned as something occurred to him. "How
did you get him to give you his key?"

"It's a duplicate from the office. Troy doesn't know I
have it. I really freaked out when you almost gave me away
tonight."

He smiled wryly. "I wish I'd known that's why you
looked so guilty."

"I only hope I can get back in his good graces. Troy is
terribly envious of you." Noelle sighed. "I guess I'm a
better dancer than an actress. He suspects that I'm
in... that I prefer your company to his."

"Slattery would lose a popularity contest to Jack the
Ripper," Roman said disdainfully. "If he tries to hit on
you again, I'll flatten him."

"No, you can't! That's exactly why I didn't want you to
know. You'll spoil everything. Since I can't find the negatives on my own, I'll have to trick him into telling me
where they are."

"Calm down, darling," he soothed.

"How can I? You know what an egotist Troy is. He won't tell me what month it is unless I flatter him silly."

"You have two chances of getting the negatives that way—little and none."

Noelle's heart sank as he confirmed her own misgivings. "I can't give up," she said doggedly.

"I don't expect you to. I only said you were going about it the wrong way. If I promise to get the negatives for you, can we stop talking about it and make love?"

"You have an idea?" she asked eagerly.

"Several of them." He took her in his arms and nibbled delicately on her ear.

She lifted her shoulder to dislodge his disturbing mouth. "This is serious, Roman."

"I couldn't agree with you more." He parted her robe while he scattered a line of kisses along her jaw.

When his head dipped to her breast, Noelle asked faintly, "You really have a plan?"

"A guaranteed one." He began to unbutton his shirt, smiling sensuously at her. "Do you have to know now, or can you wait till later?"

She had complete faith in him. Holding her arms out wide, she answered softly, "I've waited such a long time already."

Roman's lovemaking was even more wonderful than she'd imagined it would be. He aroused her to unbelievable heights with drugging kisses and a slow enjoyment of her body. She cried aloud in ecstasy when he searched out the private places that brought her the most pleasure.

"My lovely Noelle," he said huskily. "Do you know how happy it makes me to know I can bring you to life like this?"

"How did I ever find the strength to say no to you?" she marveled, running her hands over his broad shoulders.

Roman's chuckle was vibrantly male. "I should turn the tables on you to make up for all those cold showers I had to take."

Her fingers sought out and closed around the proof of his virility. "Would you do that to me?" she asked softly.

He drew in a sharp breath. "I don't have your willpower." Parting her legs, he positioned himself between them. "What little I do have just ran out."

Noelle accepted him joyfully, raising her body to meet his thrusts. The throbbing sensation filled her with such rapture that she called out his name over and over again. Roman was at the center of her universe, the source of all happiness.

Their welded bodies were taut with a passion that escalated almost unbearably. The acme was reached in a thunderous burst of power that drained away the tension. They were left with radiant pleasure that gradually subsided into a glow of contentment.

Both were totally relaxed in each other's arms. When their heartbeats returned to normal, Roman kissed Noelle tenderly, gently stroking her tousled hair.

"That was worth all the waiting," he murmured.

She smiled blissfully. "Now I regret all those other times I missed."

"I plan to make up for them tonight."

"All of them?" She laughed. "In one night?"

"Easily." He wrapped a long leg around both of hers, fitting their bodies closely together. "I could keep you in bed for a week."

"You won't be here that long." The present was starting to intrude on her idyll.

"I'll be nearby," he assured her.

"It won't be the same. A new crop of guests will be coming in Sunday night, and I won't have much free time from then on."

"I suppose I can share you for as long as it takes."

Noelle was reminded of his promise. "You were going to tell me how you plan to get the negatives. Do you really think you can?"

"Piece of cake. Before you know it we'll be back in New York."

"But you live in Chicago," she said uncertainly.

"That's something else we have to talk about. I haven't been completely candid with you, either."

A little chill of apprehension touched her spine. "What didn't you tell me?"

"My real name, to start with. It's Wilding, not Widenthal."

"Why would you...?" Her eyes widened as she made the connection. "Roman Wilding! You're the investigative reporter."

He nodded. "I'm here to do an undercover story on health spas. Naturally, I couldn't register under my own name."

Noelle scrambled out of his arms in horror. "You don't do pieces like that. Your specialty is exposés."

"Ordinarily, but I let myself be talked into this assignment." He gave her a melting smile. "Luckily, or I wouldn't have found *you*."

"Stop stonewalling, Roman! Somehow you found out about Troy's activities, and you're here to do a story on the foolish women who let themselves be duped by a man. And I played right into your hands," she said bitterly. "I guess you can add me to the list."

His face set in stern lines. "You can accuse me of that after what we just shared?"

Her suspicion evaporated as she remembered his tender, caring lovemaking. Roman wasn't a user of women. He would never do anything that underhand.

"I'm sorry," she murmured. "Troy is like an evil cloud over my head. He's even poisoned my judgment."

Roman drew her into his arms and kissed her temple. "You'll forget about him as soon as I get you out of this place."

"Why are you so sure you can find the negatives?" she asked doubtfully.

"I probably can't, so I'm not going to try. Slattery will be persuaded to give them up voluntarily."

"You can't threaten him!" Noelle's agitation returned. "That would only make things worse for Diane. Troy would carry out his threat through pure spite."

Roman put a forefinger on her lips. "Hush, sweetheart, and listen to me. Those negatives could be anywhere—in a safe-deposit box, stashed with a friend, although that's unlikely. A guy like Slattery doesn't have any friends," he said contemptuously. "The point is, there's no hope of locating them."

"So far, you're not making me feel any better."

"That part comes later." He smiled mischievously. "Unless you'd like to postpone this discussion."

"If you don't tell me soon, I'm liable to have an acute anxiety attack," she warned.

"Okay, this is the plan. Slattery is a bully who targets vulnerable women because they're not likely to fight back. Like most bullies, he isn't long on courage. If he thinks his own hide is in jeopardy, he'll fall apart like a cheap suit."

"All you'll get out of beating him up is satisfaction." Noelle was bitterly disappointed. She'd pinned her hopes on Roman.

"I don't intend to lay a finger on him. But suppose he thought he'd run afoul of organized crime? A coward like Slattery would do anything to square himself."

She gave him a puzzled frown. "But Troy isn't part of the mob. At first, I thought perhaps Sybyll was in on the blackmail scheme with him, but I'm convinced he's working alone."

"I agree with you on all counts. He's a sleazy opportunist who doesn't have guts enough for the big time. He's due for the scare of his lifetime when he discovers the heavyweights are seriously displeased with him."

"Why would they be?"

"Slattery knows your friend Diane is an ex-actress, married to a very wealthy man. What he doesn't know is that she's the sister of one of the top dons in New York City. A guy who heads up a very important family."

"You're way off base. I know all of Diane's relatives. They're lovely people. Her father is a heart specialist, and she doesn't even have a brother."

"*You* know that but Slattery is going to think he picked the wrong woman to blackmail. A mobster brother would take a very dim view of some two-bit jerk setting up his sister. He might get extremely physical—unless Slattery turned over the negatives."

Noelle's face lit with dawning excitement. "You really think Troy would fall for it?"

"Fear is a powerful incentive, and those guys play rough. I've met a few of them in my career. They've raised pain to an art form."

"You're a genius!" Her eyes sparkled with excitement. "I know a lot of out-of-work actors in New York. One of them would jump at the chance to fly out here and play the part."

"I'm sure they're competent, but I already have someone in mind."

"Don't you think I'm a better judge of acting?"

"Not for the part I have in mind. This job requires a street fighter."

"You're not going to hire a real gangster?"

"No, a detective named Mike Trinity. He's done legwork for me on some crime stories. I'll give him a call first thing in the morning."

"Couldn't you phone him right now?" she pleaded.

"Well...it's three hours later back there." Roman reconsidered after gazing at her anxious face. "Why not? This is probably the best time to catch him in." Roman picked up the phone and punched in a number.

Mike Trinity wasn't pleased at being awakened. "Yeah, what do you want?" he growled.

"That's no way to answer the telephone." Roman chuckled. "What if I were the president calling?"

"I'd tell him to do his campaigning in the daytime. In case you haven't noticed, Rome, it's two o'clock in the morning."

"It's only eleven out here. I'm in Arizona."

"Tell me about it tomorrow. I'll return your call at 8:00 a.m.—*my* time."

"Don't be such a grouch, Mike. I have a job for you. I want you to catch the first plane to Tucson in the morning."

"That's not around the corner. I can put you in touch with an operator out there a lot cheaper."

"Money is no object. This job is very important to me." Roman smiled at Noelle. "I want the best."

"I'm a pushover for flattery—along with an unlimited expense account," Mike added dryly. "What's the score?"

"I'll fill you in when you get here. Plan to stick around as long as necessary. I'll make a reservation for you at the Golden Sands Hotel under the name of... How about Johnny Scarlotti?"

"Sounds like a hood."

"You got it."

"Okay, how do I get in touch with you?" Mike asked.

"I'll pick you up at the airport. Give me a quick call before you board so I'll know your arrival time. I'll give you my number here."

After they'd concluded the arrangements, Noelle asked, "How can I ever thank you?"

Roman smiled mischievously. "I can think of a couple of ways."

She wound her arms around his neck. "Let's see if we're both thinking of the same thing."

Their lovemaking was more leisurely this time. They caressed each other with deep appreciation, delighting in discovering new ways to bring pleasure.

Gradually the kisses became more torrid as their passion escalated. The burning need for each other was evident in their straining bodies and rapid breathing. Noelle's whispered plea was gratified instantly. Roman completed their union and stoked the fire he had lit. They rode spirals of sensation to their bursting climax, then drifted down from the heights, totally satisfied.

"My beautiful love," Roman murmured. "You're mine now, and I'll never let you go."

Noelle waited expectantly the next day for Roman to return from his meeting with the detective. As the hours dragged by, she began to fret about all kinds of possible snags. When he finally appeared in the late afternoon, she was a bundle of nerves.

"Where have you been? Wasn't Mike on the plane? I knew we should have gone with a professional actor."

"Take it easy, darling," Roman soothed. "Everything's shaping up. Mike arrived on schedule and he's ready to go to work."

"You were gone for hours. I was sure there'd been a slipup. What took you so long?"

"Mike and I had a leisurely lunch. We talked over old times—all the scrapes we got in and out of." Roman smiled reminiscently. "Mike is a free spirit. He doesn't take life seriously."

"You're not exactly inspiring me with confidence."

"Believe me, you couldn't have a better man for the job."

"What did he say about the plan? Does he think it will work?"

"Like a charm. He hasn't failed me yet." Anticipating her next question, Roman said, "He'll make contact with Slattery later today."

"This waiting around is driving me up the wall," Noelle groaned. "How will I ever get through this afternoon?"

"I have a suggestion," he murmured.

Some of her tension dissipated as she gazed at his strong, handsome face. "Can you hold that thought until tonight?" she asked softly.

"If you promise me your full attention."

Noelle gave him a radiant smile. "Next time, ask for something difficult."

Mike Trinity was a tall, lanky man with medium brown hair and regular, but unremarkable features. He was the kind of person who could go unnoticed if he chose. The only truly memorable thing about him was a pair of piercing blue eyes.

That afternoon, however, he drew second glances from the guests at Carefree Dunes, where casual dress was the norm. Mike's double-breasted beige suit, navy shirt and white tie were definitely attention-getting. Ignoring the curious looks directed at him, he strolled leisurely toward the gym, following Roman's directions.

Troy came over when he noticed Mike standing by the door. "Can I help you?"

"I'm looking for Troy Slattery."

"You found him." Troy flashed a professional smile. "What can I do for you?"

Mike didn't return the smile. "We need to have a talk."

Troy frowned. "Who are you? You're not a guest here, as far as I know."

"You got that right. I'm here to have a confidential chat with you."

"What about?"

"Not here. I like privacy. You got an office?"

Troy laughed harshly. "All I've got is a fancy title—physical-fitness trainer."

"Okay, let's go for a walk."

Troy turned belligerent. "I'm working, pal. I can't just take off because you say so. What's this all about, anyhow?"

"Have it your way." Mike shrugged. "You know a lady named Diane Vanderhoff?"

Troy's eyes shifted. "Can't say I've had the pleasure."

"That's a poor choice of words, *pal*," Mike drawled.

Troy was definitely on the alert now. "Are you her husband?"

"How did you know she was married if you never met her?"

"Well, I just . . . I mean . . ."

Mike looked at him dispassionately. "I tend to get testy when people lie to me."

Troy darted a quick glance around the room. "Let's step outside for a minute." When they were outdoors he adopted a conciliatory tone. "I do remember her now—a very nice lady. I wasn't trying to stonewall. You have to understand. We get so many women in and out of here that sometimes they all run together in my mind. But Diane— Mrs. Vanderhoff—was one of the best. I mean, she had real class," he added hastily.

"You're right there." Mike gave him a disparaging look. "So, go figure women. How did she get mixed up with a jerk like you?"

Troy struggled between anger and caution. Caution won. "You got it all wrong, Mr. Vanderhoff. Nothing went on between me and your wife. I have the utmost respect for the lady."

"What makes you think I'm her husband?"

"You said . . ." Troy's surprised expression turned ugly. "Who the hell are you, and how did you find out about Diane and me?"

"Now we're getting somewhere. You admit you're blackmailing her."

"I don't admit anything. You better be careful how you fling accusations around!"

"Or what?" Mike smiled. "You'll sue me?"

"I don't need a lawyer to clean your clock." Troy jabbed Mike in the chest with his forefinger to emphasize his sneering disdain.

In a lightning instant, Mike seized Troy's wrist and twisted his arm behind his back. "You'll need a seam-stress to sew you together if you ever try that again. You're playing out of your league, lover boy." Mike didn't raise his voice, which made it all the more deadly.

"Let go!" Troy gasped in pain. "You're breaking my arm."

Mike released him. "Now that we understand each other, let's get back to Diane."

Troy sullenly massaged his arm. "I don't know how you found out, but if you think you're cutting yourself in, you're out of your gourd."

"I don't play in penny-ante games."

"Then what *do* you want?" Troy shouted.

"You have some souvenirs the lady wants."

"Up yours!" When Mike took a step toward him, Troy retreated, but his face remained stubborn. "I offered them to her. All she has to do is pay the price. It isn't like she can't afford it."

"There are two things wrong with your offer. How does she know you won't print more pictures every time you need spending money?"

"I guess she'll just have to take that chance," Troy answered insolently. "Unless she wants the world to know she sleeps around. I don't care one way or the other. Either way, I get paid."

Mike gazed at him without emotion. "You might get a different payoff than you bargained for. I said there were *two* things wrong with your proposition. The other one is, you picked the wrong mark."

"Don't try to tell me Diane isn't loaded. I know better."

"Do you also know she's the sister of Tony Mancuso, better known as the Undertaker—but not to his face. Tony hates that nickname."

"You're putting me on!"

"No, really. He goes ballistic whenever he reads it in the newspaper. You wouldn't want to be around him."

"What kind of con are you trying to pull?" Troy demanded. "You must think I'm the village idiot."

"Actually, I didn't think you were that bright." Mike unbuttoned his jacket so his shoulder holster was visible.

Troy's eyes widened as he detected the bulge made by the hidden gun. He licked his lips nervously. "How do I know you're on the level? You could be making up this entire story."

"You'll find out if you don't cough up those negatives." Mike looked him over consideringly. "A fitness trainer with smashed kneecaps would be out of a job. And a guy who depended on his looks wouldn't attract many women with a messed-up face."

"You can't scare me," Troy blustered.

Mike's smile was chilling. "It will be interesting to see just how brave you really are."

"Wait a minute!" Troy was clearly shaken. "I'm willing to make a deal. We can work out some kind of split. After all, I'm entitled to something for my trouble."

"I'll tell you what I'll do," Mike drawled. "I'll pay for the roll of film."

"Get serious!" Troy answered furiously. "You meet me halfway or it's no deal."

"You're seriously flawed on the concept, pal. The Undertaker doesn't make deals. I was sent here to get those negatives—period. Either I get them, or you get a long stay in the hospital. And don't think you'll get even by selling the pictures to the tabloids. If Diane's name appears in the newspaper, yours will, too—on the obituary page. Do I make myself clear?"

Troy stared at him in frustrated rage. Finally he snarled, "Okay, you win."

"Good. I'll take the negatives and be on my way."

"I don't have them handy." In spite of his apparent capitulation, Troy was reluctant to see his prize slip away.

Mike pinned him with a steady stare. "We can do this the easy way, or we can do it your way. I'm on straight salary, so it doesn't matter to me."

"I'm not trying to blow smoke in your ear," Troy said hastily. "I'm telling you the truth. I wouldn't leave anything that valuable lying around for the maids to pick up."

"All right. Where are they? We'll go get them."

"Well, they, uh . . . I gave them to a friend for safekeeping, but he's out of town."

"I doubt if he took your negatives along," Mike remarked dryly. "We'll go to his place and pick them up."

"I don't have a key."

"That's no problem."

"I don't know where he put them."

"Phone and ask him." Mike's voice was steely.

Troy was like a cornered animal looking for an escape. Fear and greed were waging a battle inside him. He needed time to think of a way to save both his skin and his profit.

"I know you're not going to believe me, but this guy is a nature freak. He's backpacking in the wilds of Yellowstone Park."

"You're right, I don't believe you."

"All I'm asking for is a little time," Troy whined. "Dave will be back in a week."

Mike was silent for a long time, his piercing eyes skewering the other man. "You're a lying little weasel, but I'm going to pretend to believe you. You have one week. At the end of that period, I'm going home. Where *you* go is up for grabs."

"Don't worry. I won't cross you."

"I'm not worried." Mike gazed at him thoughtfully. "I don't think you'd be dumb enough to split. You've got a nice little thing going here. But in case the thought crossed your mind, remember the old saying—you can run, but you can't hide. We have family members everywhere.'' He sauntered away without waiting for an answer.

As Mike walked leisurely to his car, he passed Roman and Noelle, who had stationed themselves near the parking lot. The two men glanced casually at each other with no hint of recognition. Only Roman could have noticed the almost imperceptible wink Mike gave him.

Chapter Seven

Noelle was impressed by the brief glimpse she got of Mike Trinity. "He certainly looks the part," she commented. "Do you think Troy bought it?"

"I'm sure of it," Roman answered. "Mike flashed me the victory sign."

"I didn't see anything."

"Trust me. We'll get the whole story tonight. I told Mike we'd meet him at the pub in the village."

"Can't we go see him now? Diane deserves some good news, but I don't want to get her hopes up until I'm sure they're justified."

"It's getting late and you have to be here for dinner," Roman reminded her.

"Not really. If Mike got the negatives, I don't have to keep up the deception anymore."

"Nothing in life is that easy. No matter how convincing Mike was, I doubt if Slattery caved in on the spot."

"You think he'll find a way to worm his way out?" she asked anxiously.

"Not a chance. By the time we get through with him, he'll be willing to *pay* to get rid of those damn negatives. You still have a part to play, however."

Noelle wrinkled her nose. "I was hoping I wouldn't have to put up with his sleazy remarks anymore."

Roman laughed. "Don't worry, *you'll* have to come on to *him*. Slattery won't be interested in anything but keeping all his body parts in working order."

"Do I have to tell him how wonderful he is?"

"Don't overdo it. The main thing is to act like you normally do, so he doesn't get suspicious."

"I can manage that. What else?"

"Mike will fill you in tonight. Meet me in the parking lot after dinner, but make sure Slattery doesn't know where you're going. It would be helpful if you could find out his plans for tonight. If he spotted you with Mike, the whole scam would be out the window."

"No problem. I already know where Troy will be tonight. Some of the men are leaving, and he has to take them to the airport."

"Couldn't be working out better." Roman kissed her briefly. "You should get back. I'll see you tonight."

Noelle hardly recognized Mike when she met him in the pub that evening. He looked completely different in a pair of jeans and a plaid shirt.

"I can't get over the change in you," she marveled after the introductions had been made. "You're like another person entirely."

He grinned. "Did you like my gangster outfit?"

"Personally, I thought that white tie was a bit much," Roman said.

"Nonsense! He was perfect. You should be an actor," Noelle told Mike.

"I guess you mean that as a compliment," he answered with amusement.

"Be careful what you say," Roman warned. "Noelle is a performer."

"That doesn't surprise me." Mike gazed at her with admiration. "You certainly know how to pick beautiful women."

Noelle was unpleasantly reminded of her competition. She concealed her feelings under a joking tone. "Does he always prefer blondes, or does he give equal time to brunettes and redheads?"

Mike slanted a laughing glance at his friend. "I don't think I'd better answer that."

"Will you kindly stop giving Noelle the impression that I'm a modern-day Casanova?" Roman complained.

She hung on to her determined smile. "I might have guessed you'd known a few women in your life."

Mike snapped his fingers. "That reminds me. Francine is looking for you."

Roman frowned. "Why would she tell *you?*"

"Because she knows we keep in touch, I suppose. She said she'd left messages on your answering machine, but you didn't return her calls."

When Noelle saw Roman's discomfort, she remarked lightly, "You men are all alike. Out of sight is out of mind."

"I wouldn't say that," he protested, then realized he was only digging himself in deeper. "I mean, I left so hurriedly that I forgot a . . . an appointment. It was an oversight, that's all."

After glancing from one to the other, Mike said in a casual voice, "I'm ready for another drink. How about you two?"

The subject was tacitly dropped, although Noelle was far from satisfied. Who was Francine, and how much did she matter to Roman? It was a good sign he'd forgotten their date, but by no means conclusive. Maybe Roman was the kind of man who could forget a woman easily. Noelle shoved the painful thought to the back of her mind when Mike began to question her about Troy.

"Could you tell if he was shook up?"

"Like a kangaroo with a bee in his pouch," she answered. "But that could have been because he was in a snit about having to play chauffeur. Troy hates being treated like a servant."

"I don't think that was his only problem tonight. But we have to keep the heat on. I gave him a week, so I can't use any more muscle yet. We hoods have a code of ethics." Mike smiled.

"If he's scared enough, maybe he won't hold out for a week," she suggested.

"Don't count on it. Without pressure, a mark starts to get his confidence back. He figures he can talk his way out, or maybe something will turn up to save his bacon. Mostly he plans to play for more time. We have to disabuse him of the idea."

"What do you have in mind?" she asked.

"This is the part where you come in. Here's what I want you to do."

It was late when Noelle and Roman returned to Carefree Dunes. They'd spent most of the evening making detailed plans for the coming week. Mike had briefed Noelle extensively on the part she was to play.

"I'll be glad when this is all over," she told Roman as they walked across the parking lot. "I'm not cut out for intrigue."

"It's a fact of life to a certain extent, whether you like it or not. People don't say what they really mean. They tell you what you want to hear, or the things that are in their best interests."

"Not the people *I* know."

"Don't be too sure."

She gave him a troubled look. This was a side of Roman she hadn't seen before. "I didn't realize you were so cynical."

"It's not a matter of cynicism. I'm a realist. You can get blindsided if you're too trusting."

"I think I'd rather take my chances."

"Then you're apt to get hurt." His expression softened as he turned his head to gaze at her. "That would be a pity."

"I'm afraid it's too late for me to change," she answered soberly.

"I don't want you to change." He framed her face between his palms and kissed her with awakening passion. "You're perfect just the way you are."

Gullible? Noelle asked herself silently. Did he really think she believed Francine was a mere business associate? She drew away from him. "Somebody might see us."

"You're right. We can't afford to take any chances at this point. Go on in and I'll come by later."

"It's been a long day and I'm kind of on edge, Roman."

"I could help you relax," he murmured.

"I doubt it."

"Okay, angel, I understand." He tucked a strand of fair hair behind her ear. "Get a good night's sleep and I'll see you in the morning."

As she got undressed, Noelle couldn't shake off her feeling of uneasiness. Had Roman revealed more than he intended to? All this week, had he told her what she wanted to hear because it was in his own best interests? Their physical relationship was awesome, but was that all he cared about?

Noelle wanted to believe she meant more to him than a brief, satisfying affair, but the seed of doubt had been planted.

The previous night's fears seemed groundless when Noelle awoke the next morning. Her natural optimism and the bright sunshine caused her spirits to soar. She and Roman planned to have the entire day to themselves!

All the men who hadn't departed the night before were leaving that day. But Roman was only going as far as Tucson. Noelle would follow in her own car, since she had to be back at the spa Monday morning.

On her way to her car, she came across Erica and Jeff saying a reluctant farewell. Noelle joined them for a moment to say goodbye.

"Have a safe trip home," she told him. "I'm sorry to see you go."

"Not half as sorry as I am to leave." He gave Erica a soulful look.

"It's only for a short time." Erica tried to console him, although she looked equally dejected.

"That's for sure! I'll make all the arrangements as soon as I get home."

Roman appeared, carrying a suitcase. "What time does your plane leave, Jeff? Can I give you a ride to the airport?"

"Thanks, but I have a rental car to turn in. When are you leaving? Maybe I'll see you in the waiting room."

"I'm staying on in Tucson for a few days," Roman answered.

"I thought you couldn't wait to get out of here."

Roman smiled at Noelle. "Women aren't the only ones who have the privilege of changing their minds."

"It doesn't take a brain surgeon to figure out what changed yours." Jeff chuckled. "Do you think they put something in our food? Romance is busting out all over."

"Actually, I used a love potion on you," Erica joked. "But I was hoping you wouldn't figure it out."

Jeff raised her chin with his forefinger and gazed deeply into her eyes. "I didn't need any help to fall in love with you."

After a misty-eyed moment she whispered, "I'll miss you."

"You won't have a chance. I'll call you every day."

Wanting to give the young couple time alone, Roman said, "Well, I have to stow my luggage in the car."

As he and Noelle walked away, she remarked, "They're so adorable together. I just love happy endings."

"You don't know yet how things will turn out."

"Yes, I do. They'll get married, have lots of babies and live happily ever after."

"That's the fairy-tale version. Erica makes a lovely Cinderella, but once Jeff gets back to his normal life, this week might seem like a charming interlude. Most likely, he'll phone her every day at first, then a couple of times a week. Finally the calls will taper off entirely."

A chill rippled down Noelle's spine. Roman could be describing their own situation. "I happen to think Jeff has more integrity than that," she said stiffly. "He wouldn't have asked Erica to marry him if he intended to dump her."

"I never said that was his intention. I'm sure he's quite sincere at the moment, but time and distance have a way of cooling youthful passion—not to mention the attractive girls back home."

"That would make Jeff a very shallow person," Noelle said evenly. "I don't think he is."

"No, just young and impulsive." They had reached Roman's car. He dropped the subject as he opened the door. "I'll meet you in the lobby of the Golden Sands."

Noelle's high anticipation was considerably dimmed as she watched Roman drive away. Did he really believe Jeff would let Erica down? Or was he sending a subtle message about himself? His warning, if that's what it was, had come a little late.

Noelle walked slowly to her car. She'd come to Carefree Dunes to save Diane from getting hurt. It would be ironic if she became the one who got hurt.

Noelle was normally an upbeat person. By the time she reached Tucson she'd decided to live for the moment and stop worrying about the future. Sitting next to Roman in his car, she was completely happy.

He turned his head to smile at her. "I thought we'd start our sight-seeing tour with a visit to Old Tucson. Is that all right with you? I was told it's the second most visited attraction in Arizona, after the Grand Canyon."

"Anything you like," she answered.

Something stirred in the depths of his gray eyes. "I'll remind you of that later."

"I'm counting on it." She smiled enchantingly.

He put the car in gear and drove away from the hotel. "We'd better get out of here or we won't see any more of Tucson than the Golden Sands Hotel."

Noelle wouldn't have minded. She was content simply to be with him. Roman made everything seem like an adventure.

He was fascinated by the open countryside bordering both sides of the road. Long stretches of desert were broken only by mesquite bushes and the sentry-shaped Joshua trees, pointing like signposts in several directions.

"I can't get over all this open space," he marveled. "In New York, some developer would have built houses all the way to the foothills."

"I hope that never happens. I've learned to appreciate nature here. I never knew there were such gorgeous sunsets or so many stars in the sky."

"It's beautiful country, all right," Roman agreed.

Noelle chuckled. "That's high praise coming from two dyed-in-the-wool New Yorkers. We both had to be coerced into coming here, and now we sound like a couple of cheerleaders."

"You look the part more than I do," he said fondly.

"Oh, I don't know." She tilted her head to gaze at him consideringly. "You have a great body—and I'm speaking from experience."

"Not a recent one. I'll be happy to turn around and refresh your memory," he said softly.

They had arrived at what looked like a small frontier village. Low wooden and adobe buildings lined the dusty street, and hawks wheeled lazily overhead in the burning-blue sky. It was a scene out of the past.

Noelle was torn between conflicting desires. "This is a slice of the Old West," she said hesitantly. "As long as we're here, we really should take a quick look."

"I never thought my rival would be a ghost town." Roman laughed as he put his arm around her shoulders. "Okay, honey, let's see how the pioneers lived."

They strolled along the wooden sidewalk, peering into shop windows displaying things like hand-operated coffee grinders and wooden churns. The dry-goods store had bolts of material on a long counter with an oil lamp next to the cash drawer.

"It's hard to imagine living without electricity or modern appliances," Noelle remarked.

"No supermarket, either. You'd have to milk the cows and churn some butter before you made breakfast."

"Why was milking the cows women's work?" she demanded. "What were the men doing, besides waiting to be fed?"

"They got to do all the good stuff, like riding in posses and getting into brawls over pretty girls at the saloon."

"I'd have been a dance-hall girl rather than a milkmaid. What would you have been?"

Roman grinned. "A steady customer at the dance hall."

While they were wandering the length of the main street, the sound of gunshots rang out. A flock of birds spiraled upward, squawking in protest as they disbursed into the blue sky.

"That must be the shootout at the Okay Corral that they stage for tourists," Noelle said.

They joined the other spectators and watched as the historic shootout was reenacted with startling reality. Six-guns smoked and cowboys fell, clutching at their "wounds." The air was acrid with gunpowder and dust from the unpaved street.

When the battle was over and the cowboys were signing autographs for the eager children in the crowd, Noelle and Roman drifted away.

"They weren't very subtle about settling their differences in those days," she remarked.

"There was a rigid code of ethics. A guy like Slattery wouldn't have lasted a week."

Noelle was unpleasantly jolted back to the present. "Don't be too sure. He's a survivor."

"Not this time. He's no match for Mike."

"It didn't occur to me before, but I guess we should have asked Mike to join us today."

"He went back to New York this morning."

Noelle gave Roman a dismayed glance. "How could he leave right in the middle of a case? We aren't really any closer to getting the negatives than we were before. You know how worthless Troy's promises are."

"Relax, darling. Mike can't do anything until next Saturday, so it would be foolish for him to hang around all week. He laid out the strategy for you, and he'll be back when he's needed."

"What if something goes wrong?"

"It won't," Roman soothed. "I should never have brought up the subject. This is *our* day." When she continued to look troubled, he said, "Let's go see The White Dove of the Desert. The guidebook says it's a Spanish mission built in the 1700s and still functioning as a church. The pictures they showed were stunning. It's stark white, with towers and tall Moorish windows, and the interior is covered with frescoes and arabesques."

Noelle smiled at his enthusiasm. "We certainly don't want to miss that, do we?"

The sun was going down as they drove back to the hotel, setting the sky ablaze and turning the mountains into purple peaks with golden crowns. By the time they were seated at a table by the swimming pool with tall, cold drinks in front of them, the first stars were beginning to twinkle overhead.

Noelle glanced around at the lovely setting. "It's been such a wonderful day."

"It isn't over yet," Roman murmured.

Anticipation had been building between them all day. It was heightened during dinner at a restaurant tucked into the hills above the city.

The food was delicious, but Noelle was more conscious of the candlelight reflected in Roman's eyes as he raised his wineglass in a toast.

"To our first dinner together," he said. "I finally have you all to myself."

"It's a special treat for me." She smiled. "You're much better company than Troy."

"I don't want you to think about him tonight. He doesn't exist," Roman said firmly.

"If only you were right." She sighed. "I've barely thought about him today, but he's like an evil presence, always lurking in the background."

"Not for much longer." Roman covered her hand with his big capable one. "Trust me."

"I do, but I still can't help wishing I could wake up and find myself back in New York."

"I can't work miracles, but if you'll let me, I can almost guarantee to take your mind off Slattery, for tonight, anyway." His voice was like deep, rich velvet.

When they returned to the hotel, Noelle waited by the elevator while Roman retrieved his key at the desk. The clerk also handed him several slips of paper, the kind phone messages are written on. That meant Roman had been in contact with people at home. He didn't know anyone out here.

Noelle's heart skipped a beat. Was he making plans to go back to New York before the week was up? She could hardly blame him; he had his own life to live. But it gave her a sinking feeling. Would she still be his first priority?

When Roman joined her, she was careful to keep her voice casual. "You're very popular," she remarked, indicating the messages.

"Not really." He stuffed the pieces of paper into his pocket and pushed the elevator button.

Noelle couldn't leave well enough alone. "You must be getting impatient to leave here."

"Do I give that impression?"

"Not today, but I know it's on your mind," she answered as they walked down the corridor.

Roman paused to unlock his door. When they were inside, he took her in his arms. "You're the only thing on my mind. You have been all day." His embrace tightened as he kissed her.

Noèlle responded wholeheartedly, even though it meant passing up the opportunity for a candid conversation. She needed to find out how serious his feelings were for her, but Roman never seemed to want to talk about the future—*their* future together. That wasn't very promising.

It would be destructive to live in a fool's paradise, but when Roman's ardent mouth took possession of hers and his hands moved over her body, nothing else mattered.

"You're like an aphrodisiac," he muttered, stringing a line of kisses down her neck. "I don't think I could ever get enough of you."

She began to unbutton his shirt. "Let's find out tonight."

"That's exactly what I had in mind." He shrugged off his shirt with a chuckle that had a rich masculine sound.

After unfastening her zipper, he slid the wide straps of the sundress off her shoulders. The soft fabric slipped sensuously down her body, almost in slow motion. Roman watched as her bare breasts were revealed, then her taut midriff and long slender legs. His breathing quickened at the enticing picture she presented, clad only in sandals and lace bikini briefs.

"You're so utterly perfect." He touched her almost reverently, like a blind man exploring an art treasure.

Noelle trembled when he stroked her breasts and circled the nipples erotically. She swayed toward him as his hands continued down her body, skimming her hips, smoothing her thighs.

As his fingertips moved under the elastic of her panties, she moaned softly. "You're driving me crazy, Roman. I need you so much."

"We need each other, sweetheart." He lifted her in his arms and carried her to the bed.

After removing her panties, he trailed a tantalizing path down her body, lingering where she was most vulnerable. His ardent kisses and caresses aroused her to such a fever pitch that she reached for the waistband of his slacks with quivering urgency.

"Make love to me, darling," she whispered. "Now!"

"With the greatest of pleasure," he answered huskily.

Roman stripped off his clothes in a blur of movement. Returning in an instant, he clasped Noelle in his arms and parted her lips hungrily. Their nude bodies met and melted together in the heat both were generating. When she moved sensuously under him, he became part of her, plunging deeply.

They rocked against each other in a dance of mounting excitement. Waves of sensation pulsed through their taut bodies as they spiraled higher and higher on a fiery path to ecstasy. When the limit of endurance was reached, Roman's hoarse cry of completion reverberated through Noelle at the same moment she reached her own peak.

Their labored breathing gradually returned to normal, but both were too languid to move. Long minutes passed before Roman stirred, and then only to kiss Noelle's temple.

She sighed happily. "What a perfect ending to a perfect day."

"What makes you think it's over?"

"You're just bragging," she teased.

"Maybe right at the moment, but I have remarkable recuperative powers."

"I know." She smoothed his hair, smiling.

"Any complaints?"

"Not a one." They kissed tenderly. "I wish we could stay here like this forever," she said wistfully. "I don't relish going back to Carefree Dunes."

"Are the women pretty hard on you?"

"Not especially. It isn't the work I mind, it's what I have to do with Troy. I keep worrying that I'll foul up and ruin everything."

"You're just suffering from stage fright," he said. "You must have been through this before. What do you usually do when it happens?"

"It only lasts for a few minutes. As soon as the music starts, I'm okay."

"You will be this time, too."

"This is different, though. Until now, I was only responsible for myself. But Diane's entire future rests on my performance."

"There's a certain amount of acting connected with your profession. You know how to play a part."

She smiled as some of her tension drained away. "Actually, I can be quite convincing. There was a dance director once who made a terrible pest of himself. He propositioned every woman he could corner, but he made me a special target."

Roman kissed the tip of her nose. "That's not surprising."

"It would have been more flattering if he didn't have a reputation for quantity rather than quality, although he was fairly successful in spite of it. A lot of dancers didn't feel they could turn him down. Kevin could have found some reason to fire them."

"You didn't feel you had to worry?" Roman shifted his position to gaze at her.

"Of course I did. He's a real sleaze-ball—not unlike Troy, now that I think of it." She sighed. "Why is that kind always attracted to *me?*"

He ignored her question for one of his own. "How did you discourage him and still keep your job?"

"I acted as if he was the most fascinating man in the world and I couldn't wait to be with him. Unfortunately something always happened to prevent it—a sick aunt who needed me, a visiting college roommate." She laughed. "You name a reason and I thought of it."

"He bought all those lame excuses?" Roman asked incredulously.

She gazed up at him through long lashes while moistening her lips provocatively. "I told you I could be convincing. A clever woman knows how to conceal her true feelings."

"That's very interesting."

His clipped tone and expressionless face finally registered. "Is something wrong?" she asked hesitantly. "I thought you'd be amused."

"I applaud your ingenuity. You're more complex than I suspected."

"Somehow that doesn't sound like a compliment." Noelle sat up against the headboard and pulled the sheet over her body. "You don't honestly think I would sleep with someone for the sake of my career, do you?"

"No, I'm sure you wouldn't."

His reply had the ring of honesty, but she wasn't satisfied. "Something's bothering you, though. I want to know what it is."

"I guess I'm not comfortable with the fact that men are so gullible."

"I didn't mean for you to take it personally," she protested.

"I'm sure you didn't."

"What does that mean?" she demanded.

A welter of emotions coursed over his strong face as he stared at her. They were replaced by a fond expression. "Nothing. It isn't worth talking about."

He reached for her, but she fended him off. "I think it is. For some reason, my story upset you. Either you don't believe I turned Kevin down, or you disapprove of me for doing it."

"You know that's not true. I've told you how I feel about men who try to victimize women. They're beneath contempt."

"Then what did I do wrong?" she asked in frustration. "And don't say nothing, because we both know that isn't so."

"It has nothing to do with the guy who hit on you. I'm proud of you for outwitting him. What shook me up was the realization that I could be as big a patsy as any other man," Roman said slowly. "When you showed me how you looked at him with those big blue eyes, I would have attended a football game in my Jockey shorts if that's what you wanted."

She stared at him incredulously. "Do you think I was putting on an act when we made love?"

His expression softened momentarily. "Nobody could be that good an actress, but..." He paused, looking troubled again.

"But what?" Noelle persisted when he didn't continue.

Roman chose his words carefully. "I was attracted to you the first time you walked in on me unexpectedly. The feeling wasn't mutual, however. You didn't even like me at first. I had to trick you into spending time with me."

"I was embarrassed, and you didn't make things easier. You kept teasing me about the incident."

"That's one explanation. Another could be that you realized you couldn't avoid me for an entire week, so you decided to make the best of it."

She let out her breath in a puff of outrage. "My job doesn't include the kind of activities we engaged in. I see now that it was a mistake to make an exception in your case. Whether you believe me or not, it was far from my normal behavior. I thought there was more than just a sexual attraction between us, but I was wrong—at least on your part."

She started to get out of bed, but Roman caught her arm. Noelle tried unsuccessfully to break his grip. He pinned her down with his body and framed her face between his hands, forcing her to look at him.

"First of all, I know you weren't faking a response when we made love. I do have some experience with women.

Part of my pleasure was watching you come to life in my arms."

"I'm glad I wasn't a disappointment," she answered bitterly.

Roman smiled wryly. "You're almost too good to be true. I guess I couldn't trust my own good fortune. When you told me how easy it is to fool a man into believing he's special, I couldn't help wondering if I wasn't simply kidding myself into thinking I was different."

"I don't understand you!" she exclaimed. "You just said you knew I wasn't pretending."

"Any unselfish man can satisfy a woman, especially one as enchanting as you. I'm glad *I* wasn't a disappointment, either." He gazed at her searchingly. "Is that all you wanted from me, Noelle?"

A little bubble of excitement started to expand deep inside her. Was he asking her to make a commitment? That meant he was ready to make one, too. Roman did love her, even if he hadn't put it into words.

Her eyes were like twin blue stars as she gazed up at him. "You're not only very special to me, you're the most exciting man I've ever known. I'd show you exactly how I feel, but I'm afraid that would only confirm your suspicions."

"I was an idiot for ever having any." He lowered his head and brushed his lips across hers. "Can you forgive me?"

She put her arms around his neck and smiled bewitchingly. "I don't approve of harboring grudges."

He clasped her in a close embrace and kissed her hungrily. Their former anger soon turned into a different kind of passion as they caressed each other with murmured words of remorse.

Roman's efforts to make amends brought cries of delight from Noelle. Tiny sparks lit a slow fire in her loins as he transferred his kisses to her breasts. The flames licked at her midsection as he moved down her body.

Roman raised his head to stare at her with incandescent eyes. "Tell me what I want to hear?"

A tiny vestige of caution prevented Noelle from handing over her heart. What if that wasn't what he was asking for? She ran her hands down his body and caressed his rampant manhood.

"You're wonderful," she answered softly.

The shadow of disappointment that crossed his face was eclipsed by a more urgent emotion. Positioning himself between her legs, he muttered under his breath, "That will have to be enough."

Roman fused their bodies, driving everything else from Noelle's mind. They responded to each other like finely tuned instruments, playing a seductive tune that grew in intensity and ended with a crescendo.

Much later, Noelle tilted her head to look up at him. "Do you realize we just had our first argument?"

"I like the way you argue," he said fondly.

"I mean before that."

"As long as they all end like this, I won't complain."

She stirred in his arms. If ever the time was right for clarifying their relationship, it was now. "You've never really told me how you feel about me," she began tentatively.

He chuckled. "I thought I gave you a couple of clues just now."

"That isn't what I mean. You—"

The telephone rang shrilly, startling both of them. "Who the devil could it be at this hour?" Roman frowned as he reached for the phone.

The woman at the other end said, "Don't tell me I finally reached you! It's Francine, in case you've forgotten."

He glanced briefly at Noelle, then half turned away. "Do you know what time it is?"

"About midnight out there. Don't tell me you were asleep."

"No, I . . . Can I call you in the morning?"

"I suppose you have some girl with you. Is she the reason you ran off without a word? She must be really hot stuff."

"I came to Arizona to do a story," Roman said evenly. "I had to leave in rather a hurry and I'm afraid I forgot to, uh, cancel our appointment."

"Appointment! What am I, a business associate?"

Noelle knew it would be courteous to go into the bathroom and let Roman take his call in private, but dynamite wouldn't have moved her. She could tell he was talking to a woman—probably that Francine. He must have called and told her where he'd be staying.

"It's late," Roman said grimly. "We'll discuss this in the morning."

Francine quickly changed her tone when his displeasure registered. "You can't blame me for being annoyed, darling. We did have a date, and you stood me up."

"I explained the circumstances."

"I know, and I understand," she said hastily. "But when you simply disappeared off the face of the earth, I was worried about you. Nobody knew where you were. I saw lots of our friends at a party at Tony Lester's tonight—that's why I'm calling so late. I just got home."

Roman sighed. "You could have waited until tomorrow."

"That's what I get for trying to do you a favor," Francine pouted. "Judson Taylor was at the party. He saw that accountant you were looking for going into an apartment building on West Sixty-third Street."

Roman sat up in bed, his body tensing. "Is he sure it was Stockwell?"

"Positive. He used to have an office in Judson's building. Stockwell was carrying a bag of groceries, so it appears he's living there."

"Francine, you're a doll! I love you."

So Roman did know how to say the words, Noelle thought bitterly. Only not to *her*. She threw back the covers and got out of bed.

Roman was abruptly reminded of her presence. "I can't thank you enough," he told the other woman. "I'll call you first thing in the morning."

"I'm more interested in seeing you. When are you coming home? I miss you, darling," Francine murmured.

"That's very... I'll have to be here for another week, but I..." He paused when Noelle shut the bathroom door sharply.

"A whole week? Can't you finish up sooner?" Francine wheedled.

"I'm afraid not, but I do appreciate your call."

"You can show me how much when you get home. Will you call me the minute you get back?"

"Yes, I'll do that."

"Promise?"

"I promise," Roman answered impatiently, watching Noelle come out of the bathroom and start to get dressed. He hung up the phone. "What are you doing?" he asked her.

"It's time for me to leave," she answered, rejecting a more biting response. Dignity was all she had left.

"I sort of took it for granted that you'd stay tonight."

"I can't." She zipped up her dress. "I have to be back at the spa early in the morning."

"I'll leave a wake-up call. We can have breakfast together," he coaxed. "I probably won't see you again for a few days."

"I'm sure you'll keep busy." Her voice was strained in spite of her efforts. She picked up her purse and started for the door.

"Noelle, wait!" Roman crossed the room in a couple of long strides and blocked her way. "Don't you think you're overreacting just a tad? It wasn't my fault the phone rang."

"You didn't seem too unhappy about it," she answered stiffly.

"Dear heart, what did you want me to do, hang up?"

"Certainly not, since you were the one who called her in the first place. Your... friend wouldn't have known where to find you, otherwise."

"I forgot we had a date," Roman explained patiently. "Doesn't that tell you how important it was? But I had to call and apologize. That's only common courtesy."

"Was it polite to fawn all over her in front of *me*?" Noelle demanded.

"What the devil are you talking about? I never fawned over Francine even when you *weren't* around!"

Noelle's eyes glittered dangerously. "Call it anything you like. I still think it's in remarkably bad taste to tell one woman you love her while you're in bed with another."

"It was only an expression!" he exclaimed. "Francine did me a big favor and I was expressing gratitude. She told me where to locate an accountant who worked for one of the failed savings and loans. My next article is going to be on that scandal."

"You don't have to explain to me," she said tautly.

"I obviously do, since you think I'm carrying on a long-distance romance with another woman behind your back."

Noelle wanted to believe otherwise, but what reason had Roman given her? The fact that he was a tender, thoughtful lover? Maybe he brought Francine the same kind of bliss. The notion caused an actual pain in her chest.

"I have to go," she said brusquely.

His jaw set. "You're being completely unreasonable. There is absolutely no reason for you to be jealous of Francine. I don't know how to say it any plainer than that."

"I am not jealous of Francine." Noelle enunciated each word clearly. "I couldn't care less about your relationship with her. You can go home tomorrow and take up where you left off for all I care."

Roman's eyes narrowed as his anger rose to meet hers. "I might just do that."

"Good. Have a nice trip. And don't bother to call before you leave. Consider this our goodbye." She stalked past him and out the door with her head held high.

Chapter Eight

Noelle had to force herself to get out of bed on Monday morning. She'd lain awake most of the night trying to get at the truth of her relationship with Roman. Was he equally insecure about her feelings for him? It didn't seem possible, but that would explain their brief argument. Unless he cared deeply for her, why would it matter whether she returned his affection or merely desired him?

Because men had giant egos, Noelle concluded sadly. *They* used women regularly, but they had to believe they were the one and only in a woman's life. Roman was a generous, stirring lover, but he wasn't immune to ego.

Noelle managed a smile when she met Erica on the way to breakfast. "Well, the vacation is over," she remarked brightly. "Time to go back to work."

"I guess so," Erica answered neutrally.

"Troy will be happy. He'll be the center of attraction again."

"No doubt."

The terse answers weren't like Erica, who was usually bubbly. Noelle had been so sunk in her own misery that she hadn't noticed at first that her friend wasn't a bundle of joy, either.

"Is something wrong?" she asked tentatively.

"No, I'm just a little tired."

"I know you miss Jeff," Noelle said sympathetically. "Have you heard from him since he got home?"

"He telephoned last night—late. He'd been to a party."

"Well, why not? You can't expect him to drop all his friends. Those are the people who will be your friends, too, after you're married."

"I hope so."

Noelle slanted a glance at her. "You're not just upset because Jeff went to a party. Did you argue about it?"

"No, it was a welcome-home party given by his mother. Jeff had to go." Erica hesitated for a moment. "He didn't call me until late—I waited by the phone all evening. And then when he did call, we talked about the times we were together and how wonderful it was."

"So what's the problem?" Noelle gave her a puzzled look. "You should be all smiles."

"Jeff didn't set a date for our wedding."

"Is *that* all? He probably didn't have a chance to talk to his mother."

"That's what he said, but I got the feeling he was hiding something from me."

"You're letting your imagination run away with you."

"I hope you're right, but Jeff couldn't wait to go home and tell his mother about us. It seems strange that he didn't get around to it."

"Perhaps he wanted her full attention when he sprang the big news. They wouldn't have had much of a chance to discuss it with a crowd of guests due to arrive any minute."

That was one explanation. Another could be that Roman was right about whirlwind romances. Was Jeff having second thoughts? Would his calls start to taper off and then cease entirely?

Noelle's private doubts were misplaced. Jeff had tried to talk to his mother about Erica, but she was more interested in hearing if he'd benefited from his stay at Carefree Dunes.

"Now you know that business isn't always conducted in the boardroom," she said. "You can make invaluable contacts by meeting important men in a social environment. I hope you made an effort to network with them."

"I didn't have much in common with any of them except a fellow from Chicago named Roman Widenthal. He was a great guy."

"Widenthal?" Estelle Mainwaring frowned. "From Chicago? What does he do for a living?"

"He owns an advertising agency, or he's the head honcho. I'm not sure which."

Her mouth thinned. "Couldn't you have struck up a friendship with someone in finance? You'd have had a lot more in common. I hope you didn't waste your entire week."

A brilliant smile lit up Jeff's face. "It changed my entire life. That's what I wanted to talk to you about."

"And I want to hear every detail just as soon as we have a chance."

"What's wrong with right now?"

"I have a surprise for you, darling. I've invited all your friends over for a welcome-home party."

"Tonight?" Jeff frowned. "I thought you and I would spend the evening together, just the two of us."

"That's very considerate of you, my dear, but I'm not one of those mothers who tries to monopolize her son. I know you're anxious to see your friends after being gone for a week."

"I wasn't in outer Mongolia," he protested. "I'm sure you meant well, but I really need to talk to you."

"We'll have a long conversation tomorrow," she promised, glancing at her watch. "Right now, you just have time enough to shower and change. The guests will be arriving in an hour."

Jeff was frustrated, but there was nothing he could do about it that night. The next morning he joined his mother for breakfast at about the same time Erica was confiding her worries to Noelle.

Estelle looked up from the newspaper and smiled at him. "Good morning, darling. It's lovely to have you home again. Did you have a nice time last night?" She rang a crystal bell next to her plate. "I'll have Gladys fix your breakfast."

"All I want is juice and coffee."

"That isn't enough to eat. Bring my son an omelet and some buttered toast," Estelle told the maid who answered her summons.

"I'm really not hungry," Jeff objected.

"Haven't I always taught you that good nutrition is important? You wouldn't expect your car to run on an empty tank, would you?"

"All right, I'll eat breakfast," he said impatiently. "Now that's settled, can we talk?"

"Of course, my dear. I've been looking forward to it. Tell me what you accomplished at Carefree Dunes."

"Quite a lot." He grinned. "I got engaged."

"I can't say I appreciate your sense of humor, Jeffrey," she said coolly.

"I'm not joking, Mother. I met the most wonderful girl in the world. We want to get married as soon as possible."

"I don't understand this at all. There were only supposed to be men at the spa. Where did you meet this girl?"

"She works as an aerobics instructor. I know you're going to love her as much as I do. Her name is Erica Jones."

Estelle stared at him with incredulity. "You want to marry an employee of a health spa?"

Jeff's smile vanished. "What's wrong with that?"

"You don't know anything about her. Who are her parents? What kind of background does she have?"

"I couldn't care less. I'd love Erica if she was found in a pumpkin patch. She's sweet and kind and beautiful. You'll see when you meet her."

"That won't be necessary. I know exactly what happened out there. You were bored and lonely, and she was available. That kind of woman is constantly on the lookout for a wealthy young man."

"I won't let you talk about Erica that way! She has absolutely no interest in my money."

Estelle's lip curled. "How naive can you be, Jeffrey? Just ask yourself how fast she would have accepted you if you'd been a truck driver or a plumber."

Jeff stared at his mother as if seeing her for the first time. "You've always stressed the importance of family, but I never realized it was because you're a snob. That's why you sent me to dancing class and private school—so I wouldn't meet anyone unacceptable."

"Do you expect me to apologize for giving you all the advantages? People are more comfortable with their own kind. Hasn't your life been pleasant?"

"It hasn't been my life—it's been an extension of yours and Dad's. With Erica, I'm a person in my own right for the first time. I'm sorry if she fails to measure up to your social and economic requirements, but I'm going to marry her as soon as I can get a license."

"I absolutely forbid it!" Estelle snapped. "I will not stand by and let you ruin your life."

"That's *your* opinion." Jeff's face firmed with a new maturity. "I've tried to be a good son. After Dad died, you said this house was too big, you were lonely, so I moved back here. I took over at the bank, even though it wasn't what I would have preferred."

"You were groomed to be your father's successor. That was understood from the time you were a teenager."

"Neither of you ever asked me if that's what I wanted," Jeff said quietly. "I went along with your wishes—rightly or wrongly—but I can't allow you to choose my wife."

"I've never tried to! I detested that little snip, Candice, you were going with, but I didn't try to break it up. I knew you'd come to your senses, and you did. You will this time, too. That's why you mustn't do anything hasty."

Jeff gazed squarely at his mother. "I intend to marry Erica. You can either be happy for us, or accept the prospect of never seeing your grandchildren." He rose and walked out of the room.

Mitzi glanced around the breakfast table and remarked, "I haven't seen this much gloom since the Donner party ran out of salt and pepper. What's the matter, Erica? Are you afraid your boyfriend will forget about you now that he's back with his fancy girlfriends?"

"How can you be so insensitive?" Noelle asked sharply. "Everything's fine between Jeff and Erica. Why don't you try being happy for them?"

Mitzi raised her eyebrows. "Aren't *we* in a snit this morning? I suppose everything's fine between you and *your* lover boy, too."

Noelle shot a quick glance at Troy, but he was scowling at his plate, ignoring everyone. "If you're talking about Roman, I was glad to see him go," she said casually. "He was getting to be a nuisance."

"I wouldn't mind being pestered by a guy like that." Mitzi looked over at the fitness trainer. "What's rattling your cage, Troy? You'd better happy up before you meet the ladies. They expect a smiling face to go with all those muscles."

Thelma laughed. "They're not interested in anything above his shoulders."

"Knock it off," Troy snarled.

"You just spoiled his illusions." Mitzi grinned. "All this time he thought they were fascinated by his mind."

"Stop picking on him. Poor Troy had to work yesterday," Noelle said to appease him. "He deserves to be in a bad mood."

"Are you for real?" Mitzi asked her. "We work twice as hard for half the pay."

"Not last week, you didn't." Troy was still smarting from the condescending treatment he'd had to suffer through. "The party's over, though. You broads better haul your buns out of here and get to work."

"Who died and made *you* führer?" Thelma demanded.

Erica glanced at the clock on the wall. "I guess it is time."

Noelle hung back to talk to Troy as the others trailed out. "Those two must have their tongues sharpened every morning," she said. "You deserve a medal for putting up with them."

"Yeah, I know." Some of the sullenness left his face. "I get tired of them, myself. Maybe you and I could get away one night, just the two of us."

His scowl was back. "Oh, I get it. Now that your rich boyfriend is out of the picture, suddenly I look better to you. Well, thanks for nothing."

"Don't be that way, Troy. I was only buttering him up the way we're supposed to. Isn't that what you do with the women?" she asked guilelessly. "It was all an act."

"Then why did you race out of my room the night he found us together?"

"Because I was rattled. It wouldn't do either of us any good if word got around that we were having an affair. Sybyll might even fire me. She knows our women guests like to fantasize about you. It would spoil the fun if they thought you were involved with someone."

"I guess you're right," he answered complacently.

"We can be friends, though, as long as we're discreet."

He looked at her with dawning lechery. "Sounds good to me. We'll leave the dining room separately tonight and meet in my room."

Noelle had gotten a faster reaction than she'd expected. "Well, we ... I was thinking about a drink in the village," she answered hastily, playing for time. Mike had told her to make her first move on Tuesday. "You know, to relax."

"Baby, if I was any more relaxed I'd be in a coma. Those freaking guys ran me ragged."

She breathed a sigh of relief. Troy had given her an out. "Then perhaps we'd better wait till tomorrow night. You need a good night's sleep."

"I'll be okay as long as I'm lying down." He smirked.

"No, I insist." She gave him a sidelong glance. "I can wait one more day."

Troy argued, but she succeeded in standing firm without alienating him. Finally she managed to get away.

Sybyll beckoned to her as Noelle was leaving the dining room. "You have a telephone call. Please make it brief—your class is waiting."

Noelle followed her into the office and picked up the phone, expecting the call to be from Diane. She received a shock when Roman's deep voice sounded at the other end.

"I expected to hear from you," he said.

"I think we covered everything," she answered stiffly.

"Not quite." His tone was clipped, anything but conciliatory. "You left in such a hurry you forgot your equipment."

"I don't know what you... Oh, no!" she exclaimed as realization hit her.

Sybyll looked up from her desk. "Is anything wrong?"

"No, I... Something just surprised me, that's all."

Roman heard her aside. "It surprised me, too. I thought that was the most important thing in your life. Certainly more important than anything *I* had to offer."

Noelle had to hide her emotions from both Sybyll and Roman, which wasn't easy. The unexpected sound of his voice made her almost light-headed. She'd never expected to hear it again.

Composing herself with an effort, she ignored his comment and asked, "Could you leave it for me at the hotel desk when you check out?"

After a pause he answered, "Are you sure you know what to do?"

"Yes. Mike explained it to me."

"He should have demonstrated. Do you know anything about the engine of a car?"

"No, but I'm not completely incompetent, simply a bad judge of character." When Sybyll tapped her pencil ominously, Noelle said, "I have to go. Just leave the package at the desk with my name on it. I'll pick it up tonight."

The day dragged by at a snail's pace. Noelle usually enjoyed her classes, but everything was drudgery now. All she wanted to do was accomplish her purpose and go home. Memories of Roman mocked her from every corner of Carefree Dunes.

At the end of the day she said to Erica, "I have to drive into Tucson. How would you like to come along and keep me company? We can have dinner at a restaurant and maybe see a movie."

"I'd like to, but I can't. Jeff might call."

"You can't sit by the telephone waiting for him to remember you exist," Noelle said sharply. She was instantly sorry when she saw the hurt in Erica's eyes. "I didn't mean that. Of course you should wait for his call. I'm just jealous. I only wish I had somebody like him."

"I thought you and Roman were starting to hit it off."

Noelle shrugged. "We were never serious about each other. We just had a few laughs together, that's all."

"I'm sorry. I liked Roman."

"Yes, women do." Noelle unlocked her door. "I have to shower and change. Say hello to Jeff for me."

Stars were starting to wink on in the sky by the time Noelle drove into the parking lot of the Golden Sands

Hotel. She ignored the couples having cocktails around the pool and walked inside to the front desk.

"I believe you have a package for me," she told the clerk. "Noelle Bartlett."

He disappeared into a back room for several minutes, then came back empty-handed. "I'm afraid there's nothing here, Ms. Bartlett."

"There must be. Roman Widenthal left it for me. He was staying here, but he checked out this morning."

"Mr. Widenthal is still with us. Would you like me to ring his room?"

"No! I mean, you must be mistaken."

The clerk shook his head. "I saw him about half an hour ago. He stopped at the desk for a paper and said he'd be in his room if anyone called."

Noelle's heart was racing rapidly. Why had Roman changed his plans? Not on her account, certainly. She couldn't go through the ordeal of seeing him again, yet she had to get the package.

When she became aware that the desk clerk was looking at her strangely, she said, "I'll just call him on the house phone."

"Room 436," the clerk told her helpfully.

"I thought you went home," she blurted when Roman answered the phone.

"I haven't finished my article yet." His voice was as distant as it had been that morning.

"Why did you give me the impression you were leaving?" she demanded.

"I don't recall doing any such thing."

"You knew that's what I thought."

"Your thought processes are incomprehensible to me," he answered coldly. "This isn't the first conclusion you've leapt to."

"I didn't come here to argue with you, Roman," she said tautly. "Will you please bring me the package? I'm downstairs in the lobby."

"You'll have to come up here and get it. I can't leave right now. I'm expecting a phone call."

"I can just imagine from whom!"

"I don't doubt that for a minute. You have a very vivid imagination. I could listen to your suppositions for hours. In fact, I *have* listened to them."

Noelle gritted her teeth. "Will you bring me the damn package?"

"Certainly. As soon as I receive my phone call." He hung up.

Noelle was furious. She wanted to tell Roman exactly what she thought of him, but not to his face. How could she go back to that room where he'd brought her such ecstasy—and then taken it away? After sitting motionless for a long moment, she squared her shoulders and walked to the elevator.

Roman opened the door wearing gray slacks and a white shirt open at the throat. He looked virile and remote. She found it difficult to imagine that hard mouth softening against hers.

He stood aside. "Come in."

"I'd rather not. May I have the package?"

"Aren't you being a little childish? We aren't exactly strangers."

"This isn't a social visit," she said curtly.

"Former lovers can still be friends."

She glanced around at a couple approaching down the hall. "I prefer not to dwell on the past."

"That's where we differ. I enjoy remembering the way you felt in my arms. You're the most responsive woman I've ever known."

Noelle stalked inside and slammed the door, her eyes sparkling with anger. "You've just hit a new low in tastelessness."

"I meant it as a compliment."

"Do I get a star by my name in your little black book? Or do you use a scale of one to ten? Just as a matter of curiosity, how does my score compare with the others?"

"You are easily the most aggravating female in this galaxy," Roman answered grimly. "If close-mindedness was figured in, you'd get a hundred percent."

"And if we were grading on deceit, you'd make the highest score ever recorded," she flared back.

"In what way did I ever deceive you?" he asked. They were standing toe-to-toe, scowling at each other.

"You let me think you cared about me."

"Dear Lord, didn't I *show* you I did?"

Her lashes fell. "I don't mean when we made love."

"What *do* you mean?"

Roman obviously had no idea of what she wanted from him, and she couldn't tell him. If she had to ask for love, it wasn't there.

She turned away wordlessly, but he hauled her back. "We're going to have this thing out once and for all. I want to know what happened between us."

"It isn't important," she murmured.

"The hell it isn't! We had something wonderful going for us, and suddenly you turned off. I can hardly believe a telephone call from another woman was the real reason."

"You wouldn't have liked it if the situation was reversed and *I* got a phone call," she said defensively.

"I'd have been jealous as the devil, but I wouldn't have walked out." He cupped her cheek in his palm. "How could you leave me?"

If only he wouldn't touch her. It made resisting him so much harder. Noelle turned her head away. "I'll admit I overreacted, but it would have happened sooner or later—with or without Francine's phone call. We simply want different things out of a relationship. Satisfying sex isn't enough for me."

"Is that how you'd describe what we shared?"

"No, it was sublime," she answered softly. "You're a wonderful lover. I didn't even know it could be like that."

"I wasn't looking for compliments. I want answers. What's wrong with out relationship?"

She couldn't see any point in evading the issue. Roman would be uncomfortable, but at least he'd stop cross-examining her. "I made the mistake of falling in love with you," she said quietly.

"You're not serious?"

She ducked her head, unable to watch the incredulity in his eyes turn to wariness, or maybe regret. "I kept hoping you'd feel the same way, but last night I realized you never would."

"Francine's call convinced you of that?"

"It was only the catalyst, a reminder of the other women in your life, and the fact that I was simply another in a long line. I had to leave. The longer I stayed with you, the harder it would have been when you found someone to take my place."

"There will never be anyone like you," he said, his voice deep with feeling.

She tried to smile. "At least we quit while we can still find good things to say about each other."

"The only thing that's over between us are the silly half-truths and evasions." He reached for her.

Noelle held him off desperately. If Roman took her in his arms she'd be back where she was before—completely under his spell. How many times could she summon the strength to walk away?

"Don't do this to me," she pleaded. "You're taking unfair advantage."

He laughed delightedly. "I need all the help I can get with you. You've had me tied up in knots for days, thinking I was only a convenient source of recreation for you."

"You couldn't have thought that! You must have guessed how I felt. I showed you often enough, hoping you'd say something."

"You also told me you were adept at making men think you cared."

"That argument we had!" Noelle exclaimed. "You *did* take it personally."

"Let's just say I thought twice about telling you I was crazy about you."

Her heart skipped a beat. "Does that mean you love me?"

"Would I put up with your terrible temper if I didn't?" he teased. When he saw that she needed to hear the words, his face filled with tenderness. "I love you more than I ever thought it was possible to love a woman. I should have told you sooner, but from now on, I intend to say it so often you'll beg me to stop."

"Never!" Noelle flung her arms around his neck.

Their kiss made up for all the hurt and frustration both had felt. Between murmured words of love and remorse, they exchanged kiss after kiss. Finally Roman carried her to an armchair and sat down with her on his lap.

She snuggled close and put her head on his shoulder. "I was so miserable when I thought I'd never see you again."

"Did you honestly think I'd give up that easily? If you hadn't forgotten the package, I'd have thought of some other way of getting you here."

"I asked Erica to come with me tonight. Just think if she'd accepted. We wouldn't be sitting here like this."

"Yes, we would. I'd have given her a quarter and sent her to the movies."

"You must have been watching old black-and-white films on television." Noelle smiled. "You can't even buy popcorn for a quarter these days."

"No matter. Erica would have known we needed to be alone. She's in love, too. Did Jeff phone and set the date?"

"He called, but he didn't say anything definite. I do hope he isn't having second thoughts. That's what you said would happen."

"I was just being cynical." Roman smiled at her. "That was probably one of the days when you were driving me to distraction."

"Would I do that to you?" she purred, tracing the inner curves of his ear with a provocative forefinger.

"You're doing it now and you know it, you little demon." He began to unfasten the buttons down the front of her shirtdress. "But two can play that game."

The evening was warm, so Noelle was wearing a pair of panties and nothing else under her cotton dress. She'd expected to drive to the hotel and right back again.

Roman's eyes glittered when her bare breasts were exposed so readily. After slipping the dress off her shoulders, he dipped his head and kissed each rosy peak.

Noelle tangled her fingers in his hair as his warm mouth stirred her blood. "What would I have done without you?" she murmured.

"I wouldn't have let you find out. You're stuck with me, because I'll never let you go."

Lifting her slightly, he removed her dress and gazed at her nearly nude body with glowing eyes. Noelle rested her head on his shoulder, feeling her very bones turn liquid as he stroked her.

"How can I feel this wonderful over and over again?" she marveled.

"You couldn't have said anything that would make me happier," he answered in a husky voice.

Parting her lips for an inflaming kiss, he removed her panties. Noelle quivered as he stroked her thighs lingeringly. She gasped when he moved higher, to the core of her desire.

"Oh, Roman, I love you so," she breathed.

When she raised her knees and curled her body around him, clinging tightly to his neck, he stood with her in his arms. Gazing deeply into her eyes, he carried her to the bed.

Their union was both passionate and tender, a reaffirmation of their love. When the physical act was over, the deep feeling remained.

After a while, Noelle stirred reluctantly. "I hate to leave."

"Do you have to?" Roman's embrace tightened.

"I can't afford to take any chances now. I'm back in Troy's good graces, but if he discovered I'd stayed out all night, I wouldn't have a chance with him. Even an egomaniac like Troy could figure out he isn't my dream date."

"I wish there was some way of nailing the creep that didn't involve you. I see red every time I think of the sexual harassment you have to put up with."

"I just consider the source. He's an object of ridicule to people who don't know how vicious he is."

"Don't worry, Slattery won't lay a glove on your friend."

"Diane will come out lucky, but how about all those other poor women he's undoubtedly blackmailing?" Noelle looked troubled. "And all his future victims. We can scare Troy into turning over Diane's negatives, but he's not about to give up his activities."

"You could tell Sybyll. The only trouble is, he'd simply go someplace else and set up shop."

"There's no guarantee that she'd even fire him. It's my word against his. The only proof I have is Diane, and I can't bring her into it."

"It's a catch-22 situation," Roman admitted. "Unless..." His eyes narrowed. "How much extra do you figure Slattery makes a year?"

"Plenty, judging by what he asked from Diane. And we both know that would have been only the first installment."

"I wonder what he does with his money," Roman mused.

"Spends a lot of it on himself. He drives a sports car that must have cost a fortune, and he mentioned owning property in California."

"Doesn't anyone wonder how he can afford all that?"

"Troy is such a blowhard that nobody believes him about the apartment buildings, and I guess they figure he puts most of his salary into horrendous payments on the car."

"The Internal Revenue Service isn't that trusting."

Noelle looked at him with dawning comprehension. "Troy doesn't pay income tax on the money."

"How could he explain where it came from?"

"Roman, you're a genius! After Diane is in the clear, we'll send an anonymous tip to the IRS."

"I can do better than that. I know a man high up in the department. I'll tell him the story in strictest confidence. The government isn't interested in ruining innocent people's lives. They just want their money."

Noelle's elation died. "What if he just pays his back taxes? We can cut into Troy's profits—which is some satisfaction—but he'll be back doing business at the same old stand in no time. He'll probably even step up his action to make up for what he lost."

"No way. The fine will be prohibitive and, in addition, he'll face criminal charges."

"They'll never get anyone to testify against him."

"I was referring to things like criminal intent to defraud. The government can get very annoyed when someone holds out on them through illegal activities. I can almost guarantee that Slattery is going to exchange his designer sweats for prison denims."

Noelle was silent for a moment as the implications set in. "Is it terrible to be happy about sending someone to prison?" she asked slowly.

"Not when he's a sea slug like Slattery."

"You're right. We're making the world a better place."

Roman scissored his legs around hers and nibbled delicately on her ear. "How about brightening a small corner of *our* world?"

"I really should start back," she said irresolutely. "I have an early morning class."

"Too bad," he murmured, caressing her lovingly.

"Oh, what the heck." Noelle's smile was radiant in the darkness. "I always did consider sleeping a waste of time."

The spa was dark and quiet when Noelle returned. Her footsteps sounded unnaturally loud in the still night, so she took off her shoes and carried them under one arm.

When she reached her room and fumbled in her shoulder bag for the key, her shoes fell with a muffled clatter. The noise shouldn't have been loud enough to wake anyone, but Erica's light went on. Noelle stiffened. Troy's room was several doors down. Surely he couldn't have heard the slight sound that far away.

Light streamed onto the concrete as Erica opened her door. "Noelle? Where have you been all this time? I was getting worried about you."

"What are you doing up at this hour?" Noelle asked.

"I couldn't sleep."

Their voices were muted, but Noelle wasn't taking any chances. "Come inside," she whispered, unlocking her door.

Erica followed her. "When it got so late, I was afraid you had an accident or something." She eyed the wrapped package Noelle put on the dresser. "What did you buy?"

"Just some things at the drugstore. I did a little shopping and then went to a movie." To forestall any more questions, Noelle yawned elaborately. "I'm really tired. I guess we should both get to bed."

"I know it's late, but I need to talk to someone." Erica looked at her appealingly. "I've been waiting all this time for you to come home."

"You're not still feeling insecure about Jeff, are you?" Noelle asked. "It's easy to imagine all sorts of things when you're miles apart, but you mustn't let yourself. I'm sure Jeff loves you."

"I know he does." Erica's face was wreathed in smiles. "That's what I wanted to tell you. He called tonight and we talked about the wedding."

"When's the big day?"

"Just as soon as I tell my parents and they can make arrangements to get away. I want them at my wedding, naturally." Erica laughed self-consciously. "I should have told them about Jeff and me right away, but I guess I was afraid to believe it myself."

"It sounds as if Jeff was able to talk his mother out of that fancy wedding neither of you wanted."

"Jeff is young, but he can be very forceful," Erica said proudly.

"Just be careful that he doesn't start ordering *you* around," Noelle teased. "You have to train them right from the beginning, I've heard."

"Anything he wants is all right with me," Erica said softly. "I'm so happy that I'm afraid I'll wake up and find this is just a dream."

"When are you going to realize there really *are* happy endings?" Noelle scolded gently.

"When I'm actually Jeff's wife." Erica laughed. "I wish you could be at our wedding. It'll only be a simple ceremony, but I'd like to have you there."

"You wouldn't know the difference." Noelle smiled. "You won't see anyone but Jeff, anyway."

"That's probably true. I don't want to lose track of you, though. I know we haven't known each other very long, but I feel really close to you."

Noelle was touched by the young woman's earnestness. "We'll keep in contact. New York is my home, and Roman gets there often, too."

Erica looked at her in surprise. "I thought you and Roman were a dead issue."

Noelle was chagrined at having automatically linked herself with Roman. She would like to have confided in her friend—actually, she wanted to announce the stupendous news over the PA system! The problem was Troy. Erica would be puzzled when she continued to cozy up to him.

"Roman and I were never a romantic item, but we got fairly friendly by the end of the week," Noelle explained carefully. "We'll probably stay in touch."

Erica continued to look at her speculatively. "Roman stayed on in Tucson after he left here, didn't he?"

"I believe that's what he planned." Noelle went to the closet and took out her robe. "I'd really love to hear more about your plans, but I'm practically walking in my sleep."

Erica rose from the foot of the bed where she'd been perched. "I'm sorry for keeping you up so late, but I wanted to tell you before I told the others."

"I'm glad you did." Noelle smothered a real yawn this time. "You ought to be able to sleep now. All of your troubles are over."

"From your lips to God's ears," Erica said with a grin as she went out the door.

Chapter Nine

Noelle's aerobics classes were always well attended. The women loved working out to show tunes from classic Broadway hits such as *West Side Story* and the like. Women who normally didn't move a muscle came out of curiosity and stayed to participate.

Erica had her following, too, but they were the ones who were more serious about keeping their bodies in shape. The "no pain, no gain" crowd.

Noelle didn't know all the women by name yet. This was a whole new group. A woman she hadn't seen before came in toward the end of the session and stood in the back of the room, simply observing. She stayed on after class was over. A few always remained to talk.

One of Noelle's most enthusiastic pupils was Betty Bradford, an outgoing, attractive woman in her early forties.

"I loved that dance routine from *Sweet Charity*," she remarked. "I hope you plan to repeat it."

"Yes, it's fun to bump and grind." Noelle smiled. "It also uses every muscle."

"If I work out faithfully, will you promise me a body like yours?"

Betty's admiration was warranted. Noelle wore a black leotard that molded to her high breasts, slim hips and flat stomach like a second skin. There wasn't a bulge or an ounce of fat on her body.

"I don't know what you're doing at a place like this," Betty continued. "You should be in show business."

"I had a taste of it once when I worked as a dancer."

"Why on earth did you give it up? You're great."

"I like having a steady income." Noelle gave her the standard excuse. "It's either feast or famine in the entertainment industry."

"Not for the people who hit it big. They make a fortune."

"They're the exceptions unfortunately."

"What do you care, as long as you're one of them? My husband is a producer at Universal Studios. I know he could get you work."

"That's awfully kind of you. I just might take you up on that," Noelle promised vaguely.

"Give it serious thought. To get ahead in this life, you have to take advantage of every opportunity that comes your way."

"I certainly try to do that."

Noelle's laughing eyes met the eyes of the woman who had come in late. There was no answering spark. The woman was inspecting her with clinical interest, the way people look at specimens in an aquarium. She was in her early fifties, with short dark hair that was impeccably groomed, yet not in a style needed to soften her strong features. She looked like one of those no-nonsense society ladies who chaired committees with an iron hand.

Noelle wasn't drawn to the woman, but as soon as Betty left, she walked over and introduced herself. "Hello. I hope you'll be joining our class."

"You're older than I expected." The woman's cultured tone didn't take any of the sting out of the rude remark. "I suppose that explains it."

"Explains what?" Noelle's eyes glinted dangerously.

The woman ignored the question, openly appraising her body. "Also the costume. Is that the way you usually parade around?"

Noelle had to remind herself that she couldn't afford to get fired yet. "This is what most of us wear when we do aerobics. If it offends you, perhaps you'd prefer to attend the lectures given at this hour."

"I'm not interested in lectures. I came here expressly to see you."

"Have we met?" Noelle looked at her searchingly without getting a clue.

"No, but we have a lot in common. I know how to get what I want, and I suspect you do, too."

"Are you selling something?" Noelle demanded. She didn't look the type, yet what other explanation could there be for this strange conversation? "Some kind of self-help course, perhaps?"

"With your equipment, my dear, you don't need any help."

"Now just a minute! You can't—"

"Noelle!" Erica came bouncing into the room, looking like a pretty teenager. Her hair was caught up in a ponytail and she wasn't wearing any makeup. "Oh, I'm sorry," she said when she noticed the older woman. "I didn't mean to interrupt, but you have a long-distance call waiting, Sybyll told me to come and get you."

"You didn't interrupt anything important." Noelle turned to the woman and said coldly, "You'll have to excuse me."

A surprised look crossed the woman's face. "You're not Erica Jones?"

"No, I am." Erica smiled at her. "How can I help you?"

"She *needs* help," Noelle muttered, turning away.

"I'm Mrs. Herbert Mainwaring, Jeffrey's mother. I want to have a talk with you."

Noelle stopped in her tracks, aware of trouble ahead. Their conversation was beginning to make sense now.

"I'm so happy to meet you!" Erica exclaimed. She checked the impulse to hug her future mother-in-law. Estelle's manner didn't invite such liberties. Still, nothing could dampen Erica's spirits. "Is Jeff with you?" she asked breathlessly.

"No, he is not. Will you please accompany me to my cottage." It wasn't a request, but an order. "We have things to discuss."

Erica's face fell. "Have you changed your mind about a big wedding? If it's really important to you, of course we'll have one, but we'd prefer to get married right away."

"There won't be any big wedding," Estelle stated.

"Oh, that's great! You don't know what this means to us. I hated the thought of being separated from Jeff for months."

"I'm sure you did. Come along and we'll talk about the two of you."

"I'll come with you," Noelle said casually. "I'd like to hear all the details firsthand."

"You have a phone call waiting," Erica reminded her.

"Whoever it is will call back," Noelle answered. She had a feeling Erica was going to need all the help she could get.

"What I have to say is private," Estelle said in a tone that brooked no argument.

Erica, at least, was cowed. "That would probably be best. I'll tell you all about our plans later," she told Noelle.

There was nothing further Noelle could do, but she was concerned. Poor Erica had no idea that Mrs. Mainwaring opposed the marriage. Could she stand up to the older woman? It wasn't exactly an even match.

"Where on earth have you been?" Sybyll asked when Noelle came into the office. "Your friend hung up. She said for you to call her back." Sybyll held out a slip of paper with a number written on it. "I asked her name, but she said you'd know who it was. Her voice sounded vaguely familiar."

"Thanks." Noelle took the piece of paper, ignoring the question in Sybyll's voice.

She called Diane from the pay phone in the lobby. "It really isn't a good idea for you to call here," she said. "It would be disastrous if anyone linked us together."

"I couldn't help it. I start to imagine all kinds of terrible things, sitting back here all alone. Drew is being difficult about the terms of the divorce. He'd jump at the chance to take Christine away from me if he had the slightest excuse."

"He won't find one. Everything's going well."

"You said that before, but you're still there."

"Not for much longer. I expect to wind things up by the weekend. I've had a few unexpected expenses, though. I hired a detective."

"You told somebody about this? How could you do such a thing, Noelle? Those people are notoriously shady.

If he does get the negatives, he'll probably blackmail me, too!''

"Relax. Mike came highly recommended by a good friend."

"My God, what did you do, take out an ad in the newspaper?''

"I did what I should have done in the first place—get professional help," Noelle answered crisply. "Without Mike, I'd end up spending my golden years at Carefree Dunes as the oldest living aerobics teacher."

"What did he come up with?''

"It's a scam, too elaborate to explain over the telephone. Just take my word for it, the nightmare is almost over."

"I hope you get results before Friday. I can't hold Troy off much longer."

"He's been pressuring you?" Noelle asked sharply. "When did you hear from his last?''

"He called me on Saturday night and he sounded furious. He said he was through being jerked around. Either I paid up or else."

Noelle's heart sank. That was after his conversation with Mike. The detective was so sure Troy was scared witless. Was he wrong?

"He also said something strange," Diane continued. "He said if I promised not to tell my brother, this was the last time I'd ever hear from him. Otherwise, he'd find a way to get back at me."

"What did you say?" Noelle asked tautly.

"I had no idea what he was talking about, but I figured I'd better agree to anything he asked. Was I right?''

"You did just fine."

Noelle relaxed. Troy's strategy was obvious. Diane wouldn't be a continuing source of income, but he could make one big score by splitting the negatives between her and Mike. Diane would never mention the incident to her supposed brother, and Mike would think his mission was accomplished. What an operator that Troy was!

"I managed to stall him one more time, but he said Friday was the absolute deadline, no more delays. Will you have the negatives by then?"

"He isn't scheduled to turn them over until Saturday, but don't worry."

"Don't worry? Do you know what Troy will do when he doesn't get the money by Friday?"

"Absolutely nothing. He's bluffing."

"I can't take that chance. I think I'd better pay him."

"You'll do no such thing," Noelle said firmly. "You're going to sit tight and wait for us to wrap this thing up. Or better yet, call your friends and go out on the town. The important thing is—don't call here again."

After Noelle had calmed Diane, she phoned Roman to tell him the latest development. She was put on hold for long minutes while they paged him.

"Where have you been?" she asked when he finally answered. "I was about to give up."

"I'm sitting by the pool, working."

"On your tan?" she asked dryly.

"For your information, I'm finishing my article. I'm glad you called. I need to ask you some questions."

She smiled. "The answer to all of them is yes."

"I consider that a promise," he said softly. "Now stop frustrating me and pay attention."

After Noelle had answered Roman's questions about some spa practices, she told him about Troy's attempted double cross. "Do you think you should alert Mike?"

"I'll tell him, but it doesn't change anything. Are you all set for tonight?"

"Unless Troy stands me up."

"I can't conceive of any man doing that," Roman answered huskily.

"Troy isn't a real man. He's a mistake that slipped through God's quality check. Getting even with him will be pure pleasure. I can't wait for tonight to get here."

"Just hang loose, darling, and everything will turn out fine." Roman's voice was soothing.

"That's what I told Diane—with the same degree of success."

"You need a massage to loosen up your tight muscles. I wish I was there to rub your back."

"Mmm, sounds heavenly." She closed her eyes and imagined his hands moving over her body. When she opened them, one of the guests was peering at her curiously through the glass partition. "I have to go, Roman. I'll call you later."

Noelle was so involved with her own problems that Erica's were driven from her mind. It was perhaps fortunate that she didn't know what was going on at that moment, because she would have barged in and spoken her mind.

Erica was nervous about her first meeting with Jeff's mother. She wanted so much for the older woman to like her. It was a good sign that Mrs. Mainwaring had come all the way to Arizona to see her, Erica told herself. They were going to have a really good relationship. She was simply more reserved than Erica's mother.

"Sit down, Miss Jones," Estelle said when they were alone in her suite. "I want to hear all about you."

"Please, call me Erica." She perched on the edge of a chair. "What would you like to know?"

"Everything. Tell me about your family, where you went to school, things like that."

"Well, I was born in Tucson and I lived there all my life until I came to work at Carefree Dunes."

"You didn't go away to college?"

Erica paused, reluctant to admit what she'd always regretted. "I didn't go to college."

"I see." Estelle nodded, as if verifying what she already suspected.

"I have three younger brothers and sisters still living at home," Erica said hurriedly. "My parents couldn't afford the tuition."

"You never considered working your way through school?"

"Times haven't been easy at home, with the recession and all. My father's been out of work off and on. I send money to help out. This job pays room and board, so when I heard of an opening, I jumped at the chance to work here."

"I don't doubt it," Estelle murmured. "What position does your father hold when he's employed?"

"He works at the Davis-Monthan Air Force Base as a civilian employee. It's a fascinating place to visit. They have rows and rows of vintage airplanes dating back to World War II. Dad used to take us to see them, and he'd tell us about all the battles they were in." Erica's lovely face was flushed with animation.

"What exactly does he do at the base?"

"He works on the planes."

"In other words, he's a mechanic."

"Well, yes, I guess so," Erica answered slowly. Mrs. Mainwaring had made the job sound menial. "His official title is maintenance supervisor."

Estelle's raised eyebrows dismissed the euphemism. "So you went to work right after high school. That meant you weren't able to travel. Marriage to my son would afford you that opportunity, correct? You wouldn't have to work, either."

Erica sat up straighter in her chair. "Are you suggesting I fell in love with Jeff because he's rich?"

"Or you think he is. Jeffrey has a small trust fund, but he doesn't come into the bulk of his inheritance until he's thirty-five. That's a long time to wait."

"I don't care if he doesn't have a dime!" Erica answered angrily.

"A noble sentiment, but you'll pardon me if I don't believe a word of it. This is a classic example of a poor girl setting her sights on a rich man."

Erica rose from her chair. "I don't see any point in continuing this conversation," she said with dignity.

"I notice you didn't deny my allegation."

"What good would it do? You've already made up your mind about me. I'm not good enough for you because I come from a working-class family and I haven't had your advantages. All that is true, but being poor isn't a crime."

"Neither is trying to better yourself, but I don't intend to let you use my son to do it."

"I wish you'd given me a chance before condemning me as a fortune hunter, but it doesn't change anything." Erica's body was taut. "Jeff and I love each other. We're going to get married, with or without your blessing."

"I wouldn't count on it. Jeffrey has always been a dutiful son. He knows I have his best interests at heart, and he'll think twice about going against my wishes."

Erica smiled scornfully. "Don't count on it. He might feel a sense of duty toward you, but he *loves* me. Which one of us do you think he'll choose?"

Estelle's stare was coldly contemptuous. "All right. How much do you want?"

"Are you offering me money?" Erica asked incredulously.

"Spare me the histrionics and let's cut to the bottom line," Estelle said curtly. "How does twenty-five thousand sound?"

"I wouldn't give Jeff up for a million!" Erica declared passionately.

"Fifty thousand, and that's my top price. Don't make the mistake of being too greedy. Take the money, or I warn you, you'll wind up with nothing."

"I'll have Jeff. He's all I want."

"Don't try to bluff me. I hold all the cards. If you persist in marrying my son, I'll see that he's fired. I'm the majority stockholder in our bank. I'll also have him blacklisted in the financial community. He won't be able to get a job in the only field he's experienced in. You'll live in a walk-up apartment, struggling to pay the rent."

Erica looked at the older woman in a kind of horror. "You'd do that to your own son?"

"To bring him to his senses? In an instant. You wouldn't stay with him long. That isn't the kind of life you planned on."

"If this is what money does to a person, I'm glad we won't have any," Erica said. "I come from a home where we all care about each other and try to help out. We don't bargain for anything, least of all love. Keep your money, Mrs. Mainwaring. From what I can see, it's all you have."

As she walked to the door, Estelle called, "Erica, wait!"

"We don't have anything more to say to each other."

"I do. I owe you an apology."

Erica turned to look at her uncertainly. "I'm not sure I can ever forgive the things you said to me."

"Try to understand, my dear. This was all such a surprise. Jeffrey came home and told me he wanted to marry a girl he'd known only a week. What was I to think?"

"You didn't have to rush to judgment."

"That's true, and I'm terribly ashamed of myself. I believe you really do love my son."

"Does this mean you won't oppose our marriage?" Erica asked slowly.

Estelle hesitated. "As you rightly pointed out, I can't stop it. I'm deeply troubled, however—for you, as well as my son. You seem to be a lovely young girl. I don't want to see you get hurt."

"How could I? I adore Jeff!"

"That's just the point. If the marriage fails, you'll be the one who will suffer. It's still a man's world, my dear. There will be any number of women waiting to console him, but if I judge you correctly, you'd be heartbroken."

"Of course I would! But our marriage won't fail. It isn't just a physical attraction between us," Erica said earnestly. "We like the same food, the same music. We both want lots of children. We're completely compatible."

"Your life-styles have been markedly different. Jeffrey was educated at the finest schools. He's comfortable in the most elegant hotels and restaurants. He's traveled widely."

"You think I wouldn't know how to act?"

Estelle chose her words carefully. "I think you might be uncomfortable with Jeffrey's friends. They wouldn't mean to be unkind, but they do share the same experiences. You're sure to feel left out of the conversation."

"Jeff and I will store up our own memories, from our own experiences," Erica answered confidently.

"You intend to estrange him from his friends?"

"No, I . . . Certainly not. But we can make new friends, too, people we both have something in common with."

"In other words, Jeffrey will be persuaded to simplify his standard of living to make *you* happy."

"That isn't what I mean at all," Erica protested. "I wouldn't try to change his life. It might not be what I'm used to, but I'll do whatever he wants."

"You're going to be a very busy young woman. To fit into my son's world, you'll have to take lessons in golf, bridge and sailing, to begin with. Those are all skills he and his friends learned as youngsters."

Erica tried to cover her dismay with a flip reply. "Anything else?"

"You'd better enjoy the ballet, symphony and opera. Those are important social events in New York City."

"I can learn whatever I have to," Erica said doggedly.

Estelle quickly masked her look of annoyance. "I suppose that's possible—in time. You'll be thrown into the social whirl immediately, however. Everyone will want to entertain for you. What will you say when you're seated next to a United States senator at a dinner party? Or to a psychiatrist or an eminent criminal attorney?"

Erica's eyes widened. "Jeff knows those kind of people?"

"They've been guests in our home since he was a little boy."

"He never said anything," Erica said falteringly. "He seemed to be having a good time just going to the pub in the village. It isn't very fancy. Everybody comes in jeans, and most of the time we dance to tunes on the jukebox."

"I imagine it was quite a novelty for him."

"I guess so," Erica answered in a muted voice.

Estelle's gaze was shrewd, but her voice was gentle. "I can see why Jeffrey fell in love with you. You're a charming, unspoiled young woman. If he had been the boy next door, you could have had a happy life together. But oil and water don't mix. Deep down, you know that, don't you?''

"No! None of those differences matter when two people love each other."

"Not at first, but when the initial passion dies down, Jeffrey will find out how little you have in common. It will start to bother him when you say something unfortunate and his friends exchange amused looks, or when he has to refuse a golf date because you don't play well enough. He'll be secretly impatient with you and you'll argue. You won't have anyone to turn to, but he will—a man always does. Either he'll leave you, or he'll make the best of a bad bargain and be coolly indifferent. Is that the way you want to live?"

A shudder passed through Erica's slim body. "Jeff would never treat me that way."

"How well do you know him after one week?" Estelle asked softly. "He really hasn't told you anything about himself. He hasn't shared the important things with you, and he never will." When Erica gave her a stricken look, the older woman said urgently, "Give him up for both your sakes. Can you be happy if he's miserable?"

"I . . . I'll have to think about it."

"That's all I ask. I want you to make up your own mind. Don't tell Jeffrey about our little talk. This is your decision and no one else's. Whatever it is, I'll accept it."

Noelle remembered Erica and her problems when she heard her moving around in the room next door. Erica answered her knock, looking forlorn.

"I gather the wicked witch of the east gave you a bad time," Noelle observed.

"Come in." Erica opened the door wider.

"Did she tell you that Jeff could have his pick of women?"

"Something like that. How did you guess?"

"I got a dose of her winning personality when she confused me with you. She won't be the easiest mother-in-law in the world."

Erica smoothed an imaginary wrinkle in her leotard. "Mrs. Mainwaring is a widow and Jeff is an only child. I guess it's natural she's concerned about his welfare."

"I have a feeling she wouldn't like anybody Jeff picked out, so don't take it personally. She's lucky he picked somebody like you."

"I'm beginning to wonder why he did," Erica answered soberly.

Noelle smiled. "It's called love—that peculiar state of mind that makes you feel wonderful and do goofy things."

Erica gave her a strange look, but the telephone rang before she could reply. Her expression didn't lighten after she picked up the receiver. "Oh... hi, Jeff."

Noelle rose. "Come over to my room when you finish," she whispered, going out the door.

"I miss you, darling," Jeff was saying.

"I miss you, too," Erica answered woodenly.

"The only thing that keeps me going is the thought that we'll be together soon. Did you tell Sybyll you're leaving?"

"No, I... Not yet."

"Why not? She has to get someone to take your place."

"Oh, well, she has a whole list of girls dying to work here. That's no problem."

"Good, then let's talk about our wedding. Are your parents coming?"

"I haven't... I mean, I don't know yet. It's such short notice. Maybe we should wait a while."

"No way! A *week* is too long for me," Jeff declared. "I thought you felt the same way."

"I do, but perhaps we're rushing things," she answered carefully. "We haven't had time to make any plans."

"Like what? I have the license and the ring. That's all we need."

"Not really. We have to decide where to live, and…and things like that."

"No problem. We'll rent an apartment and move in."

"You don't just rent an apartment like you buy a new dress," she protested.

"What's wrong, Erica?" Jeff asked quietly. "Are you having second thoughts?"

"We met and fell in love so fast," she said slowly. "We didn't really talk about a lot of important things. What if we're not right for each other?"

"Answer me one question. Do you love me?"

Tears sprang to her eyes. "With all my heart."

"Then that's all that matters. If you try to change your mind I'll come out there and kidnap you. Decide what day you want to leave, because I have to buy your ticket. You can tell me when I phone tomorrow."

After she hung up, Erica was more confused than ever. She stared at the telephone for a long time, then went next door to Noelle's room.

"Don't look so woebegone." Noelle smiled. "You and Jeff will be together soon."

"That's what he wants."

Noelle stared at her in surprise. "Don't you?"

"More than anything in the world." There was no mistaking the fervor in Erica's voice.

"Then why all the gloom and doom?"

"I never realized before what different lives we lead," Erica said slowly. "Jeff is used to servants and the best tables in restaurants. When he travels, it's to the most expensive resorts. I'm used to working in one.''

Noelle chuckled. ''You'll find the lap of luxury very comfortable.''

''Will I?'' Erica looked down at her fingernails. ''Or will I make a fool of myself because I don't know which fork to use or how to dress?''

''That's utterly ridiculous. Everybody will love you. Why shouldn't they? You're a wonderful person.''

Erica shook her head. ''I haven't been anyplace or accomplished anything. What if Jeff gets bored with me because I can't play golf or bridge with him and his friends? They're expert at all kinds of things I've never done.''

''Wait a minute.'' Noelle's eyes narrowed. ''I smell a large rat named Mrs. Mainwaring. Did Jeff's mother convince you that you're not good enough for her precious son? You'd have to be out of your mind to believe her!''

''She was right about a lot of things. I'm not familiar with many operas, and I've never been to the ballet. Those are the kinds of places Jeff goes to in New York. Out here it wasn't any strain because we just went to the pub to dance.''

''That's the sort of thing he does at home, too. I guarantee you that most of his dates involved a movie and a hamburger afterward.''

Erica looked doubtful. ''Mrs. Mainwaring told me—''

Noelle cut her off. ''Mrs. Mainwaring is a selfish, spoiled woman who will use any dirty trick to hang on to her only son. You can't let her get away with it. Jeff loves you and you love him. That's all that matters, not whether you know how to pour tea or butter a crumpet.''

Erica gazed at her with relief. ''You really think so?''

''I'm sure of it,'' Noelle stated firmly.

Erica threw her arms around her. "Thanks for setting me straight. I'm going to call Jeff back and tell him I love him."

A maid answered the telephone. "Mr. Mainwaring is dressing to go out. May I take a message?"

"No, this is very important. Tell him it's Erica. I'll wait."

A few moments later, Jeff picked up the phone. "Darling, what a nice surprise. I'm glad I hadn't left yet."

"Where are you going?"

"To a cotillion. That's a stupid formal ball where debutantes get introduced to society—meaning the people they've known all their lives."

"I know what a cotillion is," Erica said sharply. "Are you taking a date?"

"It was unavoidable," he answered ruefully. "I would have gotten out of it if I could, but I promised months ago to escort Judge Baldwin's daughter. He sits on the state Supreme Court, so I don't want to offend him." Jeff laughed. "I'm only kidding. He's an old friend of the family, and I couldn't drop out at the last minute, anyway."

"No, of course not," Erica answered mechanically.

"I knew you'd understand. Why did you call, darling? Did you decide when you want to leave?"

"No, I just wanted to hear your voice," she said quietly.

"That's sweet. It's good hearing yours, too. I have to run, but I'll call you tomorrow when we can talk longer."

Erica sat motionless for a long time, too desolate even to cry. Jeff was farther away than New York. He was in a different world.

* * *

Noelle was emotionally charged for a different reason. What she had to do next was critical and involved precision timing. She stood by the window, peeking out until she saw Troy cross the lawn on his way to the dining room.

As soon as he was out of sight, she slipped out and headed for the employee parking lot, taking care not to be seen. Whenever she heard footsteps or voices, she ducked behind a tree or the corner of a building.

The parking lot was deserted, as she'd fervently hoped. The maintenance people had left for the day and the employees were all at dinner.

Troy's red sports car would have stood out anywhere, but amid the other small, somewhat battered vehicles, it gleamed like a peacock among sparrows. The paint was pristine, as if he polished it every day, which he undoubtedly did. Troy's slovenliness didn't extend to his car.

Noelle had trouble getting the hood open. She broke a fingernail and swore a lot before she figured out how to do it. The engine was awesome. It had pipes, coils and gadgets that defied description, mostly connected to a large round contraption that was flat on top.

She fished Mike's diagram out of her pocket and tried to find something in the machinery that even faintly resembled his squiggles. By the time she located it, perspiration was dewing her forehead as she worried about being seen.

Her hands shook as she unwrapped the object she'd brought, a small square box with some wires sticking out. Placing it between a thick coil and a metal pipe, she quickly twisted the wires around the coil. Her work was now done except for lowering the hood, but not closing it completely.

Noelle's sigh of relief was premature. When she tried to open the passenger door, it was locked. Of course it would be! Why hadn't Mike thought of that? Either it slipped his mind, or he figured Troy didn't need to lock his car in the employee lot. He didn't know Troy wouldn't trust a priest!

Her stomach churned as she clutched the note she'd taken from her purse. Time was slipping by. If she was too tardy for dinner, Troy might make the connection later on. Finally she folded the note several times and wedged it tightly into the jamb of the door. If worse came to worst and the note got dislodged, she planned to have a duplicate in her purse.

Everything had gone off without a serious hitch so far. Noelle crossed her fingers and took off at a trot for the dining room.

Chapter Ten

Everybody looked up when Noelle arrived, breathless.

"It's a good thing you got here," Mitzi said. "We had to fight off one of the guests to save your roll and butter. She saw it sitting by an empty place and got a crazed look in her eyes."

"We could go into business selling underground cheeseburgers for fifty bucks a pop," Thelma remarked. "We'd make a fortune."

"That's chickenfeed," Troy said smugly. "If you want to set up a sideline, pick one that makes real money."

"Are you starting to charge?" Mitzi asked disgustedly. "There's a name for guys like you."

"Yeah—irresistible," he answered, looking pleased with himself.

"Let's start a pool to see who Troy will hit on this week," Thelma suggested.

"Dibs on Stephanie Martin," Mitzi said. "She's a real fox and she has that friendly look in her eyes."

"Isn't she married to Moose Martin, the football player? He'll break Troy in half."

"Hey, don't start any rumors," he ordered. "She's just a paying customer."

Thelma grinned. "That's what I said."

"Knock it off! So I get a few presents from grateful guests. That isn't payment," he protested with belated caution.

"What are they grateful for?"

"My expertise. Stephanie just wants to perfect her backhand."

"That's a new name for it," Mitzi snorted.

"You can come watch us. I'm giving her a lesson after dinner."

Noelle gripped her napkin in dismay. Everything was all set. He couldn't slip through her fingers now! She tried to catch Troy's eye, but he didn't look in her direction.

Eventually the two women tired of trading barbs with him. Noelle and Erica had remained silent. Finally Mitzi commented on the fact.

"You two have been awfully quiet. How come?"

"You were so busy bashing Troy we couldn't get a word in," Noelle answered.

"Feel free to join us. Just jump right in."

"No thanks." Noelle gave him a meaningful glance.

"Your taste in men is weird," Mitzi said disgustedly.

"Except for the handsome hunk from Chicago," Thelma reminded her. "He and Noelle had quite a thing going. Too bad he left at the end of the week."

Noelle held her breath, but Erica wasn't listening. She was too sunk in her own misery.

"That's the story of our lives." Mitzi sighed. "The prize catches go home, and we're left with a flounder."

"I told you before, there was nothing between Roman and me," Noelle said quickly. "Actually, he was pretty boring. I just kidded him along to break the monotony."

"Sure, you did!" Mitzi and Thelma replied in unison.

"What do you think of this week's crop of guests?" Noelle asked to distract them. "Betty Bradford is nice. You'd never know her husband is such a big shot."

"What does he do?" Thelma asked.

The conversation became general as Noelle had hoped. When dinner was over and everyone dispersed, she hurried to catch up with Troy.

"I thought we had a date tonight."

"You should have taken your chance while you had it. I'm in big demand," he said smugly. "I have to spread myself around."

"You looked so tired last night." She gave him a glance through lowered lashes.

"Baby, I'm never *that* tired."

"Give me another chance, Troy," she coaxed. "I've been looking forward to our date all day."

"No can do. I got to put business before pleasure. The lady is a paying customer, and she has first call on my services."

Noelle flattered and cajoled, but Troy was adamant. Finally she was forced to give up—for the moment. As he left her to change into tennis shorts, Noelle's eyes narrowed in thought.

Half an hour later, Noelle strolled over to the tennis court. Stephanie Martin and Troy were there, but they weren't playing tennis. Both were dressed for the sport, although Stephanie's tight T-shirt and very brief shorts weren't exactly Wimbledon attire. She and Troy were deep in conversation.

Noelle approached them with a smile. "Isn't it a glorious night? I always think this is the best time to play tennis."

"Yes, I... It's too hot for me during the day," Stephanie answered.

"You're married to Moose Martin, aren't you?" Noelle asked, oblivious to Troy's scowl of annoyance. "I'm a big fan of his."

"I must remember to tell him," Stephanie replied.

"He's absolutely awesome on the field," Noelle continued. "When he tackles someone, you can almost hear bones breaking."

"It's a rough sport." Stephanie bounced a tennis ball and glanced at Troy.

"I'm trying to give Mrs. Martin a lesson," he grated.

"Oh, dear, and I'm keeping you from it," Noelle said apologetically. "Go right ahead. I'll shag balls for you."

They exchanged a glance. "That won't be necessary," Troy said through gritted teeth.

"No trouble. I'll enjoy watching."

After an imperceptible pause, Stephanie said impatiently, "Come on, let's get started."

Troy purposely smashed balls out of bounds, running Noelle ragged. If he hoped she'd get tired and leave, he was due for a disappointment. Noelle was prepared to stay as long as they did. Eventually Stephanie was the one who called it quits.

"That was quite a workout," she said, walking off the court and picking up a towel to mop her face. "I'll sleep well tonight."

"Your backhand is definitely improving." He picked up her duffel bag. "I'll carry this to your room for you."

Stephanie glanced at Noelle, who was looking on with interest. "No thanks, it isn't heavy. I can carry it."

When she was out of hearing, Troy turned on Noelle furiously. "Why the hell did you have to butt in? A moron would know when she wasn't wanted!"

"What did I do wrong?" Noelle asked in an injured voice. "I was only helping out."

"The hell you were! You were getting even with me for breaking our date."

"Well, it did leave me with nothing to do."

"If you ever pull a stunt like that again, you'll be damn sorry."

She stared at him coldly. "You're acting as if I broke up a hot date. Is it true what the others say about you? I thought it was just a running joke, but now I'm starting to wonder. *Are* you sleeping with the the women guests?"

His belligerence faded. "You know better than that. It's all a gag, like you said. The women expect me to play up to them, so I oblige. That's all there is to it."

"Oh, really? Then why did you throw such a temper tantrum when Stephanie wouldn't let you carry her books home from school?" Noelle asked sarcastically.

"These women don't like to share me. I mean, they want my full attention," he corrected himself hastily.

"She can have it," Noelle said haughtily. "After all, she is a *paying* customer. You just better hope you don't get caught fooling around with the wrong woman."

"What do you mean by that?" he asked sharply.

"A husband like Moose Martin could make confetti out of you." She looked him up and down with a contempt that didn't need to be feigned. "Frankly, I hope he does." She turned and stalked away.

Troy fell into step with her. "Hey, what are you getting so steamed about? Those women are a joke. Most of them are neglected broads who just want a man to notice them. I play their game, but you couldn't pay me to lay a finger on them."

Noelle gazed at him uncertainly. "I don't know. They say, where there's smoke, there's fire."

He chuckled suggestively. "I've got plenty of fire, baby, but it isn't for any of those old bags."

"You didn't mind breaking our date for one of them." She pouted. "Of course, Stephanie isn't an old bag."

"You think I'd fool around with Moose Martin's wife? I'll tell you what—we can still have our date. We'll go down to the pub and have a few laughs, just like we planned."

She hesitated. "I *would* like to get out for a while."

"Me, too. Come to my room with me while I shower and change."

"I want to change, too," Noelle said.

His eyes swept over her jeans and checked shirt. "Nobody dresses up at the pub. You look fine."

"I want to comb my hair and put on different shoes. Knock on my door when you're ready." She disappeared into her own room and closed the door.

Noelle was quite proud of her acting job and the results it had produced. Breaking up Troy's date with Stephanie hadn't been difficult, but she'd anticipated trouble talking him around afterward. It was a stroke of luck that she'd maneuvered *him* into suggesting a drink in the village.

As they neared the spa parking lot, Noelle hoped the second phase of her scam would go as smoothly. The curtain was going up on the most important role she'd ever played.

"I've seen your car in the lot," she remarked. "It's fabulous."

"It should be for what it cost," he answered complacently.

"You certainly keep it in good condition." The low red sports car glittered under one of the light standards that illuminated the lot. "The hood is like a mirror. I'll bet I could see my face in it."

"I believe in taking care of things. If you—" He broke off sharply. "Somebody's been tampering with my car."

"No one here would touch it."

"Don't kid yourself! But it could have been anybody. I told Sybyll we should have guards patrolling the grounds."

"That would make the place feel like a prison," Noelle protested. "It was probably kids. I've heard they steal hood ornaments and stuff off luxury cars. You'd better check to be sure they didn't branch out into stealing parts."

"If I ever get my hands on them!" he muttered.

As he reached for the hood, she said, "I'll get in."

"The door's locked. I'll open it in a minute."

Noelle walked around to the passenger side and waited expectantly. After a moment she called, "What's taking you so long?"

When he didn't answer, she walked back to the front of the car. Troy was standing rooted to the spot, staring in frozen horror under the hood. A rattlesnake couldn't have shocked him more.

"Did they do any damage?" she asked.

"Somebody put a bomb in my car," he answered in a strangled voice.

"Oh, Troy, stop kidding around," she said impatiently. "Are we going to the pub, or aren't we?"

"I'm telling you there's a bomb in there!" He pointed with a shaking finger.

"I don't know anything about cars, but it looks fine to me. I think you've been watching too much television."

He grabbed her arm and jerked her closer. "You see that square box with the wires coming out of it?"

"What about it? Isn't that part of the engine?" she asked innocently.

"If I'd turned on the ignition, I'd have been blown sky-high."

It was typical that he said "I" instead of "we," Noelle thought ironically. She masked her disgust under a look of uncertainty. "You're not joking, are you? Troy, this is awful! We have to call the police."

His expression changed. "No police. You're not to tell anyone about this."

"Why not? If somebody is trying to kill you, we have to go to the authorities."

"It would be bad publicity for the spa. Sybyll would have a fit."

"You can't worry about that when your life is in danger. Who would do a terrible thing like this? Do you have any idea?"

Troy's eyes shifted. "It was probably some low-life bum who's jealous of other people's success."

"That doesn't give us much of a clue." She glanced down at the folded paper in her hand, as if just then remembering it. "This was stuck in the door. Do you think it has any connection?"

He snatched the note from her hand and smoothed it out. Noelle looked over his shoulder, reading along with him. The words were printed with a black marking pen, making them stand out starkly against the white paper. The message read:

The bomb in your car is only a dummy. It was put there to show you how easy it would be. If you have any idea of pulling a double-cross, forget it. Next time you won't get any warning.

"What do you think it means?" Noelle asked when Troy stood motionless.

"I..." He moistened his lips. "It's just a practical joke."

"Are you sure? It sounds like a threat to me. You can't simply ignore it."

"Some kids were fooling around, that's all." He crumpled the paper in his fist.

"But suppose they try something else? Next time it might not be harmless."

"Will you forget about it?" Troy's face was pale under his tan.

"Well, sure, if you say so. Let's have that drink. I think we both need it."

"I'm not in the mood anymore. We'll do it some other time."

"I understand," Noelle said soothingly. "Even if this was only a prank, it's scary to think what could happen if somebody actually had it in for you."

"Nothing's going to happen to me," he answered grimly.

"I certainly hope not! But as long as everything turned out okay, I must admit this has all been very exciting. Nothing out of the ordinary ever happens at Carefree Dunes. The most we can look forward to is seeing one of the top-flight celebrities. And then, often as not, they barely speak to us." She chattered on nonstop as they walked back to their rooms, pretending not to notice Troy's strained preoccupation.

* * *

Noelle phoned Roman as soon as she got into her room. "It worked like a charm!" she crowed. "Troy spotted the raised hood right away. I didn't have to point it out to him. I did have a bad moment worrying that he wouldn't recognize the dummy bomb. I was prepared to ask him what the funny box with the wires was, but it worked better this way."

"He's probably familiar with every spark plug and piston," Roman remarked.

"*I* sure wasn't. I broke out in a cold sweat trying to decipher Mike's diagram. Does a car really need all those gadgets to make it run?"

"Probably not, but people who fork over that kind of money expect a lot of bells and whistles. The important thing is, everything went off without a hitch."

"Due to a little ingenuity on my part." Noelle told him about Troy's unexpected date with Stephanie. "Do you think he could be up to his old tricks so soon?"

"I wouldn't put it past him. But it's more likely he was simply getting in a little extracurricular activity. I've seen Moose Martin's wife—the TV camera always shows a shot of her in the stands during his games. She's one good-looking female."

"If you like the obvious type," Noelle sniffed.

Roman chuckled. "She couldn't fill your leotard."

"Yes, she could, with a lot left over. You should have seen her tonight in short shorts and a tight T-shirt."

"I'd rather see you without either one," he murmured. "Do you feel like taking a ride?"

"I can't leave here. I'm sure Troy won't be able to sleep. If he knocks on my door for any reason, I'd better be here."

"You've done your part for tonight," Roman said sharply. "You're not to let him anywhere near you."

She laughed. "Don't worry, Madonna couldn't get a rise out of Troy right now. I only meant he might stop by to borrow an aspirin, or a book maybe."

"Who would he get to read it to him?" Roman's voice turned coaxing. "I could come to you. It wouldn't take me long to get there."

"No, don't do that. This is no time to take chances. I miss you, too, darling, but we'll just have to settle for talking on the phone a lot."

"If you think I intend to let a week go by without seeing you, you're badly mistaken. I'm only sticking around to wrap this thing up."

"I know, and I'm grateful," she said soothingly.

"I don't want gratitude, I want *you*. Tomorrow we're going to have lunch together at least."

"I only get an hour for lunch. It takes that long to drive to Tucson and back."

"I wasn't suggesting that. I'll meet you in the village."

"That's not a good idea, either. Everybody there knows the people who work at the spa. Someone might mention to Troy that I was goofing off in the middle of the day with a tall, gorgeous stranger. He'd know it was you immediately," she said fondly.

"If you're trying to distract me, it won't work. There's a solution to every problem. I'll have the hotel pack a picnic lunch and we'll meet in that little grove where we went riding last week. What fault can you find with *that* plan?"

"Not a one," she answered softly. "I can hardly wait."

"We'd better hang up, or you won't have to," Roman said huskily.

Noelle stopped by the gym when she had a break the next morning. Troy was making the rounds of the exercise machines, giving encouragement mechanically. His usual ingratiating manner was missing.

She waited to catch his eye, then beckoned him over. "I'm going into the village for lunch," she said to explain her absence.

"What do you want, my permission?"

Ignoring his sarcastic tone, she said, "I thought you might want to come with me." Noelle was sure he was in no mood to agree, but she stifled a sigh of relief when he refused.

"I'll pass. I plan to skip lunch and sack out for an hour. I didn't sleep very well last night."

"It's understandable. You must have been really shook up by that unfunny incident."

"That had nothing to do with it," he said in annoyance. "I just have a lot on my mind these days—some investments that went sour."

"Trouble comes in bunches, doesn't it?" she asked sympathetically. "I've been thinking about what happened last night."

"I told you to forget it," he growled.

"I think you're taking the entire matter too lightly. Suppose it wasn't kids? If somebody has a grudge against you, they won't stop now. I saw a movie like that once. This man wanted revenge against a guy who ruined his daughter's life. The man kept playing practical jokes on him, but some of them weren't harmless. One time he put just enough poison in the guy's food to make him deathly ill. He didn't want to kill him that time, see, only make him suffer a lot."

"Thanks for sharing that with me." Troy's smile was a mere contortion of his facial muscles.

"I'm not suggesting a cold-blooded psychopath is after you, but I do think you should be careful."

"I intend to be," he answered somberly.

She glanced at her watch. "Well, I guess I'd better get back to work. Sorry you won't have lunch with me."

Roman was already at the meeting place when Noelle arrived. He got out to greet her as she pulled her car off the road next to his.

"I'm sorry I'm late," she said. "I was all set to leave when Betty Bradford cornered me. Her husband is a movie producer and she wants to discover me."

Roman took her in his arms. "Tell her I already did."

After a most satisfactory kiss, Noelle glanced over her shoulder at the road. "I think we'd better continue this somewhere more private."

"I'll drink to that." He reached into the car and took out a bottle of wine and a picnic basket.

With their arms around each other's waists, they crossed the bridle path to the narrow strip of lawn and trees on the other side. As soon as they reached comparative privacy, Roman pulled her close.

"How do you manage to get more beautiful every time I see you?" he asked in a husky voice.

"You're responsible. You make me feel beautiful," she answered softly.

He clasped her tightly and buried his face in her neck. "I can't wait to get you out of here so we can be together all the time."

"I'm ready." She stroked his hair lovingly.

"I don't think I can be patient much longer. I want to go to sleep with you in my arms every night and wake up to find you there in the morning."

He captured her mouth for a deep kiss that awakened all the dormant passion that was always present between them. They murmured unintelligible words of love and caressed each other with increasing urgency.

Sinking to the grass with their mouths still joined, Roman pillowed her head on his arm and began to chart a wandering path over her body. Noelle moved restlessly as he stroked her bare thigh, then traced erotic patterns under the hem of her shorts.

"Not here," she whispered.

"I know," he groaned. "All I'm doing is frustrating both of us, but I can't leave you alone."

"I wish you didn't have to."

His intimate caresses were testing her willpower. Arching her body into his, she slid her hands inside the low-slung waistband of his jeans. The supple smoothness of his skin destroyed her remaining inhibitions. Digging her fingers into his buttocks, she urged their hips closer together.

Roman's reaction was immediate and unmistakable. "I want to make love to you right now!" he said hoarsely.

As she was about to agree, a car with a blaring radio went by on the highway. The jarring noise brought Noelle to her senses.

When she started to draw away, Roman stopped her. "Don't go. No one can see us from the road. Just let me hold you."

She smiled up at him. "We both know what that will lead to."

"Is that so bad?" he murmured. As his head dipped toward hers, they heard voices and the sound of horses hooves in the distance. Roman sat up with a sound of annoyance. "What is this, a main thoroughfare?"

Noelle couldn't help laughing. "Maybe it's your ten-derfoot tourists coming back. Or should that be tender-*feet?*"

"Whoever it is, I hope they get tender *bottoms,*" he groused. "Why aren't they out swimming or playing ten-nis?"

"Because they woke up this morning and said to them-selves, 'What can I do to ruin Roman Wilding's day?'" she teased.

He returned her smile wryly. "They should be happy to know they succeeded beyond their wildest dreams."

Noelle waved at the passing horseback riders in re-sponse to their greeting. "Can we have lunch now?" she asked Roman. "Or did you just lure me out here to have your way with me?"

"A fat lot of good it did," he grumbled good-naturedly.

Noelle sat with her back against a tree while he took sandwiches out of the hamper and uncorked the wine. Gazing off at the majestic mountains in the distance, she sighed happily.

"I'm really going to miss this place. It's beautiful coun-try, and I made a good friend here."

"Is that the highest rating I get?" he asked in mock outrage. "Friend?"

"I meant Erica." Noelle's face sobered. "She has a tough road ahead of her."

"Did their love song hit a discordant note?"

"A very sour one." She told him about Jeff's mother. "Poor Erica, she had no idea of what was coming. It was painful to watch. That woman could intimidate a drill sergeant—without raising her cultured voice."

"I must say, I'm not surprised."

"How could you know a nice guy like Jeff would have a mother who rides around on a broomstick?"

"From the little bit he told me about her, and Jeff, himself."

"He's nothing like his mother," Noelle protested.

"No, but he lets her run his life. Jeff didn't want to come here, but Mama said it would be good for him, so he came. Obviously she's a strong woman."

Noelle was silent for a moment. "He has to learn to assert himself, or their marriage could run into trouble before it has a chance to succeed."

"*If* they ever get married. Jeff would be hurt and disillusioned if his mother coerced Erica into breaking the engagement."

"She almost succeeded until I gave Erica a pep talk," Noelle said angrily. "Erica will make Jeff a wonderful wife. He's a lucky man."

"So am I." Roman brought her hand to his mouth and kissed the palm.

They forgot about the problems of the other couple and concentrated on each other. All too soon, Noelle had to leave.

The rest of the afternoon flew by. Noelle was kept so busy she didn't see Erica until dinnertime.

"You look as if something's bothering you," she commented as they walked to the dining room together. "Did that old...did Mrs. Mainwaring have another go at you?"

"No, I haven't seen her today," Erica answered listlessly.

"Then what's the matter?"

"I phoned Jeff after I left you yesterday." Erica's lashes hid her eyes. "He was going out on a date."

"I'm sure you misunderstood!"

"No, he said he was going to a formal ball with a judge's daughter."

Noelle paused. "Oh, one of those things. Well, he probably made the date weeks ago. He couldn't very well cancel out at the last minute."

"I suppose you're right," Erica answered politely.

"Of course I am. Now is not the time to add jealousy to all your other troubles." Noelle wanted to bite her tongue as soon as the candid words were out.

Erica smiled faintly at her friend's chagrined expression. "It's all right. I'm not kidding myself anymore."

"I hope that doesn't mean what it sounds like."

Before Erica could answer, they were joined by Thelma. Any chance of a private conversation was impossible as they straggled into the dining room.

Troy came in after all the others were seated. He pulled out a chair without a word to anyone.

"Oh, goody, the entertainment is here," Mitzi observed. "Dinner just isn't the same without Troy's smiling face."

"Knock it off," he snarled. "I'm not in the mood tonight."

"Did you strike out with one of the guests?" she asked.

"That's another thing. I'm tired of having you circulate rumors about me," he grated. "You won't be happy until you get me in trouble."

"You don't need any help in that department," Mitzi said.

"What's that supposed to mean?" He turned his head to glare at Noelle. "Have you been shooting off your mouth?"

"I didn't say a word!" she protested.

"About what?" Thelma asked avidly.

"Nothing. Forget the whole thing." Troy's scowl included the entire table. "Couldn't we have just one meal without discussing my personal life? Is that too much to ask?''

"You never minded before," Mitzi answered.

"Well, I do now. Get it?"

Noelle was afraid the added pressure from his colleagues would blow Troy right out of the dining room, so she stepped in hastily. "You could lighten up a little," she told Mitzi.

"Tell *him* that! He's as cranky as a vampire on a vegetarian diet."

"Speaking of vegetables—" Noelle changed the subject determinedly "—what is this stuff?" She indicated a small mound on her plate. "It's delicious, but I can't tell what it is."

"Eggplant." Erica joined in for the first time. "You can make it a lot of different ways and it tastes different each time."

"I can't believe I'm eating eggplant," Noelle said. "I wouldn't touch it when I was a youngster."

"Your tastes change when you grow up," Thelma remarked. "I was a very picky eater as a child, but now I like everything."

"Not me." Mitzi poked a fork at the food on her plate. "I wish they wouldn't serve coleslaw so often."

"It's delicious," Thelma told her. "Especially tonight. They put something different in it."

"You may call it delicious," Mitzi answered. "I say it tastes funny."

Noelle stole a look at Troy while the others were talking. He was staring at his plate.

Suddenly he pushed it away and stood. "I'm finished. I don't want any dessert."

"What got into him?" Mitzi asked, staring as he went out the door. "He hardly touched his dinner."

"That *is* strange," Thelma agreed. "Usually Troy eats everything but the design on the plate."

"I guess something affected his appetite," Noelle remarked innocently.

Mitzi shrugged, dismissing his problem. "Who wants to go to a movie tonight? They changed the bill at the theater in the village."

"It's about time," Thelma commented. "The last one played for a month."

"Tell me this one isn't a Western," Noelle pleaded. "I couldn't stand to see another cowboy kiss his horse."

"You Easterners aren't happy unless one of them has an emotional problem," Mitzi said. "Out here we keep our plots simple."

"Any cowpoke who's in love with his horse isn't only simple, he's sick," Noelle answered.

"Even if you don't like the movie, the popcorn will make up for it. They make it fresh every Wednesday, whether it's stale or not." Mitzi looked at her watch. "Let's get going. We just have time to get there for the first show."

Erica remained seated as they all got up to leave. When Noelle realized it, she turned back. "Aren't you coming with us?"

Erica gave her a forced smile. "I think I'll pass. I'm not crazy about Westerns, either, with or without neurotic horses."

"It'll be fun," Noelle coaxed. "A real no-brainer. The good guys are always the ones in the white hats."

Erica's smile faltered. "Too bad life isn't that cut-and-dried."

"You don't have to make it more complicated. Jeff loves you," Noelle said urgently. "You can't let his mother spoil something wonderful."

"She loves him, too," Erica said quietly. "She wouldn't try to break us up if she thought I could make him happy."

"You *are* naive," Noelle groaned. "Women like Mrs. Mainwaring don't know the true meaning of the word 'love.' They do what's right for *them,* and then rationalize it in their own mind. Her objections to your marriage have nothing to do with you. *Any* woman would be a threat."

"Noelle, what's keeping you?" Mitzi called impatiently. "Are you coming or aren't you?"

"Go ahead," Erica said. "I'll be all right."

"Why don't you reconsider and come with us? It will do you good to get away for a couple of hours."

"I honestly don't feel like it."

"Then I'll stay with you," Noelle said. "We'll talk this out and get you back on track."

"No. I've listened to all of you. Now I have to make up my own mind," Erica answered with calm maturity.

Noelle left her reluctantly when Mitzi's insistent voice summoned her again.

After everyone left, Erica wandered around the spa by herself. The beauty of the night contrasted with her inner turmoil. She was being pulled in three directions—by Jeff, his mother and her own heart. Which one should she listen to? If only the scales would tilt one way or the other. She needed some indication of what to do, a divine signal, perhaps. But the stars winked down coldly, indifferent to her problem.

Eventually Erica returned to her room. Was she unconsciously trying to avoid Jeff's phone call? If so, she'd wasted her time. The telephone rang almost as soon as she got in.

"Where the heck have you been?" Jeff demanded. "I've been calling every fifteen minutes."

"Oh, well, I was . . . with Noelle."

"What were you doing all this time? Never mind, you're here now. Do you miss me?"

"You know I do. Do you miss *me?*" she asked yearningly.

"Need you ask?"

Erica paused. "How was your date last night?"

"It wasn't a date," Jeff protested. "I told you why I had to go. You're not upset about it, are you, darling?"

"No. Did you have a good time?"

"How could I enjoy myself without you?" he asked in a melting voice.

"What time did you get home?"

He hesitated. "Well, it was kind of late. Tiffany wanted to go on to a couple of parties. You know how kids are."

"You're not that much older than she is," Erica remarked.

"I feel as if light-years separate us. Do you know how long it's been since I've done something as zany as riding from party to party in a hansom cab drawn by a horse wearing a flowered hat?"

"It sounds like fun," Erica said in a neutral voice.

"It wasn't fun when someone stole the horse while we were inside Le Petit Renard having breakfast." He named one of the toniest restaurants in New York.

"I've read about the celebrities who go there for dinner. Does a place like Le Petit Renard stay open for breakfast?"

"Not ordinarily. A few of us chipped in to make it worth their while."

"Wasn't that terribly expensive?"

"That's what money's for," Jeff said dismissively. "To have fun with."

"I thought you said you didn't enjoy yourself." Erica knew she was being quarrelsome, but she couldn't help it.

Jeff stifled a sigh. "Erica, dearest, you can't possibly be jealous of Tiffany. She's a bubbleheaded little debutante. She wouldn't even have gotten into a decent college without her father's influence."

"I guess that's important," Erica said in a muted voice.

"Well, sure, it's—" He stopped abruptly, belatedly aware of her sensibilities. "You're not comparing yourself to Tiffany, are you? She'd have to go to school twice as long to be half as smart as you are, my love."

"You don't have to say that, Jeff. I know about the differences in our backgrounds. They're pretty obvious."

"That's nonsense! It doesn't matter where you went to school—or didn't go," he added quickly. "You're absolutely perfect just the way you are."

"Suppose everybody doesn't agree with you?" she asked hesitantly, wondering if she should tell him about his mother's visit.

"They will. I can't imagine anyone not loving you like I do."

"But if they didn't?" she persisted.

"What are you trying to say, Erica?"

After a moment's pause she said, "Nothing. I guess I'm just on edge tonight."

Forcing Jeff to choose between his mother and her would only jeopardize their future chance for happiness. At this point he would probably choose her, but his mother's objections had to make an impression. He'd remember them if she didn't turn out to be the perfect wife he expected.

"This is a difficult time for both of us," Jeff said soothingly. "It's hell being separated. But it's only for a few more days, honey. Get some rest and I'll call you tomorrow night."

Erica hung up the phone slowly. Why hadn't she told Jeff she couldn't marry him? What was the point in prolonging this misery? Tomorrow night she'd have to end it.

Chapter Eleven

Noelle didn't think Troy needed any further incentive to turn over the negatives. But since Mike's plan had succeeded brilliantly so far, she followed his instructions and carried out the last step.

In the middle of the morning on Thursday, she checked on Troy's whereabouts. He was giving a tennis lesson, which had started ten minutes earlier. That meant she could count on his being occupied for another twenty minutes. She only needed five.

After making a brief stop at her own room to get something, she let herself into Troy's room with the duplicate key she'd used before. It no longer mattered if anyone discovered it missing from the office. Troy would assume Mike was responsible.

Troy's bed was unmade as usual. Noelle reached gingerly into the paper bag she'd brought and took out a large, lethal-looking fake rattlesnake. It was so remarkably lifelike she hated to touch the thing. Dropping it onto the sheet, she slid a block-printed note under it, then hurriedly pulled the blanket over the loathsome object. A few minutes later she was leading her aerobics class.

Noelle hadn't expected Troy to discover his surprise until he went to bed that evening, but he returned to his room at noon. His appetite was off and he wasn't sleeping well at night, so he decided to take a short rest.

Troy was so used to disorder that he didn't notice the covers were pulled up, instead of flung aside. He flopped on his back on the narrow bed, one forearm shielding his eyes.

It took a few moments until the lump under the covers began to annoy him. After squirming ineffectually to get comfortable, he swore pungently and got up to dislodge whatever it was. A bloodcurdling scream reverberated through the staff quarters when he saw the snake.

One of the gardeners was working nearby. He rushed over, calling out, "What's happening in there? Did somebody have an accident?"

Troy came barreling out the door. "It's in my bed!" he shouted. "I could have died!"

Joe, the gardener, grabbed his arm. "Calm down, man, and tell me what's wrong."

"There's a rattlesnake in my bed. I was lying right on top of it! In another second it would have bitten me." Troy was gibbering with fear.

"Let's take a look."

"I'm not going back in that room! There's no telling where that thing's gotten to by now. It could be curled up waiting to strike."

"We have to find it. We can't just leave it loose here in the grounds."

"Wild horses couldn't drag me back in there," Troy stated adamantly.

"Okay, I'll have a look." Joe picked up a long-handled edger he'd been using and went inside.

Troy waited tensely, poised to run. He flinched when he heard a series of whacking sounds, as Joe presumably located the rattlesnake. Then, after a moment of silence, laughter filtered out the open door.

"You can come in now," the gardener called. "He put up a helluva fight, but I got him."

Troy went inside cautiously, recoiling at the sight of the snake dangling from the wheel of the edger. Both the head and tail were swaying back and forth.

"Watch out! It isn't dead yet," he shouted.

"It's as dead as it will ever be." Joe chuckled. "You sure got weird friends. Somebody put this in your bed as a gag."

That took a moment to sink in. "He wouldn't," Troy muttered. "Not a live rattlesnake."

"This one isn't real. Sure could fool most anyone, though. I guess *you* could swear to that."

"Are you certain it's not a real snake?"

"Here, I'll show you." Joe grasped the head and held it out. "Go ahead, see for yourself."

Troy backed up instead. "I'll take your word for it."

"Your jokester left a note for you." Joe gestured toward the bed. "Some people think this kind of thing is funny, but it could give a man a heart attack. Me, I'd get a new set of friends." He dropped the snake into a wastebasket and went out the door, shaking his head.

Troy approached the bed slowly. Picking up the piece of paper as if it were alive, he read the message:

Just a reminder of our appointment on Saturday. Have the merchandise ready, or next time won't be a game.

Troy waited till his breathing returned to normal, then he crumpled the note and picked up the telephone.

Noelle had just finished her class when Sybyll buzzed her on the intercom to tell her she'd had a phone call.

"I took a message this time because I didn't know when your class would be over. You can stop by the office and pick it up."

Noelle raced to the office, hoping the call hadn't been from Diane. The hope was in vain.

"It was from that same woman who called you before," Sybyll said, handing her a slip of paper with the phone number. "It's funny that she never leaves her name. I swear I've heard that voice before. Has she ever been a guest here?"

"No, she couldn't afford this place."

"She can afford plenty of long-distance calls," Sybyll answered crisply.

Noelle managed a laugh. "The phone company doesn't charge what Carefree Dunes does."

"What's your friend's name?" Sybyll asked directly, since hinting hadn't gotten her anywhere.

"It's, uh, Carole Bradford."

"Oh? Is she related to Betty Bradford?"

Noelle was furious with herself for not thinking faster. Sybyll's cross-examination had rattled her and that was the first name that popped into her mind, probably because she'd just been chatting with Betty.

"Carole doesn't have any relatives out West. I guess Bradford is a fairly common name."

Sybyll eyed her speculatively. "I never knew anyone else with that name."

"Well, now you do." Noelle smiled nervously. "I'd better call her back." She hurried out of the office.

"Didn't I tell you not to phone here again?" Noelle demanded when she reached Diane. "Sybyll thinks she knows you. How much time did you spend with her when you were here?"

"Quite a bit," Diane admitted. "My television conked out the first night, and the maintenance man had gone home. There was a program I wanted to see, so Sybyll invited me to watch it in her apartment. We got fairly friendly."

"Oh, great! Didn't it occur to you she might recognize your voice?"

"They get a new contingent of guests there every week. I didn't think she'd remember me," Diane answered defensively. "I didn't see as much of her after a while." An uncomfortable silence ensued as they both recalled the reason.

"I only hope there's no harm done," Noelle said finally. "I expect to get the negatives on Saturday. It would be heartbreaking if you jeopardized everything by your impatience."

"Oh, God! I'll simply die if I did!"

"Don't get excited. Even if Sybyll finally places you, there's no reason for her to mention it to Troy. All we need is one more day. Just don't call here again, no matter how nervous you get."

"That's not why I called today," Diane said. "I really intended to wait until you got in touch with me, but I received the strangest phone call from Troy. I thought you should know about it."

"I can't believe he's still pressing you for money! Either he's the world's greatest actor, or he has more courage than we gave him credit for."

"I have no idea what's going on out there. Troy called me about half an hour ago and pleaded with me to ask my brother to call off his dog. Troy said he's ready to deliver the merchandise if the man will contact him tonight."

"What did you answer?" Noelle asked urgently.

"You told me you were working some kind of a sting, so I figured that had to be part of it. I said it was out of my hands now."

Noelle breathed a sigh of relief. "Fantastic! You couldn't have done better. Then what did Troy say?"

"He apologized—can you believe it? He claimed he was desperate. That he never would have done such a despicable thing if he hadn't been head over heels in debt. And *then* he had the nerve to say he hoped I understood and would forgive him."

"The man is unbelievable! But at least it shows how scared he is. It's over, Diane. We've won!"

"I'll believe it when you call and tell me you have the negatives."

"You'll hear from me on Saturday. Just promise you won't phone here again. If you absolutely have to get in touch with me, call Roman Widenthal at the Golden Sands Hotel and leave a message. He'll relay it to me."

"Should I use my real name? How much does he know about me?" Diane asked anxiously. "I wish you hadn't told so many people."

"Roman and Mike are the only ones who know, and they're solely interested in nailing Troy."

"Why would this Roman person care about my troubles? He doesn't even know me."

Noelle smiled bewitchingly. "Chalk it up as a favor to me."

Diane laughed reluctantly. "You little devil. I've been feeling sorry for putting you through an ordeal and, instead, you've been having the time of your life."

"I wouldn't say that, but it hasn't been all bad."

Diane caught the softened note in Noelle's voice. "Are you serious about this man? Where does he live? Is he in show business?"

"I'll tell you all about him when I see you. Right now I have to concentrate on winding things up here so I can come home."

"You'll never know how grateful I am," Diane said soberly. "I don't know how I'll ever repay you."

"Just consider us even," Noelle answered softly.

Noelle's euphoric mood took a nosedive when she came out of the phone booth and noticed Troy standing over Sybyll's desk. His tension was obvious even from a distance. Whatever she was telling him had produced a strong reaction. Noelle's stomach was churning as she raced into the office, prepared to do damage control. If only it wasn't too late!

"Oh, Troy, I've been looking everywhere for you!" she said breathlessly. "Stephanie Martin wants to see you. I told her I'd send you over to the gym right away."

"What does she want?"

"I didn't ask her, but you'd better hurry. She's not the patient type."

He frowned. "What am I, a bellhop you snap your fingers for?"

"She *is* a guest of the spa."

"Since when are you running this place? Stephanie can wait a few minutes. I'm talking to Sybyll about something."

"The conversation is over," Sybyll said. "I am not going to hire security guards. It's totally unnecessary."

Noelle's stomach muscles relaxed. Her worries were for nothing.

"You're being shortsighted, Sybyll." Troy refused to give up. "We get a lot of rich women here. They have diamonds that would choke a horse. A thief could make quite a haul.''

"We're insured and so are they."

"How about the safety factor? Under our present setup, a thug could get in here and do God knows what."

"You're being paranoid," Sybyll answered impatiently. "I am not going to turn this place into a fortress because you've been watching too much scary television. The subject is closed," she said firmly, turning her attention to Noelle. "I couldn't get your friend out of my mind, and I think I know why her voice seemed familiar. She sounds like a guest we had here recently."

Sybyll's first words chilled Noelle. She had to keep her from mentioning Diane's name. "I'm hoping Carole can come and visit me some day. She's never been out West and I know she'd love it. I certainly do. Of course New York has a lot to offer, too." Noelle babbled on in the desperate hope Troy would leave.

He merely gave her an annoyed look and continued to press Sybyll. "At least think about what I said. It's better to be safe than sorry."

"I wish you'd get going, Troy," Noelle urged. "Stephanie will be sure to think I didn't give you her message."

"When did you start to care that much about Stephanie Martin?"

"Are you still ticked off about the other night? I didn't mean to break up your date with her," Noelle said defensively. "How was I to know you two wanted to be alone?"

"What's all this?" Sybyll asked sharply.

Troy slanted an uncomfortable look at his boss. "Noelle is just clowning around. I didn't have a date with Mrs. Martin. I was only giving her a tennis lesson."

Sybyll continued to stare at him. "I expect all of our employees to be accommodating to the guests—but within the boundaries of good taste."

"You don't have to tell *me* that." Troy smiled nervously. "Well, I'd better see what Mrs. Martin wants. Probably another lesson. She's a real tennis nut." He left hastily.

Noelle was limp with relief. "I have to go, too. My next class starts in ten minutes."

Noelle couldn't get in touch with Roman immediately as she'd hoped. He didn't return her calls until late afternoon.

"Where have you been all day?" she asked. "I needed you."

"The feeling is entirely mutual," he answered in a honeyed voice. "Just tell me where and when."

"Business before pleasure." She told him about Troy's phone call to Diane. "He's ready to throw in the towel, but now it's too late for Mike to get here tonight. You'll have to tell him to catch the first plane in the morning."

"I think it's wiser to stick to our original timetable. It only involves one more day."

"That one day could be our undoing." She told him how Sybyll had almost blown their entire plan to bits. "If she brings up Diane's name in front of Troy, he won't pass it off as a coincidence, not now when he's so jumpy."

"Sybyll has no reason to think Troy would be interested in a former guest. There's only a chance in a million she'd mention Diane when he's around."

"It's that one chance that bothers me," Noelle said grimly. "I won't relax until I'm out of here."

"That can't be too soon for me. I miss you like crazy. What if I come over after midnight? We can go skinny-dipping in the pool."

"Are you trying to make me miserable?" she demanded.

Roman chuckled richly. "Just the opposite." His voice deepened. "Remember the last time we went swimming together?"

"No. I refuse to think about it."

"That's where we differ. I enjoy the memory. You looked like an enchanting wood nymph poised at the edge of the pool, naked in the moonlight."

"I had on a bathing suit," she protested.

"I couldn't tell. All I could see were the lovely curves of your breasts and your long, beautiful legs."

"You were the one who was naked that night," she murmured.

He laughed softly. "Too bad you weren't interested."

"If you'd only known!"

Her first encounter with his supple nude body would stay with Noelle forever. She'd wanted to strip off her own suit and experience the full power he so obviously possessed. Where had she found the strength to resist?

As if reading her mind, Roman said, "We have some unfinished business."

She groaned. "You know we can't take the risk."

"You're right again." He sighed. "Okay, angel, I'll stop pestering you. But when Saturday gets here, I don't expect to hear any excuses."

"You won't," she promised. "What time is Mike meeting Troy?"

"I don't know that he set a specific time. I'll phone him and let you know what I find out."

Troy waylaid Noelle outside the dining room that night. "What the devil are you up to?" he asked angrily.

Her heart skipped a beat. "I don't know what you're talking about."

"Don't hand me that! Stephanie wasn't in the gym when I got there."

"She probably got tired of waiting for you. Did you go look for her?" Noelle asked casually. That had been a worry, but it was the lesser of two evils.

"How could I, after the number you did on me with Sybyll? Why did you make her think I was having a thing with Stephanie?"

"If I did, you deserved it." Noelle decided to go on the offensive. Not only because it wasn't credible that anyone would continue to take his abuse without eventually striking back, but because she was fed up with him. "You've been on my case since I broke up your date with that blond bimbo! If you *are* having an affair with her, why should I protect you?"

Troy gritted his teeth. "I never laid a finger on her."

"You don't have to tell *me*. I couldn't care less," Noelle answered coolly.

"Just stay out of my business from now on, do you hear me? I've got enough trouble without you starting more for me."

Noelle dropped her distant manner for pretended concern. "Is something wrong, Troy?"

"Nothing serious." He gave her a sidelong glance. "Have you seen any strangers hanging around here?"

She shook her head. "We never get new guests this late in the week."

"I wasn't talking about guests. I meant a guy—tall, kind of lanky, wearing wraparound shades."

"No, I haven't seen anybody who fits that description. But men's week is over. What would a man be doing here now?"

"I just thought you might have seen him," Troy said, ignoring her question. "Somebody played another practical joke on me."

So Troy had discovered his surprise earlier than expected. That explained his panicky call to Diane. Noelle gazed up at him, wide-eyed. "You know who did it?"

"Yeah. What really ticks me off is the way he gets in and out of here like a shadow. You can't protect yourself. Damn it, I'm going to talk to Sybyll again!"

"No!"

When Troy stared at her, surprised by her vehemence, Noelle added hastily, "She already turned you down flat, and you know how hardnosed Sybyll is. She'd never back down after taking a stand. Let me try to talk her around."

"That might work," he agreed. "You gals stick together. Just don't tell her about my, uh, little mishaps."

"Why not?" Noelle asked ingenuously. "That might convince her we need some security around here."

"I told you no!" he ordered. "I'd be the butt of all kinds of jokes if it got blabbed around."

"Okay, whatever you say."

Noelle and Troy weren't the only ones on edge. Erica was wound to the breaking point. The last person in the world she wanted to see was Mrs. Mainwaring, but the older woman was waiting for her after Erica finished her final class.

"It's been two days since our little talk. I was wondering if you'd come to a decision," Estelle said.

"Yes, I guess so," Erica answered hesitantly.

Estelle's nails bit into her palms, but her face was outwardly serene. "May I ask what it is?"

"I thought a lot about what you said. I love Jeff very much, and I want him to be happy."

"Then how can you go ahead with this unsuitable marriage? It will never work, I tell you. You'll both be miserable!"

"I'm afraid you're right," Erica said sadly.

"You're going to give him up?" Triumph blazed for an instant in Estelle's eyes. "That's very wise of you, my dear. You'll find someone more suitable, and I know you'll be happy."

"I don't feel very happy," Erica said forlornly.

"Perhaps not now, but in time you'll see that it was all for the best." Estelle paused imperceptibly. "Have you told Jeffrey?"

"I intend to tell him when he phones tonight."

"I hope you won't say I pressured you in any way. As I stressed when we had our talk, I want this to be solely your decision. My son can be a little stubborn at times. He might insist on going through with the marriage if he thought I'd influenced you."

Erica looked at the other woman squarely. "I know you came here to break us up. I'm not stupid, no matter what you think. Your motive was selfish, but I'm giving Jeff up because his happiness means more to me than my own, and I'm afraid I wouldn't make him happy."

"That's all you need to tell him," Estelle said earnestly.

Erica's lip curled. "You don't have to worry. I have no intention of spoiling your relationship with him. That wouldn't make any of us happy."

Estelle couldn't hide her relief. "You're a very generous girl. I'd like to show my gratitude. Not with money," she added hastily at the look on Erica's face. "I was thinking of a new car, or perhaps a lovely piece of jewelry—whatever you want."

"What I want doesn't have a price tag on it." Erica walked away with her head held high.

Everyone was nervous and keyed up on Friday. Troy kept looking over his shoulder and jumping if a tree rustled.

Stephanie commented on it in the gym that morning. "What's the matter with you, Troy? You haven't been listening to a word I said."

"Sure I have." He forced a smile.

"Okay, what were we talking about?" she demanded.

"We'll pick it up when I get back. I have to make a phone call." He left her abruptly.

That was only one of many calls he placed to Diane that day without reaching her. Noelle had told her to have the maid answer and say she was out. Mike couldn't get there till Saturday, anyway, since he was involved in another case. Noelle was counting off the minutes.

Erica was equally tense. Jeff hadn't phoned the night before, after she'd been all primed for a painful argument. By the time she realized he wasn't going to call, it was too late to call *him*. He probably wasn't home, anyway. Jeff had resumed his social life with a vengeance, she thought drearily.

When the day was finally over, all three were emotionally drained. Noelle and Troy went to their rooms to watch television, and Erica sat by the phone in her own room, preparing herself. As she reached for the slip of paper with his number on it, the phone rang.

After expressing the usual loving sentiments, Jeff said, "I'm sorry I didn't call you last night. I had a meeting at the bank that ran late, and then everybody wanted to go out for a drink. I couldn't very well refuse. We'd just financed a big merger."

"You could have called me when you got home," Erica said in a small voice.

"Well, the thing is, I didn't go right home. After a couple of drinks we were all hungry, especially me. I didn't have lunch. So we went to Le Petite Renard again for dinner. I can't wait to take you there, darling. Their escargots are superb—not too garlicky—and they make a roast truffled capon that's as good as anything Paris has to offer."

"I didn't know you liked that sort of thing," she said slowly. "You said the hamburgers and fries in the village were your kind of food."

"I eat anything that's put in front of me." He chuckled. "I was the only kid in prep school who asked for seconds. You won't have any trouble cooking for me."

"We have to talk," she said abruptly.

"What's on your mind, sweetheart?" he asked when she didn't continue.

"I can't marry you," she blurted out. It was a bald statement of fact, but there was no easy way to say it.

"Don't even joke about a thing like that!"

"I'm serious, Jeff. I'm really sorry, but I made a mistake. Try to understand."

"I can't believe what I'm hearing! Everything was fine the last time we talked." His voice sharpened. "Are you angry because I didn't phone last night? Is that it?"

"It has nothing to do with that. I should have told you sooner, but I . . . I just couldn't."

"Are you saying you're not in love with me?"

Why did he have to ask that? Could she force herself to lie? "I'm very fond of you," she answered carefully. "But we simply aren't right for each other."

"There were never two people more perfectly suited. I love you, darling. If you're having an attack of the jitters, I understand," he said soothingly. "I rushed you into something and now you're getting scared. But you have nothing to worry about. I'm going to devote my life to making you happy."

"I want *you* to be happy, too," she replied desperately.

"If I were any happier they'd throw a net over me." He laughed. "This separation is for the birds, though. I can tell you to the minute how long it's been since I held you in my arms."

"Marriage is more than just sex," she said soberly. "When the bells stop ringing, a lot of things become important."

"In the first place, they won't ever stop for us. But that's not the only reason I want to marry you, sweetheart. You're everything I've been looking for in a woman. I want to share my life with you and watch our children grow up. I want to grow old with you."

Erica wavered. She wanted desperately to believe him. "I'm so afraid it won't work out," she whispered.

"Darling little Erica, how can you doubt it?" he asked indulgently. "We'll have a wonderful life together. I've told all my friends about you and they can't wait to meet you. They've planned a round of parties for us, and you'll be invited to join the Junior League."

The picture he was painting was the same one Mrs. Mainwaring had outlined. But Jeff thought she could fit right in without any of the experience that came with privilege. What would happen when she failed the test? The stars in his eyes prevented him from seeing clearly, but Erica couldn't bear to watch the dream die.

"That's your life, Jeff," she said quietly. "It isn't mine."

"You don't have to do anything you don't want to, sweetheart. I just thought you were worried about being lonesome in New York."

"I'm sure I would be. That's just one of the problems that would arise."

When he realized she was serious, his high spirits plummeted. "I guess every couple has problems, but we can work them out," he said slowly.

"Jeff, you have to listen to me. I can't marry you. I thought I could, but I can't go through with it."

"That's a strange way of putting it." His voice cooled. "You make our marriage sound like a business investment that isn't worth the cost. *I* was marrying for love. Was I just a high-priced meal ticket to *you?*"

"You know better than that," she answered in a low voice.

"I'm beginning to think I don't know you at all. You said you loved me. I was on cloud nine. Now you pull the rug out from under me. What's going on, Erica? I'd hate to think any of my suspicions were valid."

Erica was drowning in misery. "Let's stop this, Jeff. We're only hurting each other, and I'm sure neither of us wants to. You're angry now, but in time you'll thank me. Can't we just leave it at that?"

"I suppose there's nothing else I *can* do." He sounded hurt and confused. "Goodbye, Erica. It was fun while it lasted."

"Goodbye, my love," she murmured after replacing the receiver. "No one will ever take your place."

Mike Trinity took an early-morning plane from New York on Saturday and drove directly to Carefree Dunes. But because of the time difference, he didn't arrive until late afternoon. Noelle hovered around the parking lot, waiting on pins and needles.

She rushed over to the car when he finally pulled in. "I thought you'd never get here!"

"Relax, kid. I'll have this wrapped up in ten minutes. You did a great job, incidentally. Rome filled me in on the details."

"Your plan was brilliant. Troy is coming unglued. The rattlesnake pushed him over the edge."

"I thought it might. Send him to me and we'll get this over with. I'll bring the negatives to you afterward."

"My room is in that building over there." She pointed. "Number nine."

"I know." Mike smiled. "Rome told me."

Saturday was traditionally a slow day at the spa. Most of the guests had either lost the weight they'd hoped to or given up. They usually spent their last afternoon in relaxation. Noelle found Troy alone in the gym, checking the equipment.

"I just saw him, your practical-joker friend," she said breathlessly.

Troy stiffened. "Where is he?"

"In the parking lot. I went out to see if I'd left my sunglasses in my car. I'm always misplacing the darn things, and in this—"

His hands bit into her forearms. "Did he say anything to you?"

"He told me to send you to him on the double."

Troy didn't wait to question her further. He raced out the door with Noelle following.

"He looked kind of scary. Maybe it was those dark glasses," she panted. "I like to see somebody's eyes when I talk to him."

Troy stopped in his tracks, realizing she intended to go with him. "I've got personal business with this guy. Buzz off."

She gave him an indignant glare. "I thought you'd want moral support, but this is it! I've had it with you, Troy."

Noelle waited a suitable time, then followed him. From a sheltered spot behind a grove of oleanders, she watched the meeting between Troy and Mike.

"I've been trying to get in touch with you since Thursday," Troy told the detective. "I managed to get the negatives sooner than I expected."

Mike lounged against the side of the car with his arms crossed over his chest. "I got your message, but I was doing another job for the boss."

"You didn't have to put that rattlesnake in my bed. I damn near had a stroke."

Mike grinned. "Guys like you are apt to die in bed—one way or another. Do you have the merchandise with you?"

Troy handed over an envelope. When the detective merely put it in his pocket, he asked, "Aren't you going to look at them?"

"I trust you." Mike took off his sunglasses to give the other man a steely look. "If they aren't what we agreed on or you held on to a couple, I'll be back."

"They're all there, I swear!"

"Good, because if I do come back, I won't be nearly as friendly." Mike straightened. "Let me give you a word of advice. Get into another business."

When Mike knocked on Noelle's door a short time later, Roman was standing beside him, holding a bottle of champagne.

"I was waiting around the corner, out of sight," Roman explained. "Too bad we both had to miss all the fun."

"I wish all my jobs were this easy. The guy unraveled like a cheap sweater." Mike chuckled, handing Noelle the envelope.

"Did you look at them?" she asked hesitantly.

"No, I thought your friend would prefer to check them out herself. I'm sure they're what she wanted, though."

"Diane doesn't need to go through any more. I intend to burn them."

Noelle took out the negatives and walked over to the window to hold them up to the light. Even in miniature, the pictures were vulgarly graphic. Troy was even more despicable than she'd thought. Poor Diane. Noelle hoped she didn't remember much of what had gone on that night.

Roman came up behind her and curved his hand around her neck. With his other hand he held out a book of matches. "First we'll have a bonfire, then we'll open the champagne."

They stood around the dresser, watching as Noelle dropped the packet of films into a ceramic soap dish and touched a match to it.

When only a residue of ashes remained, Roman said, "Now all that's left is taking out the garbage. I spoke to my friend in Washington. Troy will be hearing from the IRS very soon."

"I can't think of anything I'd rather drink to," she said. "I'll get some glasses."

Mike shook his head. "Not for me. I have to get back to the airport. I'm taking the next plane back to New York."

After he left, Noelle said, "I guess we'll have to celebrate without him."

"That's the best way." Roman took her in his arms and kissed her. "I want you all to myself."

His mouth slid across her cheek to her ear. While he probed sensuously with his tongue, his hands slid under her shorts to caress her bottom. She moved against him with a small sound of pleasure.

"You know what I like best about Carefree Dunes?" he murmured. "You wear so few clothes."

"And you have on too many." Their smiling eyes held as she reached up to unbutton his sport shirt. She had only unfastened the first button when a knock sounded at the door.

"Don't answer it and they'll go away," Roman growled.

She might have done just that, but Erica's soft voice called, "Noelle? I need to talk to you."

She sounded so plaintive that Noelle gave Roman a rueful look. "I have to see what she wants."

Erica's face was mournful. "I wasn't going to talk about it, but I—" She stopped when she saw Roman. "I didn't know you were still in town."

"I won't be for long, and neither will Noelle. She's coming back to New York with me."

Erica looked confused. "I thought your home was in Chicago."

"It's a long story that I won't go into now." Noelle gave Roman a laughing glance. "When are *you* leaving?"

"I'm not." Erica bit her lip. "I've decided not to marry Jeff."

"You let his mother break it up? Oh, Erica, you're making a big mistake! What did Jeff say when you told him?"

"He wasn't hard to convince," Erica answered bitterly. "He thought I was after his money, too."

"I can't believe that!"

When another knock came at the door, Roman commented, "This is a busy place."

Noelle's abstracted expression changed when she opened the door and found Jeff standing outside. "Jeff! What are you doing here?"

"I came to talk to Erica," he replied grimly. "She isn't in the gym or her room. I hoped you could tell me where to find her." His face became charged with emotion when Erica appeared from behind Noelle.

"You shouldn't have come, Jeff," Erica said in a low voice. "We've already said everything we had to say to each other."

"Everything but the truth." He came inside and slammed the door. "I want to know why you changed your mind about marrying me. I don't believe for one second that you stopped loving me. What we felt for each other doesn't vanish overnight."

"That's not the way you talked last night," she answered tautly. "You accused me of having dollar signs in my eyes."

"I was hurt and angry. I barely knew what I was saying." His voice dropped to a pleading note. "Don't cut me out of your life, sweetheart. I don't know what I did to make you doubt me, but whatever it is, I'll change."

Tears welled up in her eyes. "You're not the one who needs to change," she whispered. "I am."

"I don't want you to change. You couldn't be more perfect."

When she shook her head mutely, Noelle exclaimed, "Oh, for Pete's sake, *tell* him!" When Erica still remained silent, Noelle turned to Jeff. "Your mother convinced her she isn't good enough for you. Maybe you can talk some sense into her. I can't."

He gave her a blank look. "Erica has never even met my mother."

"I don't know where Mama told you she was going, but she's right here at Carefree Dunes. After the number she did on Erica, the poor kid is convinced she'd ruin your life."

Jeff stared at Erica. "Is this true?"

"She told me things about you I didn't realize before. I could never fit into your life," Erica said sadly.

His strained expression turned to relief. "I don't have a life without you, my love. If something displeases you, we'll change it. And if my mother doesn't like it, that's tough. You and I are getting married tomorrow."

"No, Jeff, we can't! She said she'd fire you and have you blacklisted in the banking business if we got married."

He laughed. "That's one way of getting out. Frankly, I never liked banking."

Roman had been looking on approvingly. Now he spoke up. "I can get you a job in public relations if you find yourself looking for work. You'd be a natural at it."

"I might take you up on that." Jeff put his arm around a dazzled-looking Erica and steered her toward the door. "If you'll excuse us, we have a little talking to do and a lot of serious kissing."

Roman smiled. "I was thinking along those same lines myself." As soon as they were gone, he said to Noelle, "Quick, close the drapes before the rest of Carefree Dunes stops by with their problems."

"You don't mean that. You're as happy for Erica and Jeff as I am. He'll straighten her out."

Roman drew Noelle into his arms. "I'm also pretty delighted about the way things turned out for you and me." He chuckled unexpectedly. "I came here to do a story and got a bride as a bonus."

She became very still in his arms. This was what she'd dreamed about all along. "Are you asking me to marry you?"

"That's a strange question." He drew back to look at her with a slight frown. "I thought it was understood."

The spreading happiness inside her was like the glow from a thousand candles. "A woman likes to be asked."

"Okay, consider yourself asked."

"That isn't very romantic, but consider yourself accepted." Noelle smiled ecstatically as Roman embraced her tenderly.

The kiss they exchanged held romance and love, and the promise of a lifetime of happiness.

* * * * *

Silhouette

SPECIAL EDITION

™

It takes a very
special man to win

That **SPECIAL** *Woman!*

She's friend, wife, mother—she's you! And beside each Special Woman stands a wonderfully *special* man. It's a celebration of our heroines— and the men who become part of their lives.

Look for these exciting titles from Silhouette Special Edition:

April **FALLING FOR RACHEL** by Nora Roberts
Heroine: Rachel Stanislaski—a woman dedicated to her career discovers romance adds spice to life.

May **THE FOREVER NIGHT** by Myrna Temte
Heroine: Ginny Bradford—a woman who thought she'd never love again finds the man of her dreams.

June **A WINTER'S ROSE** by Erica Spindler
Heroine: Bently Cunningham—a woman with a blue-blooded background falls for one red-hot man.

July **KATE'S VOW** by Sherryl Woods
Heroine: Kate Newton—a woman who viewed love as a mere fairy tale meets her own Prince Charming.

Don't miss THAT SPECIAL WOMAN! each month—from some of your special authors! Only from Silhouette Special Edition! And for the most special woman of all—you, our loyal reader—we have a wonderful gift: a beautiful journal to record all of your special moments. Look for details in this month's THAT SPECIAL WOMAN! title, available at your favorite retail outlet.

TSW2

MORGAN'S MERCENARIES
Lindsay McKenna

Morgan Trayhern has returned and he's set up a company
full of best pals in adventure. Three men who've been to hell
and back are about to fight the toughest battle
of all... love!

Be sure to catch this exciting new trilogy
because you won't want to miss out on these
incredible heroes:

Wolf Harding in HEART OF THE WOLF (SE #818),
available in June.
Appearing in July is Sean Killian, a.k.a. THE ROGUE
(SE #824).
And in August it's COMMANDO with hero Jake Randolph.
(SE #830)

These are men you'll love and stories you'll
treasure... only
from Silhouette Special Edition!

Fifty red-blooded, white-hot, true-blue hunks from every State in the Union!

Beginning in May, look for MEN MADE IN AMERICA! Written by some of our most popular authors, these stories feature fifty of the strongest, sexiest men, each from a different state in the union!

Two titles available every other month at your favorite retail outlet.

In July, look for:

CALL IT DESTINY by Jayne Ann Krentz (Arizona)
ANOTHER KIND OF LOVE by Mary Lynn Baxter (Arkansas)

In September, look for:

DECEPTIONS by Annette Broadrick (California)
STORMWALKER by Dallas Schulze (Colorado)

You won't be able to resist MEN MADE IN AMERICA!

New York Times Bestselling Author

Sandra Brown

Tomorrow's Promise

**She cherished the memory
of love but was consumed
by a new passion too
fierce to ignore.**

For Keely Preston, the memory of her husband
Mark has been frozen in time since the day he was
listed as missing in action. And now, twelve years
later, twenty-six men listed as MIA have been
found.

Keely's torn between hope for Mark and despair
for herself. Because now, after all the years of
waiting, she has met another man!

**Don't miss TOMORROW'S PROMISE by
SANDRA BROWN.**

**Available in June wherever Harlequin
books are sold.**

TP

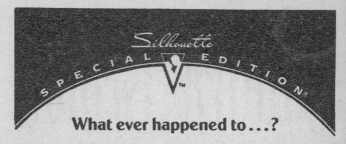

Silhouette
SPECIAL EDITION™

What ever happened to...?

Have you been wondering when a much-loved character will finally get their own story? Well, have we got a lineup for you! Silhouette Special Edition is proud to present a *Spin-off Spectacular!* Be sure to catch these exciting titles from some of your favorite authors.

TRUE BLUE HEARTS (SE #805 April) *Curtiss Ann Matlock* will have you falling in love with another Breen man. Watch out for Rory!

FALLING FOR RACHEL (SE #810 April) *Those Wild Ukrainians* are back as *Nora Roberts* continues the story of the Stanislaski siblings.

LIVE, LAUGH, LOVE (SE #808 April) *Ada Steward* brings you the lovely story of Jessica, Rebecca's twin from *Hot Wind in Eden* (SE #759).

GRADY'S WEDDING (SE #813 May) In this spin-off to her *Wedding Duet*, *Patricia McLinn* has bachelor Grady Roberts waiting at the altar.

THE FOREVER NIGHT (SE #816 May) *Myrna Temte's* popular *Cowboy Country* series is back, and Sheriff Andy Johnson has his own romance!

WHEN SOMEBODY WANTS YOU (SE #822 June) *Trisha Alexander* returns to Louisiana with another tale of love set in the bayou.

KATE'S VOW (SE #823 July) Kate Newton finds her own man to love, honor and cherish in this spin-off of *Sherryl Woods's Vows* series.

WORTH WAITING FOR (SE #825 July) *Bay Matthews* is back and so are some wonderful characters from *Laughter on the Wind* (SE #613).

Don't miss these wonderful titles, only for our readers—only from Silhouette Special Edition!